Dimwater's Demons

By

Sam Ferguson

This is a work of fiction. All of the characters,
organizations, and events portrayed in this book are either
products of the author's imagination or are used fictitiously.

Dimwater's Demons

For Y.C.T. & F.T.

Other Books by Sam Ferguson

The Sorceress of Aspenwood
Dimwater's Dragon
Dimwater's Demons
Dimwater's Dagger

The Dragon's Champion series
The Dragon's Champion
The Warlock Senator
The Dragon's Test
Erik and the Dragon
The Immortal Mystic
Return of the Dragon

The Netherworld Gate Series
The Tomni'Tai Scroll
The King's Ring
Son of the Dragon

The Dragons of Kendualdern
Ascension
Dominion

The Fur Trader

The Wealth of Kings

CONTENTS

CHAPTER 1

Feberik Orres pulled short on the reins and his horse slowed to a lazy pace. A servant was out front of the manor, chopping wood and tossing it onto a careless pile. As Feberik approached, another two servants emerged from the manor and grabbed wood, stacking it into their arms and hustling it inside.

Feberik's horse nickered and the servants looked up at him curiously.

"The master isn't seeing visitors today," one of them called out.

Feberik smiled and slid off his horse. He was an imposing young man by any measure. Wide shoulders, a barrel-like chest, arms thicker than most men's legs, and a voice deep and stern enough to wake the dead during normal conversation. Even without his sword, he likely would have scared the three servants up close, but as it was, the large claymore was currently resting in a harness upon his meaty back, the handle sticking up a few inches over his head and the point dangling just above his ankles. The servants kept glancing from Feberik's chest to the sword over his back, not sure where the threat was going to come from.

"You know who I am?" Feberik asked in his thunderous voice.

One of the servants dropped his armload of wood and dashed into the manor. The other two stayed in place.

The servant with the axe, a younger man with a decent build and thick arms, though nowhere near as thick as Feberik's, tossed the axe down and moved to stand in front of

Feberik.

"The master isn't entertaining any visitors. He's in mourning."

Feberik looked up to the window of the southern parlor, a room he had been in only the summer before to discuss Kyra's dowry. Now he saw it filled with people. Men and women were mixing about in the room, and appeared to be drinking and making themselves merry with a bit of dancing as well.

The large man turned and looked over at the stables. There were many extra horses there today, and it appeared as though at least one coach was parked around the back of the building, for Feberik could see one of the oversized wheels from where he stood.

"I didn't realize mourning went hand in hand with parties," Feberik said sourly.

"My master won't tolerate an intrusion," the servant said as he reached up and placed a hand on Feberik's chest.

Feberik felt a sweltering heat rise up through his neck and head. His fists clenched, almost involuntarily. For weeks the man had debated whether to come to Caspen Manor. He had wanted to wait for the appropriate amount of time before paying a visit to Kyra's father, even convincing the administration at Kuldiga Academy to allow Kyra to continue living at the school through the summer term on good faith until Lord Caspen, still her legal guardian, was out of mourning and in the right frame of mind to make proper, legal arrangements for her year-round accommodations. Now he felt the fool for caring enough about the worm to worry about timing.

Though the academy had sent over the necessary paperwork three times to formalize the decision to make Kyra a ward of the school since the day Lord Caspen had verbally disowned Kyra as his child, the man had never returned the signed documents. Now Feberik was here both as a representative of the school, tasked with getting the necessary signatures, and as a man who had a personal contract to settle with Lord Caspen. By the terms of the betrothal contract that had been agreed to the last time Feberik was here at the manor, he already had legal standing as an in-law, until such time as Lord Caspen might dissolve the contract and formally disown Kyra. Feberik intended to do what he could today to convince Lord Caspen that he had acted rashly that day in the headmaster's office, using the leverage of his own agreement with the man to convince him to fulfill his obligations. Now he felt his own temper beginning to get the better of him.

Feberik reached out in one swift move with his left arm. He yanked the servant forward and off to the side to land in the dirt. The young man crashed into the ground and pushed up, shaking the dust from his face.

"I'm going inside," Feberik said. He had only to eye the last remaining servant to dissolve any resolution that man may have had to fight. The servant dropped his armload of wood and backed away, holding his hands up in the air.

"Don't want any trouble," the servant said quickly.

Feberik marched to the front steps leading up to the wide porch. No sooner had he stepped upon the first stair than the front doors opened and a trio of armed spearmen emerged, with the first servant right behind them.

"That's him! That's him!" The servant was already closing the door behind the guards as he pointed Feberik out to them.

"The master isn't seeing visitors today," the first guard said as they formed a line in front of the door and stamped their spears upon the porch.

"What about his daughter's fiancé?" Feberik asked as he continued up the stairs. He sized up the guards. They were not knights. By the looks of their simple chainmail sleeves sticking out from under their tan tunics they were nothing more than mercenaries hired on by Lord Caspen. Caspen Manor had never been large enough to warrant a standing army before, nor had Feberik ever seen any guards on the premises.

The middle guard was the largest, but even he was nowhere near as large as Feberik, except in height. The other two were several inches under six feet, and Feberik was confident he could convince all three of them to let him in easily enough. At that moment, a small voice entered his mind and asked if it was the right thing to do. He knew he *could* force his way in, but *should* he?

Fate helped him decide when one of the guests opened the window to the parlor off to the left. Feberik looked over just as a busty woman with too much rouge on her cheeks leaned out and shouted at the guards.

"Trounce that louse! Go on, let's have us a show!" She was waving a drink in her hand. A man leaned out behind her, wrapping one arm around her waist and smiling blissfully at Feberik.

"I've got five gold on the guards," the man called out.

Out from the window came the boisterous laughter and music from inside the parlor.

That was it. Feberik's rage boiled beyond what he could control.

He stormed up the steps and socked the middle guard dead in the nose. The man flew back, blood trailing out of his nose and mouth, and crashed into the door before sliding down to his rump.

The guard on the right leveled his spear, but Feberik was not only strong and large, he was fast. With blinding speed, his right arm shot out and he seized the spear, pulling it out and causing the guard to stumble. Then he reached out with his left so he had both hands on the weapon. He spun mightily and the guard sailed out over the steps and fell to the ground in a heap.

The last guard rushed in, but Feberik spun out of the way, stuck the spear he was holding down in front of the guard's feet, and let gravity handle the rest. The third guard tripped and flailed wildly before slamming into his comrade at the bottom of the steps. The two connected first with their heads, and they both hardly moved afterwards.

Feberik then turned back around to face the first guard, who was sliding up the door as his legs pushed him back upright.

"You can't go in," the guard said dopily, the strength gone from his voice.

Feberik tossed the spear aside and launched a massive front kick that connected with the guard's chest and blasted him through the front door.

He could hear people screaming and shouting as he entered the manor. His boots thumped heavily upon the marble floor as his anger propelled him down the short hall to the left and into the parlor.

Most of the people inside the room cowered against the walls. The women screamed and shouted at him, but Feberik locked his eyes on Lord Caspen and moved steadily toward him.

A large man stepped in front of Feberik and swung his fist.

Feberik blocked it, snaked his hand around the back of the attacker's neck, and then pulled in as he gave the man a heavy head-butt that dropped him to the floor.

A second man drew a dirk and rushed forward, screaming and shouting obscenities.

Feberik grabbed him and tossed him out through a closed window like a rag doll.

No one else dared move.

Lord Caspen cowered in the corner near the hearth, sitting upon a cushy chair with a woman in a green dress sitting in his lap. The woman was obviously too frozen with fear to think of moving. Her lower lip quivered and the glass in her hand trembled violently as she looked up with wide, brown eyes.

Feberik reached down and grabbed her by the wrist, yanking her up before shoving her away.

"Everyone out," Feberik ordered. "Party's over."

No one argued with him. The guests all scrambled out of the parlor and ran down the hallway, some of the more drunken guests tripping and falling in the hallway as they screamed and shouted from all the excitement.

"Now, Feberik, don't do anything stupid," Lord Caspen

said.

Feberik struck out with a back-handed slap across Lord Caspen's face. Whether it was the force of the blow, or the sheer panic that had seized Lord Caspen, Feberik didn't know, but the man lost consciousness right there in the chair, along with his ability to hold his bladder.

Feberik turned and helped usher the last of the guests out, literally tossing two of the drunken men out onto the front porch, and then went back to the parlor, closing the door to the room behind himself. He went to the couch, which was pushed up against the wall with the windows, and picked up the piece of furniture to place it back where it had been the last time he was in the home. He looked through the windows to see that carriages and horses were filing out along the main road, and then he sat down and waited for Lord Caspen to wake up.

In the hour he sat there, he helped himself to a snifter of brandy to try and calm his nerves. Mad as he was, he knew he was already likely in trouble. He only hoped that his status as in-law would be sufficient justification for a certain amount of…liberty to be taken inside of this home.

As the nobleman began to wake up, he mumbled a few things. Something about a woman named Geraldine, and a few things that threatened to stoke the fires in Feberik's soul. However, not everything the nobleman jabbered about in his unconscious state drew ire from the hulking man. Lord Caspen also mentioned something about dark creatures in the woods, and appeared genuinely afraid of them as his body shook and he thrashed about.

It was during a particularly violent episode that Lord Caspen woke, screaming in horror and calling out for help. The nobleman then seemed to recover, wiping a hand over his face and taking in a few breaths. When the man's hand slid down his face and touched upon his reddened jaw, his eyes flicked up and about the room, wide and filled with fear. The orbs fell upon his guest as Feberik took his last drink from the snifter before tossing the glass down at Lord Caspen's feet, shattering it to pieces.

"What do you want?" Lord Caspen asked as he tried to sink back into the chair and melt away.

Feberik stood and picked up the couch with one hand, setting it just a couple of feet away from Lord Caspen before sitting down and leaning forward, glaring into the nobleman's eyes. Lord Caspen's color drained from his face and small beads of sweat formed upon his brow.

"I didn't know," Lord Caspen said. "I had no way of knowing she wasn't mine! You have to believe me. I would never have dishonored you—"

"Dishonored me?" Feberik echoed as he narrowed his eyes on Lord Caspen. "You think that is why I am here?"

Lord Caspen shrugged, pulling his legs up and hugging them into his chest. "You're going to kill me, aren't you? Guards! Guards! HELP!"

Feberik sighed and leaned back, shifting his large claymore so it wouldn't be in his way. "I came to discuss Kyra's support, and her dowry." He produced the school papers from a pocket inside his vest and waved them at Lord Caspen.

Lord Caspen nodded quickly. "Of course. The wedding is off! I understand. Keep the dowry. I'll sign the dissolution papers. No harm done."

Feberik reached up and scratched the corner of his mouth with his left hand. "Shut up," he said calmly.

The words may as well have been daggers, for Lord Caspen ceased breathing and sat helplessly, terrified.

"These are not papers to dissolve our contract. I came to tell you that I still intend to marry Kyra once she becomes of age. I've come to get your signature on Kyra's school papers, and to convince you to abandon this ridiculous notion of disowning her."

"You...what?" Lord Caspen said. His brow drew in close and he narrowed his eyes on Feberik. "But why? Wouldn't that dishonor the Orres family?"

Feberik leaned forward and grabbed a fistful of Lord

Caspen's shirt, pulling the man in close. "I do not need lessons in honor from a man who is gallivanting around with whores and drunkards instead of mourning for his departed wife. That isn't even mentioning the fact that you have abandoned your daughter."

"She isn't mine!" Lord Caspen squeaked.

"You raised her for fourteen years as though she were. That makes her yours. You have no right to punish her for something that isn't her fault." Feberik rose from his seat, picking up Lord Caspen and holding him above the urine-stained chair. "I was going to come to convince you to return to Kuldiga Academy. Your daughter is in pain. She has lost everything she has ever loved. I was hoping you would have a heart large enough to swallow your pride and help her."

Feberik glanced around the room, his anger rising once more with each glass and bottle he saw.

"Okay, I can do that," Lord Caspen said. "I can help her."

Feberik shook his head. "No, you can't. You have neither a heart, nor a spine. I was wrong to think you could offer her anything." Feberik roughly tossed Lord Caspen back to the chair, which would have toppled over backward with the sudden impact had it not been for the wall behind it. He retrieved the school papers from the couch where he had been sitting and thunked them down on a short end table that he dragged into place before Lord Caspen. He retrieved a quill and ink from a desk in the corner of the room and pushed them into the quivering man's hands. After glancing momentarily at Feberik's stony face, Lord Caspen signed each of the papers, and then pointed meekly with trembling hands back to the desk.

"M-m-my sealing wax," he stuttered weakly. Feberik retrieved the wax and a candle with which to melt it, and stood right near Lord Caspen's shoulder as he used the ring on his left hand to properly seal the final document. Then he pushed the man back into his chair and retrieved the papers, placing them back into his vest pocket once the wax was sufficiently dry. He turned back to Lord Caspen, who was now shifting uncomfortably in his chair, undoubtedly bothered by the cold, dampness of his clothing. He pointed a stern finger at Lord Caspen and leaned in closely.

"Stay away from her. Better she never know the cad you have become."

Lord Caspen nodded with a whimper.

Feberik looked down at the man's wet pants and shook his head. "Kyra is now a ward of Kuldiga Academy," he patted the place on his chest where the papers were now held, "however, you will contribute to her care. I have the dowry to offer her, but you will pay for her tuition. Maybe in that way you can atone for some of your worthlessness while not adding injury to Kyra. I will inform the administration at the academy to expect to receive payments the first of each month."

"Sure," Lord Caspen said with a quick nod of his head. "Anything you say."

Feberik reached up and drew his claymore. The sword ground against the scabbard and filled the room with a terrible *schring!*

Lord Caspen looked to the blade and began to cry and shake his head. "No, please, I'll pay, I swear it by Icadion!"

Feberik nodded. "Kyra is boarding at the school for each summer as well. I expect you to pay every month of the year."

Lord Caspen nodded as tears streamed down his red face. The noble's eyes were locked on the shining blade. "I'll do as you say."

"And make sure you stay away forever. If you should come looking for her, or if you should ever miss a payment…" Feberik stabbed the blade through the chair just an inch away from the left side of Lord Caspen's face. The nobleman's eyes rolled into the back of his head and his body went limp.

Feberik turned and replaced his sword. With a sniff he wondered what the headmaster and the local magistrate would say when and if they received word from Lord Caspen about the manner in which this visit had been conducted. What he had just done was far more than what he should have. He had come only to have a discussion after all. Still, he couldn't help but hope that perhaps somewhere in the plane of the dead, Kyra's mother was smiling, appreciative of his actions. As he left the parlor he caught sight of the servants he had encountered when he first arrived. He offered them a limp salute and a tight-lipped smile that likely betrayed too much amusement for the potential consequences of this visit.

Climbing atop his horse, Feberik made a decision. Though the young girl didn't yet care for him, he would watch over her in any way he could. Perhaps one day she would see that his efforts on her behalf were worthy of her affection. For now, though, it was enough to know that Lord Caspen had been chastened.

CHAPTER 2

Kyra walked through the tall pines, taking in a breath of warm, summer air. The first full week of summer term had finally come, and she couldn't help but feel utterly relieved that most of the other students who attended Kuldiga Academy had gone home until regular classes would reconvene in the fall. She could finally move through the corridors, eat in the dining hall, and wander the school grounds without hearing whispered conversations that featured her name, or catching stray glances from unfriendly faces everywhere she went.

Since her encounter with a shade, a dark creature not unlike a vampire that drained a person's life force and magical essence instead of blood, the hostility toward her had become different from what she had faced shortly after initially arriving at the academy for the first year of sorcery training. At first she had been teased because of the rumors that had cropped up as a result of too frequent visits from her overly attentive fiancé, a man twenty years Kyra's senior to whom Kyra had been betrothed by her father just before her 14th birthday. A man who, to Kyra's chagrin, had taken up a teaching post at the academy. However, the treatment she had received as a result of her relationship with Feberik had melted away once word had spread that she had needed to be interviewed by a tribunal of priests from Valtuu Temple after surviving a battle with a shade. The news of Kyra's true identity as the daughter of a vampire had somehow been leaked as well.

As a result of these two bits of supposedly confidential information becoming widespread knowledge, a general fear and awe for Kyra had overtaken the disdain and teasing she had previously thought to be the most unbearable of treatment from her peers. Instead of openly bothering her, they whispered quietly whenever she entered a room, and were quick to look away if she glanced at them. Now she found herself fantasizing about how much easier it would have been to complete the next three years of schooling if the only peer difficulties she had to deal with were a few pranks and some childish teasing about her fiancé.

Even Lady Gerrigan, who had comforted Kyra after her mother's murder, now scrutinized the young apprentice with narrow eyes whenever she passed by. Kyra knew better than to hope for any amount of comfort from Lady Gerrigan now. That woman had even once muttered the words 'half-blood' while staring at Kyra and talking to another one of the instructors.

Given these developments, Kyra might have left the school if not for Cyrus. He was the one shining beacon of hope in an otherwise dreary school. He was always the optimist.

"We must train to find the shade once more," the old wizard had said whenever Kyra would get discouraged.

True to his word, that is exactly what they had begun focusing on once she was healed up enough from her battle to return to her classes with him. Despite having gone into battle with a dragon on her side, Kyra had been grossly outmatched by the Shade, and had been lucky to come away with scarcely more than a broken ankle. Her dragon friend, Leatherback, and she had been pinned down by a host of illusionary shades, each able to cast its own spell, and would surely have been done for had Cyrus not arrived just when he did, banishing the shade, and returning Kyra, unconscious, to her room at the academy.

Now that summer had come, she was looking forward to enjoying her time at the school, reading, pursuing her own studies, and working with Cyrus to prepare to defeat her mother's murderer. She especially was looking forward to spending more time with Leatherback in his secret aspenwood grove where the taint of Nagar's Blight, a terrible curse that promised to overtake the mind of any dragon still found in the middle kingdom, so far had been unable to find him. It was strange to think that, except for the daily lesson with Cyrus, she would be entirely self-directing her use of time this summer.

There would be no summer festivals to attend, no travels to other parts of the middle kingdom to occupy weeks of time, and no stuffy dinners to attend with other noble families. She didn't mind the lack of structure, but she did desperately miss her mother, and was almost happy not to be returning to the home she had grown up in, where she would certainly be confronted with hundreds of things that would remind her that her mother was gone forever.

As Kyra had been disowned by the man she had grown up thinking of as her father, she had been given permission to stay on at Kuldiga Academy for the term of her enrollment. Though she wasn't sure who was paying for it all, it seemed her room and board were being handled through the school. She had been allowed to stay in the same room on the top floor of the school to which she had been assigned after first arriving at the academy, and had still not been re-assigned roommates since having them transferred away after the death of her mother.

She had been happy to be rid of those first roommates – girls with whom she had nothing in common, and who had never taken up her defense when the rumors had begun about her and Feberik, even though they had been there each time he had come to call. The private room had also afforded her the necessary privacy to magically open a portal whenever she had needed to last term, and travel through it to visit Leatherback. Now that the summer was setting in, she wondered how much longer she would be so lucky in her housing situation. Perhaps by next year they would require her to take on a roommate. It would be strange to share her little place with someone. She smirked at herself for a moment, realizing that she had come to look upon her dorm room as her own private little apartment, as though she would be able to remain there for the rest of her life.

While most other students and half of the faculty went home for the summer, Kyra was already at home. Though she despised the news that she would be expected to attend weekly dinners with her fiancé Feberik and his brother Janik, she did enjoy knowing that it seemed this would be the most she would have to see Feberik, as he had been assigned a summer cohort of third and fourth year apprentices of the sword who would be staying on for extended training during the summer. With the reduced faculty during the summer, as many of them were sent away on assignments for the king, Feberik would be with his students almost constantly, supervising their training and helping them grow accustomed to the regimented life of a soldier.

There had been some discussion of putting her with a similar summer cohort of sorcery students to keep her out of trouble. But when word of her potentially being re-integrated with the other students had gotten out, the few sorcery candidates there had been had mysteriously all chosen to spend their summer months at home. As a result, all of the sorcery faculty had also been sent out on assignment for the summer, and there was now no worry in her mind of being paired with a hostile instructor.

Her ankle had healed nicely, thanks to the priests from Valtuu Temple. Still, she had hated having them around so close in the weeks and months since the fight with the shade. And now, despite the marvelous ways in which her dragon, Leatherback, had been developing, the older priests were still always trying to convince her that Leatherback was not to be trusted. Their rhetoric was much like Njar's when she had first met the Satyr, but there was something about the way the priests said it that made it more insulting somehow.

Worse than this, though, was the fact that they could see her aura from a great distance. It had never been overly difficult to sneak out of the academy before, but now, having these priests tasked with watching over her, it was much more complicated than she would have liked.

Then there were the semi-weekly visits with the priests. They would examine her aura and then go to see Leatherback. She hated those days. Kyra knew they meant well, but it felt like they were judging her value as a person each and every time they stared at her with those dull, gray eyes. She could only imagine what Leatherback must feel like. She wondered whether the dragon knew that the priests would condemn him to death if they saw the slightest hint of what they called "the taint" in his aura.

Kyra shook her head and sighed. This was not how she had imagined spending the next few years of her life. Fortunately, she had completed the first year of four that she would spend as an apprentice at Kuldiga Academy. Well, four years was the normal course of study for the average apprentice at any rate. She wondered whether she would be expected to complete the terms as normal from here on out. Ever since the winter festival last year, she had only had one-on-one instruction with Cyrus following an incident with a teacher against whom Kyra had defended herself. Unbeknownst to Kyra, Lady Priscilla had been with child, and when Kyra's wind spell had caused the teacher to fly back into a wall, it had put both mother and child in serious danger.

Kyra sighed, remembering the incident. If only Feberik could have let her be that first term! His incessant visits had spoiled any chances she might have had to make friends, or at least quietly complete her terms while teaching herself spells from the book her mother had snuck into her bag the day she had left home. She closed her eyes and clenched her teeth for a moment before blasting an old stump with a fireball as the memory of that little spell book brought a flood of memories and emotions rushing into her mind. Kyra picked up the pace, knowing that the sooner she could get to Leatherback, the sooner she would have something positive to focus her energy on.

Just the thought of her friend put a smile on Kyra's lips. Perhaps she would learn enough from Cyrus to leave with Leatherback in the next year or so, if he grew enough to make the flight across the sea to the north. It all depended on him. Then he would be safe from Nagar's Blight, and she would be free of the rumors of her half blood, the priests, and most of all, she would be free from the engagement which loomed over her.

Continuing to tromp along, Kyra began her ascent up the second hill from the academy. She needed to put enough distance between herself and the priests and faculty members who may be curious about her adventures before she could conjure the portal that would ultimately take her to the aspen wood. Not wanting the priests to suspect that she had the ability to magically travel away from her dorm room, she began most of her visits to Leatherback these days with a long hike across the hilly terrain. She always made sure to wait until she was safely over the third ridge from the school before travelling the rest of the distance in a single leap.

She was nearly to the place where she normally conjured the portal when she heard something. She stopped and glanced to the right. She didn't see anything there.

"Heading off to see your pet dragon again?" a familiar voice called from behind her.

"Kathair!" Kyra shouted disapprovingly.

Kathair Lepkin stepped out from behind a large oak and gave a flourish of his right arm and a mock bow. His blue eyes seemed to sparkle as he stepped toward her. "You know, I have mentioned before that I don't really care for my first name. You really should call me Lepkin."

Kyra shook her head. "And I have told *you* that I disapprove of being followed."

Lepkin held a finger in the air and his boyish grin stretched as he seemed to wrestle with himself over letting the next words out of his mouth. He settled on saying, "Fair enough. But what else am I supposed to do with my free time? Though the dragon slayers are excellent company," he began sarcastically, "and I need something else to occupy my free time when I am not in classes."

"It's summer, there aren't any classes," Kyra replied

evenly.

"*Exactly!*" Kathair said, pointing at her emphatically. "Classes aren't even going on. As boring as they might be, at least it would be something. When I recovered and learned that the other students that… caused the problem," Kathair seemed unwilling to fully recall just how badly he had been beaten by the gang of students who had attacked him in his dorm room last term, "had been expelled from the academy, I thought it would be good to come back. But arriving the last week of the term was so strange. Everyone was finishing exams and packing up to go home."

Kathair's eyes dulled a bit and his smile faded. "And I, well, I guess I don't really have a place to go home to for the summer. I'm welcome in Tualdern, of course, but I'm not an elf. I guess I thought I might spend the summer better up here, with you." The words hung in the air as they both shared a brief glance. Then, his boyish grin came back, flashing those dazzling white teeth of his as he swept his arm out to the side. "Besides, the dragon slayers are staying around too. I figure they might let me go on a few of their hunting trips if I play my cards right."

"Hunting trips?" Kyra echoed. "They're looking for Leatherback?"

Kathair shook his head. "No, something else. They are being awfully secretive about it, but I think it has something to do with that creature you fought."

"You mean the shade," Kyra said. "They'll have to find him before I do," she said through gritted teeth. Then after a moment she realized that Kathair might actually be angling to accompany her to see Leatherback. "You know I can't take you there," Kyra said quickly. "I know you wouldn't hurt him, but if the other dragon slayers found out you knew where he was, they might pressure you into talking."

Kathair waved off the notion. "My field training is a bit sporadic now, anyway," he said. "They have bigger issues to deal with than me. I don't think it would even cross their minds."

"Kath—" Kyra began, but abruptly changed what she was saying when Kathair began to take in a deep breath, "Lepkin, what you need is a project. You know, something that can really capture your interest."

"Yeah, but not everyone can just wander out into the woods and find a dragon egg to raise up." The two of them stood for a moment in silence. "Well, I won't keep you," Kathair said suddenly. "If you ever want to study together in the library sometime, maybe I can help you out. I have learned a lot with the dragon slayers, you know. I'm decent with a sword too."

Kyra nodded and smiled. If it were any other boy in Kuldiga Academy, she would think he was boasting to be impressive, but she knew better in this case. She remembered clearly the trouncing he had dished out to the group of students —not to mention their instructor— that had caught him in the courtyard last year.

"Maybe I'll see you there soon. Cyrus gives me a lot of materials to read."

"Excellent," Kathair said with a widened smile and bright eyes. "Try to stay out of trouble, will you?" With that, Kathair Lepkin disappeared behind the tree again and was gone.

Kyra tried to see which way he went, but there was no sign of the boy anywhere. It was as if he vanished into the air. The young sorcery apprentice moved around the tree and scanned the area for him, but she never saw so much as a wiggling branch. Kyra thought it must have been a trick he learned from the elves who raised him, for she had never seen a human so easily disappear into a forest before.

She waited for a few moments, just to ensure that Lepkin had actually gone and was not hiding somewhere just to follow her to Leatherback. She knew better than that though. Kathair wouldn't want to risk Leatherback being discovered by the dragon slayers any more than she did.

Taking one last look around to ensure that there were no prying eyes, Kyra opened the magical portal that Njar had taught her to use as the surest way to the aspen wood and smiled when she finally saw the green and golden leaves flittering about in the summer breeze. After quickly closing the portal behind her, the young woman turned sideways as she slithered through the tangled mess of white trunks and grinned wide when Leatherback noticed her coming into the secret glade.

His tail flicked up and thumped the soft grass as what could only be described as a joyful grin stretched his lips over his fangs. His sky-blue eyes twinkled and his nostrils flared as he lifted his head.

"Hello Kyra," Leatherback greeted.

"Hello, dear friend," Kyra replied. "Is Njar around today?" she asked.

Leatherback shook his massive head slowly. "Already gone." A wisp of smoke slithered out from his nostrils as he spoke. The dragon stretched his neck forward and rested his head down upon the ground in front of his forelegs. "Story?"

Kyra shook her head and crossed the grassy ground to pet the top of his scaly snout. "I'm afraid not today. I just came to see you, and ask how you were feeling."

"Priests today?" Leatherback asked, his grin diminishing somewhat.

"Not today," Kyra answered. "Just me."

"Good." Leatherback closed his eyes and let Kyra scratch the area of his neck just behind his jaw.

He emitted a sound akin to a cat's purr, only it was much louder and vibrated throughout the glade.

"I know it's been hard having those priests around all the time," Kyra said as she ceased stroking the dragon and curled up next to his head, leaning back into the sturdy neck. "I think I might have a great idea of how we can just forget about them for a day."

The eye closest to Kyra popped open as Leatherback asked, "What idea?"

"I thought we might find out whether or not you have any of Gorliad's talent in the water." At this suggestion, both of Leatherback's eyes opened wide and he stood so abruptly that Kyra had to twist quickly to avoid being swept up by the large horn which protruded from the side of his head. Kyra had read Gorliad's story, Ascension, to Leatherback while he had still been in his egg, and again after he was old enough to understand the story. Having received it and its companion volumes from her mother for her fourteenth birthday, she had worked hard to translate it from the Old Peish it had originally been written in.

"Swim?" He cried, a hint of a roar escaping from the back of his throat in his excitement.

"Well, yes. We will have to get a bit creative to make a place for you, but the trout stream in the forest over there does have a deep eddy that we might be able to widen," she smiled mischievously and ignited a small fire ball in her hand, "and deepen. We are far enough away from the school. What do you say to a little target practice?"

Leatherback snatched up Kyra's aspenwood staff and dropped it into her waiting hands. "Go now!" he said eagerly. Kyra made her way through the aspens as Leatherback, now entirely too big to wind his way through the close-growing trees, flew up and over the outer ring of the aspen wood, and landed to wait for her amongst the oaks and pines that generally made up the rest of the forest. They walked the short distance together to the stream and then followed it until they came to a waist-high waterfall where the terrain descended for a short distance, and then levelled out again, causing the stream to have naturally formed a wider, deeper section that Leatherback had discovered early on was an excellent place for catching trout.

"We'll make a fantastic mess, but I think that if we can carve out a place right in here," she indicated the section of stream from the waterfall to a spot downstream," and pile the rock and dirt around as we go, we just might be able to make enough of a pond for you to use. At least until you grow to your full size," she added, looking up to his head which already towered over her.

She paced back and forth on the bank of the stream for a

few moments, trying to decide the best way to get started on the project. She had just taken a step back to try and visualize where the edges would be when Leatherback suddenly let loose a fireball that blasted into the opposite bank, sending mud and water flying everywhere. She was so surprised she jumped back half a foot while emitting a shriek. She shot a reproving look at Leatherback as she put a hand over her thumping heart. Leatherback gurgled in his throat, laughing at her.

"You said, 'fantastic mess.'" And with that he shot twice more in rapid succession, causing a small amount of mud to rain down on her hair. Kyra lost no time to retaliate. She sent a large fireball of her own right into the water nearest to where Leatherback was standing and laughed heartily when the water caught him full in the mouth as he had opened up to release another blast of his own. He shook his massive head in displeasure as smoke leaked out of the side of his mouth and his nostrils, apparently having been quenched quickly when Leatherback had abruptly snapped his mouth closed.

After that, any thought of analytically approaching the project and completing it in a calculated fashion was lost entirely. The two of them took turns blasting new sections of bank away in turn, trying to shower the other with as much debris as possible. It was fortunate that Kyra was so proficient at ward spells, as several times there had been large chunks of rock blown up from the bottom of the stream bed, and she had quickly needed to protect herself from certain damage.

Once she began to feel tired from the expenditure of magic, she held her hands up to him in surrender. "We really should take a break. The water isn't even remotely pooling in the way we need it to." She looked about them and realized they had come closer to creating a miniature swamp than anything that resembled a swimming hole. "Why don't we try to deepen what we have here? Or rather, *you* can start digging to deepen it while I," she started wringing mud out of her hair, "see if I can get any of this muck out of my hair!" With that, she playfully tossed a handful of the sticky stuff at Leatherback, succeeding only in catching the outside of his wing as he blocked her. "Even Gorliad was willing to get his claws dirty excavating his home, remember?"

Leatherback happily stepped to the center of what had, only an hour before, been a quiet mountain stream, and began pulling out chunks of water logged mud and rock with his claws. Kyra laughed as she headed upstream to where the water still flowed clean, and bent down to wash her long, black hair in the stream as best she could. Whoever lived downstream would not be happy about the disruption in flow for the day, but this was the most fun she had had since she had come to school. She and her mother had often enjoyed silly activities together as her mother tried to find inventive ways to teach Kyra spells and creative applications for them.

The first time Kyra had successfully cast a simple ward at age six, they had been in the large kitchen at Caspen Manor. Her mother had sent the servants out for the day, and had spent the afternoon helping Kyra to hand mix a warm, sticky mess of any ingredient Kyra chose to add to the large batch of bread dough the cook had left behind to rise. When the dough was so discolored, and so full of strong, spiced aromas that her mother assured her it was completely inedible, her mother had begun tossing bits of it at her, giving her instructions before each throw to help her try and deflect the sticky blob with a ward. They had been laughing so hard, tears had been making their way out of her mother's eyes, but when Kyra unexpectedly conjured the ward, she had dropped the entire bowl of dough on the floor in her motherly excitement. Kyra's hair had been full of sticky substance that day too.

The memory brought a smile to her lips, but also made her whole chest ache. How would she ever stop missing her mother? At this moment, it felt like that empty feeling in her chest would be there forever, and the thought made her angry all of a sudden. She was going to find the shade who had killed her mother. She was going to find him, and she was going to destroy him and any other creature that might have been working with him. In answer to the anger inside of her, she inadvertently conjured a little spark of lightning and gave herself a little shock when she closed her fist as she imagined pummeling anything that got in her way. She jumped a little at the sensation and then stood up and decidedly wrung her hair out.

When she returned to the place where she had left Leatherback to work, she was amazed at the progress he had made in such a short amount of time. Piles of mud and rock as tall as she was had been thrown up all around the place where the eddy had been. She came up on Leatherback from the middle of the stream, rather than trying to scale the slippery mounds of streambed that would otherwise have separated her from his work space.

"Been having fun?" She asked with a sweep of her arm, indicating the area which now seemed expansive enough to accommodate Leatherback's length twice over, and, if it held water, would allow him to swim a little as long as he tucked his legs up under him.

"I could ready my own mountain. Like Gorliad," he said proudly, stretching his wings out and shooting a single flare of fire into the air.

"I believe that! Maybe someday we will find you a mountain. For today though, we may need to be done." She looked at the water that was beginning to pool up around Leatherback's feet and realized that they would have a proper mess if there wasn't an outlet for the water that would allow it to follow its original path down the mountain. More than that, they might have someone miss the water downstream who would follow the stream back up to them and cause trouble.

"Let's put our fire to work over here and see if we can't make a proper outlet for the water. It will probably take it the better part of a week to fill up at this rate," she looked behind her at the water which was trickling down what was left of the little waterfall, "but then we will need a place for the extra water to go." She waded through the water to the far end of the pool and showed Leatherback where she thought they should focus their work. When she was satisfied that the water would be able to escape in a controlled manner after filling the pool, she tapped on Leatherback's leg. He lowered his head to her and allowed her to climb on up behind the crown of horns that grew from the base of his skull.

"I'm frozen, let's head back to the aspen wood so I can dry out!"

CHAPTER 3

In a dark hovel, a young girl sat at the edge of her mother's bed. Torn blankets covered the doorway and the dirt floor was littered with the stalks and husks of various plants that had been recommended for a healing poultice that had ultimately proved to be ineffective. Eleanor now cursed the time she had spent gathering the herbs and flowers instead of tending to her mother, and watched as she coughed into a stained, brown rag again and again.

"It's all right mother, the physician is coming," Eleanor said. Her thin hand reached out and stroked her mother's leg over the thickest, best blanket they owned. Her mother was barely lucid. Sweat dripped down her forehead, and her hands shook even when she wasn't coughing. Small circles of blood soaked into the rag she held in her hand.

Eleanor had gone hours ago for the physician. He said he would be there soon, but no one had come. The young girl of fourteen watched as her mother slipped back into a fitful sleep. Once she was sure the coughing fit had ended, Eleanor stood up and crossed the room in four steps, nearly tripping over the chamber pot as she went to the doorway. She pulled back the blankets and poked her head outside. It was still raining. Gray and black clouds filled the sky above, and mud ran through the streets below.

Across the street, a young boy played in the mud, shaping clumps into balls and stacking them together. Down to the right, a pair of young girls splashed in the puddles along with their dog, a mangy, wire-haired mutt. Up to the left, the street was empty, save for the rainwater rushing down the sides of the street and threatening to overflow into the houses. No matter which way she looked, there was no physician.

"I paid you already," Eleanor mumbled under her breath as she continued to look up and down the street. Indeed, she had given the man four coppers, the last bit of money she knew of.

He kept it and never arrived.

Eleanor left the doorway when the last bit of light left the sky. There were no lamps in this part of the town. As the shadows crept through the street, so too did the mice and the stray cats, among other things that were much worse. The young girl went back inside and grabbed the rough cloth in her right hand, stretching it back across the doorway and hooking it over a large nail that acted as an anchor for the covering. Then she turned and grabbed the large, hollow crate and pulled it into the doorway behind the blanket. It wasn't a complete door, but it helped keep some of the animals out.

The burglars and miscreants wouldn't come into the shelter, so there was no fear from them. They would set in the shadows outside, waiting to pounce upon any fortunate enough to be returning from a day's labor in the fields or the mines to the east. It wasn't uncommon for such muggings to end with a body in the street the next day either, and the blankets over the doorway did little to keep her sheltered from the screams in the night.

Still, none of that worried her tonight.

Eleanor looked back to her mother's pale face, matted with hair stuck to her scalp with sweat. Even in the most peaceful times of sleep now, her mother's breathing came in short, struggling spurts. She tried to rouse her mother just enough for dinner.

"I made soup, mum," Eleanor said with a cheery voice as she brought a clay bowl over to her mother. In truth, it was barely more than tepid water with a couple of cubed carrots and a third of an onion, but it was more than they had had the day before.

Normally it wasn't as bad as all of this. Eleanor's mother

had a friend who sent them money each week. It was never much, but it had been enough to buy food and clothes through the years. Unfortunately, Eleanor's mother had taken ill in late spring, coughing up blood and riddled with fevers. That ate up the money they had been saving. Eleanor's mother had always said there would be a special surprise on Eleanor's fourteenth birthday.

That day had come and gone over a month ago, but her mother was too sick to disclose what the surprise was.

Then, two weeks ago, the money stopped. Eleanor stretched it as best she could, but she wasn't old enough to earn money with the day laborers, nor could she leave her mother alone for long.

"Mum, come on, we have to keep your strength up," Eleanor said as she settled in at her mother's bedside with the soup.

Her mother opened her green eyes and smiled lucidly for the first time that day.

"My little bumblebee," she said softly. "You made dinner?"

Eleanor beamed proudly. "I did," she said. She raised the bowl to her mother and helped her drink the broth.

"It's good," her mother said. "But, where is yours?"

"I already ate, while you were sleeping," Eleanor lied.

Her mother nodded and continued drinking the soup from the bowl, stopping to chew the bits of carrot and onion as they came into her mouth. Then, once it was gone, she pushed herself up on shaking elbows.

"Mum, you should rest," Eleanor said as she moved to block her mother.

"I'm all right. Listen to me for a bit."

Eleanor scooted in close and her mother stroked her hair. "I never got to give you your present," she said as she reached under her pillow for a white comb and moved to separate the tangles in Eleanor's sandy hair. "I have it ready now, but before I give it to you, I want you to promise me something."

"Anything, mum," Eleanor said. She winced as her

mother pulled at a knot in her hair with the comb that yanked on her scalp.

"I want you to promise to do whatever Horace Bagman tells you to do tomorrow."

Eleanor's brow drew into a knot above the bridge of her narrow nose and she pulled away to look at her mother. "Why should I do that, mum?"

"Uh-uh, you promised to do something for me. You can't go back on it now."

"I had my fingers crossed, you know, in case I didn't like it." Eleanor hurried to cross her fingers and then triumphantly display them to her mother. "So, I can change my mind now if I want to."

Eleanor's mother sighed and shook her head. She opened her mouth to speak, but was cut short by a fit of four coughs, each one more intense than the last until the woman was nearly doubled over.

"Are you okay?" Eleanor asked.

Her mother nodded her head and wiped her mouth. Eleanor didn't miss the new, bright spots of blood on the rag.

"Promise me you will do what Horace says."

"All right, mum, if it means that much to you. I will do what he wants me to do."

Her mother nodded appreciatively. "That is as it should be. Now, take this to him tomorrow in the morning, and he will give you your present."

"Your comb?" Eleanor asked as she looked at her mother's comb. "But you said this was a gift from my father."

Her mother winced at the mention of her father, and tried to hide the oncoming tears in a cough as she looked away before replying.

"It's made of ivory," she said. "This comb is going to Horace Bagman so that your father and I can give you one last birthday gift. You are fourteen now, and you deserve a proper gift. Something fitting a young lady. You be a good girl and do whatever Horace tells you, you hear?"

Eleanor nodded and took the comb when her mother

pressed it into her chest. "All right, mum, I'll do as he says."

Her mother reached out and caressed her cheek with her hand. A single tear dripped down her bony cheek and she smiled once more before lying down upon the bed. "I love you, Eleanor, my little bumblebee. Remember to keep your chin up."

"I will mum," Eleanor said.

Her mother closed her eyes and drifted back to sleep.

Eleanor slid off the bed and pulled a smaller blanket out from under the bed. She curled up on the floor next to her mother. She reached out and extinguished the candle, casting the room into near-total darkness, and went to sleep.

The next morning, Eleanor woke to the sound of a crowing rooster. Unfortunately, imagining the rooster made her stomach growl angrily. As she pressed up from the dirt floor, she rubbed her tummy and thought whether it was worth chancing Farmer McKnought's wrath to try and steal a chicken, or maybe just an egg or two.

"Mum, what would you do if I stole an egg for us today?" Eleanor asked aloud. "Would you mind much if your little bumblebee turned to a life of crime?" An impish smile crept across her face and she turned to see if her mother had woken and heard her joke.

Her mother was very still, and very quiet.

"Mum? You awake?" Eleanor asked. No answer. She thought it was perhaps better to let her sleep. It was rare these days that her mother could sleep without waking up and coughing every few minutes.

Eleanor got up and went to the doorway. She poked her head outside. The rain was gone and the sun was out. The mud was still thick in the streets, but at least the day would be bright and warm. She moved the crate out of the doorway and then peeled back the wet blanket to let the light in.

It's going to be a good day today. Eleanor let her hand wrap around the comb that she had tucked into her one pocket on the side of her trousers. She pulled it out and looked at it in the sunlight. She had heard of ivory before, but had never seen it.

Or, at least she never realized that she had seen it. She just thought her mother's comb was a nice trinket from her father. She had no idea that it was such an expensive item. She smiled as she ran her fingers over the fine teeth.

She was definitely going to take it with her today, but she was not trading it to Horace Bagman for any silly presents. No, she was going to find a real physician, and buy medicine too. She would probably even have enough left over to buy food. Maybe they could buy a chicken from Farmer McKnought!

Eleanor didn't want to disappoint her mother, but she also didn't need any silly toys. She was a young woman now, after all. She turned back to give her mother a goodbye kiss. She stepped across the room in four steps and started to bend down, but then noticed that her mother's face was much paler than ever before. It was a ghastly grayish-white.

Eleanor sucked in a quick breath and shook her head as she bent low to her mother. She couldn't hear her mother's breath.

"Mum?" Eleanor said as she dropped her ear down to rest upon her mother's breast. There was no breath, nor was there any heartbeat.

Eleanor dropped to her knees. Her mouth fell open and tears filled her eyes. If only she had known that last night was going to be the last. She would have stayed awake and rested beside her mother. She would have held her hand. She would have kissed her on the cheek and told her goodnight.

She looked down through her tears and studied the comb in her hand.

Why hadn't her mother let her sell it long ago? Maybe it could have saved her. Now there was nothing the young woman could do. Her mother was gone, and was never going to wake.

She sat there, in a silent stupor, staring at her mother's body. She reached up and slipped her hand in her mother's and then rested her head upon her mother's shoulder. She didn't want to move, ever.

There was no way for her to know how long it was.

Perhaps an hour or two had passed. Then, a tap came at the doorway.

"Hello to the house," an old man said.

Eleanor turned and saw the physician she had hired the day before. He used his cane to keep the blanket moved to the side as he ducked low to enter. His black over cloak was caked with mud along the bottom, and water was soaking up past his ankles.

"Terribly sorry, young lady, but the Shiftens had their baby yesterday. It took some time, but they had a nice, healthy baby boy. He and mother are doing just fine, but by the time it was over..." he looked up and saw Eleanor. His eyes flicked to her mother and his pleasant smile faded. "Oh, I see." He reached up and removed his hat, revealing a head of snow-white hair neatly combed to the side. "I'm terribly sorry."

Maybe it was the insult that the physician had arrived after it was too late to do anything for her mother. Perhaps it was the cruel joke played by the gods that another family should have life brought into their family on the same night her mother died. Whatever it was, it put her over the edge. The tears fell and the anger rose. Before she even knew what happened she was up, crossing the room, and kicking the physician directly in the groin.

"You should have come!" she screamed as she kicked the man again.

Somehow, she ended up in his arms. The physician hugged her close, holding her tightly and leaning in with his head. She tried to wrestle free, but it was no use.

"Shh, quiet now, child." The physician held her tighter as he spoke. "It's all right, you go on and let it out."

"I hate you!" Eleanor shouted through tears. Then she broke down into sobs and melted into the man. He continued to hold her, loosening his grip just slightly and turning the embrace into a more comforting one.

"That's all right," he said softly. "That's all right."

After a while, she pushed away and wiped her eyes. Somewhere deep inside herself she knew she should apologize, but the words never found their way to her mouth. She just glared at the man and crossed her arms.

The physician fished in his pocket and pulled out a few coins.

"I don't have any copper on me, but I have some silver pieces. Take these, it's the least I can do."

"Take them and eat them for all I care, they won't do me any good," Eleanor spat.

The physician sighed. "All right. I'll just set them on the crate over here." He moved to the crate and dropped all of the silver coins onto the crate. Then he turned and offered a smile. "If you need someone to talk to, my door is always open."

"Just go," Eleanor shouted. She knew it wasn't his fault. The physician had told her days before that there wasn't much he could do anymore. Consumption was not an easy disease to fight. Still, he was the closest object onto which she could project her sadness and anger, so that is what she did.

She stared at the doorway for at least an hour before she finally was able to calm down enough to think. She looked back to her mother and thought of the last conversation they had had together. Eleanor moved to her mother and kissed her cold forehead, and then she left, taking the six silver coins with her.

Before she made her way to Horace Bagman's house, she found Mr. Gib, the local mortician.

He was a short, fat man who lived just on the outskirts of the slums where the dirt road met the cobblestone and the shanties became proper, small houses. He was outside, nailing a new coffin together as she approached.

"'Ello, Eleanor. What can I do for you?" he asked with his bright hazel eyes beaming over his round, bearded cheeks.

"How much does it cost for a burial and a proper coffin?"

Mr. Gib's smile changed to an expression of confusion and the man wiped his hands and set his hammer down. "Now, why should that question cross your mind?" he asked.

"My mother passed away last night," Eleanor said, choking back the tears and doing her best to hold her head high.

Mr. Gib sighed and shook his head. "I heard she was sick," he said. "I'm sorry to hear she's gone." He turned around and put a hand on his head while he sighed again, this time it went out through his teeth and made a slight, sad whistle. "Eleanor, I'll tell you what, I can give her a proper burial. I won't charge for the coffin, deary, okay?"

Eleanor shook her head. "I don't want her in a pauper's grave," Eleanor said. "She deserves better than that."

Mr. Gib nodded. "Most people do, your mother especially."

"How much for a proper grave and a proper burial?" Eleanor pressed.

Mr. Gib pursed his lips and scratched his chin. "How much do you have?" he asked after a moment.

Eleanor held up the six silver coins and the ivory comb. "This is all I have."

Mr. Gib shook his head. "No, no, that comb is for you. Your mother was firm on that."

Eleanor scrunched up her face. "What do you know about it?"

Mr. Gib pointed down the road. "Mr. Tavers, the merchant who deals with fine jewelry, tried to buy it a year or two ago. I know, because I was there when he made the offer. That was back when your mother worked in the inn serving coffee and such to travelers. Well, your mother told him in no uncertain terms that it belonged to you and was going to be the one thing she would leave to you no matter what."

Eleanor looked down to the comb, confused why it should matter so much to her mother.

Mr. Gib put on a friendly smile and knelt in front of her. He gently took the comb and then slipped it into her pants pocket. "You don't show this to anybody, you understand? This is yours, from your mother."

"She told me to give it to Horace Bagman last night," Eleanor said without thinking.

Mr. Gib's left brow shot up and he cocked his head to the

side. "Well then, I suppose you should do as your mother told you, but don't flash it around, not in this town, you hear? You keep it safe and hidden in your pocket. You give it to Horace then, but no one else."

Eleanor nodded.

"Also," he continued, "I only need three silver coins to take care of your mother."

Eleanor's eyes went up to the two display coffins outside the house. The sign on the simple pine coffin said five silver. Even at fourteen, she knew the man was cutting her a deal he couldn't afford. She held her hand out, with all six coins.

"I want her buried right," Eleanor said.

Mr. Gib plucked three coins out of her small hand and smiled. "For your mother, I'll get it done right for three silver. Now you get on over to Horace's house. I bet your mother had something special planned for you."

Eleanor nodded her thanks and watched the man move back to the coffins. His wife came out from the house just then and talked to him. Eleanor watched as they talked for a minute and then Mrs. Gib put her hand over her mouth and closed her eyes, dropping her head and shaking it slightly as Mr. Gib pulled her into an embrace.

Seeing the grief in another person was too much for her. She turned and made her way down the cobblestone street, headed for Horace Bagman's house.

She turned twice to the left, and once to the right. When she came to the corner of Mercer and Beauregard streets, Eleanor turned to face a tall, skinny building made of brown brick. She went to the door and pushed it inward. A small brass bell jangled above her, bouncing on a type of spring and swinging back and forth. The room was well appointed, a fine woven tapestry hanging on each of the two side walls, both depicting large dragons entangled in battle. Upon the floor was a blue and silver rug with a floral pattern woven into it. Alongside the rug were two long cases of glass that displayed fine pieces of jewelry.

The whole scene made her quite anxious. Eleanor bit her

lip and fidgeted with her fingers as she stepped into the room. A short, balding man sat behind the far counter with a strange apparatus hanging around the crown of his head by a long strap that secured it in place. He looked up, one of his brown eyes covered by a series of round magnifying lenses. He reached up and slipped the strange hat off, setting it onto the table next to a ring that was held in some sort of metal vice.

"Come in, come in," Horace said as he stood up and placed a hand on the small of his back, leaning into a stretch and groaning. "You are little Miss Eleanor Hughes, aren't you?" Horace said with a wagging finger. "I've been expecting you."

Eleanor approached the counter and stared up at the man. He smiled wide from ear to ear, but somehow it seemed less sincere than anyone else's smile she had seen lately. Even the physician had appeared to be more genuine. Horace had shifty eyes that hardly stayed upon Eleanor. They constantly flicked back up to the doorway, or over to the window as he leaned over the counter and spoke to her.

"I have something for you," he said quietly.

Eleanor nodded. "Yes, my mum told me," she said.

Horace nodded and narrowed his eyes on her. "How is your mother?"

Eleanor didn't want to answer Horace. Each time she acknowledged what had happened, it felt as if it made it more final. Somewhere inside of her, there remained a sliver of hope that perhaps she could yet wake from this horrid day, and that maybe it was all just a terrible nightmare.

"What's the matter, cat got your tongue?" Horace asked.

"She's dead," Eleanor answered dully, wincing as she felt that sliver of hope deep within herself shrink a bit more.

Horace nodded and tapped the counter with a finger. "I see," he said flatly. His eyes ceased shifting around the room and he bent forward to gently take Eleanor's shoulders in each of his hands. "Keep your chin up, yeah? That's what she would want you to do."

Eleanor didn't need a lecture from Horace. She pulled

back and reached into her pocket. "My mum said to give you this. Then she said you would have instructions for me." She fished out the ivory comb and set it upon the counter.

Horace's greedy eyes lit up, sparkling wildly as his smile returned. This time, Eleanor believed the expression to be genuine.

"Did you know that in the Middle Kingdom, ivory is more valuable than gold? It is only found in the Eastern Wilds, and even there it is a rare thing to find, and usually comes at a high cost of life," Horace said.

Horace had always had a hunger for expensive items that most people found unhealthy. He wasn't a cheat, but he was always sure to play any bargain to his favor, and he never seemed to be pleased with his fortune. It was one of the reasons someone of his wealth dealt with people from the slums. Sometimes he preyed upon their desperation, other times he conspired with someone down on their luck to acquire items in a less than honorable fashion. Despite the rumors, Horace had never been caught by the authorities. Even when his first wife left him and threatened to have him arrested, nothing ever happened to Horace. That was why he was called Lucky Bagman.

The man held up the comb and quickly turned to lock it into a silver chest that sat upon a shelf over his workstation. He was still smiling when he turned back to Eleanor.

"Wait here a moment, will you?" he said before disappearing into a door that led to a back room. Eleanor could hear the scrape of a box being pulled from a shelf somewhere in the other room. A metallic click was then followed by a squeaky hinge and the rustling of papers. Horace returned seconds later, a small bundle wrapped in brown paper in his hands and sealed with twine.

"What is this?" Eleanor said as she held out her hand.

Horace held the package back and shook his head. "First, the instructions." Horace walked out from around the counter and went to the front door. He locked it and then came back to kneel before Eleanor. "This is something your mother was working on for quite some time. Inside this bundle is everything you need for your new life."

"My new life?" Eleanor echoed.

Bagman sighed impatiently. "I don't have time to explain everything twice. Keep your mouth closed and your ears open, understand?"

Eleanor nodded.

"Good." Horace grabbed one of her hands and set the package into it. "Inside this bundle is everything you need. You will find a nobleman's family pedigree tied to your name. You will also find your new family history. You must memorize everything in this manual and forget about your life here in the slums. You are no longer Eleanor Hughes from Brighton. You are Miss Linny Ravia, a young noblewoman from Nortwyn Abbey. Can you remember your new name?"

Eleanor nodded. "Sure, my mum used to call me Linny when I was younger."

"Good girl. Now, the first paper you will find is a note to a driver. I have hired a coach to take you to Kuldiga Academy. Your travel charter and your school enrollment papers are all included. Also, in the coach you will find a trunk with clothes, and a wand."

"Kuldiga Academy?" Eleanor asked.

Horace nodded emphatically. "You have magic in your veins, little Eleanor. Your mother did too, but she never was able to develop it. She lacked the funds for that, you see. She's been working hard on this for years. She wanted to make sure that you would have the chance she never did. Make us proud little Eleanor."

"How can I pay for tuition?" Eleanor said. "I can pretend to be anyone I want, but I can't afford to study there."

Horace reached out, set his right hand on her shoulder, and gave her a wink. "Eleanor, if I can forge a new life for you, don't you think I could arrange to make it look like your education had already been paid in full?"

Eleanor's eyes teared up as she realized why her mother had never sold the ivory comb before. It could have bought life-saving medicine, but her mother was bent on saving another life. "I'll make her proud," Eleanor said.

CHAPTER 4

Kyra slipped her textbook back into her bag as Cyrus wiped the chalkboard clean. The lesson today had been dry and boring, but Cyrus had insisted upon going through each painful detail of the first recorded encounter with a wraith. Truth be told, it wasn't much different from her own. A young wizard had been out in the woods, plying his magic to the fish in a stream, when a wraith came upon him and nearly killed him. The main difference from Kyra's own encounter was that the young wizard's tutor was near enough by to come running in and save the young man. Kyra had had to rescue herself, though it had rendered her unconscious.

She must have sighed a bit too loudly, for Cyrus turned back from the chalkboard and raised a snowy brow as he cast his eyes upon her.

"What did you learn today?" he asked in his raspy voice.

Kyra shook her head and gave her honest assessment. "Nothing I didn't already learn for myself out in the woods."

Cyrus nodded and stepped around his desk before leaning back upon it. "You see no value in the text we studied today?"

Kyra shook her head. "Gamel didn't even fight the wraith that attacked him. He just froze and shouted for help. It was Master Coen who banished the wraith."

Cyrus nodded and smiled. "Ah, and so there is nothing for you to learn from his encounter because it wasn't as exciting as yours, is that it?"

Kyra sighed.

The old wizard moved toward her and slowly slipped into the seat next to hers. "Did you find it odd that the wraith suddenly appeared?"

Kyra shrugged. "No," she said.

"So, I suppose you also failed to question why the wraith chose to attack the young wizard, even despite Master Coen's close proximity."

"What difference does it make *why* it attacked? What matters is how to fight them."

Cyrus laughed and nodded as he stroked his beard. "I might have said the same thing many years ago. However, in order to fight your enemy, you must understand them."

"It doesn't say why the wraith attacked," Kyra said impatiently. "It just says what happened, where it happened, and how they banished it."

Cyrus nodded. "That is why we are studying this account. It is a prime example of why we must stretch our minds beyond the plain text." He reached out with a bony finger and gently poked her forehead. "You should put yourself there, and ask yourself why the creature attacked. What did it want? What did it hope to gain? Why the boy?" He then indicated the bag with his finger and shook his head. "If all you ever learn to put in your brain are the accounts written by historians, then you will fail to see clearly. Each historian has his or her own bias. They present a passage the way they see fit, sometimes omitting or embellishing truths that ultimately twist or altogether hide the true lesson to be gained from the experience."

"So what should I learn from this?"

Cyrus shook his head. "We are out of time today. Go and think on it. We will discuss it together tomorrow. Hopefully by then you will have figured the answers out for yourself." Cyrus then rose and went back to pack his books into his own bag.

Kyra might have argued the point, but she was anxious to get to Leatherback. The priests would be coming today, so she wanted to read to him and calm him before their visit.

She rushed out from the room and through the empty corridors until she made the field outside the southern exit. A pair of instructors wearing green robes stood near a large, smooth-topped stump, but they hardly glanced at her as she ran past.

Kyra didn't have to worry about escaping from the priests today. Since they were coming later anyway, they expected her to run on ahead. So long as she didn't try to interfere once they arrived, they didn't mind her extra time with Leatherback.

She found him resting in the glade, sunning himself lazily on his side with his neck stretched upward and his eyes closed.

Leatherback smiled when he saw her coming toward him, and rolled over to his stomach.

"Story?" he asked.

Kyra nodded. "I brought a fun one today," she said. "One that should help us with the shade."

The dragon snorted a puff of smoke and blue flame through his nostrils to show his disgust for the dark creature they had fought together.

"No worries," Kyra said as she settled in next to his front right shoulder. "It looks like it will be a fun read as well as informative. I've skimmed through this book already, and I'm pleased to say I've found us a historian who took the time to tell the story well, and not just report the events. I found it in the library in the same section with the books about dragons. A friend at the school told me about the section last year, and that is how I was able to learn what a special egg I had found when I first came across your nest. The section is full of books about rare and extinct creatures. The story I'm going to read is the only one that talks about a garunda beast at all, so it seems like pure luck that it was filed right in the place I usually go to read, but I think you will like it."

Leatherback brought his neck around and rested his head before Kyra's feet, effectively wrapping her into a protective embrace.

"This is the tale of Ravenel and the Garunda," Kyra said. "The foreword in the book says it is a favorite among the cities of southern Landale. It comes from the second century of the Era of Kings and is the first encounter with a garunda recorded in all of Terramyr." She lifted the book and peered at the dragon's sky-blue eye from under the book. "The garunda may be our key to slaying the shade," she said with a grin.

Leatherback purred and his lips stretched back into a smile.

Kyra continued, quoting from the last sentence in the foreword. "The garunda is a rare creature. It's elusive and savage, and this tale actually is one of the best texts to understanding the monster even today." She snuggled into Leatherback's shoulder. "All right, here we go," she said.

"Ravenel fidgeted with his bow and glanced around the room to the eyes that now were fixed upon him. 'I fear there has been a mistake,' Ravenel said as he crossed his arms over his chest. 'I am a simple hunter.' His fingers tapped on his bow as he looked around the room once more.

Princess Lirian, who had summoned him to her court, nodded and smiled. 'Yes, I know, that' Lirian replied with another nod of her head that seemed to make her golden hair dance softly about her face. 'From what I hear, you are also among the best archers to live in our land.' She looked up from the table then and her gaze met that of his deep blue eyes. 'Your valor in the Battle of Detean is legendary,' she added.

"'Even so, I have been living a life of peace in the forests since then. This creature you describe to me is strange, and I have never encountered such, nor do I wish to,' Ravenel announced."

Leatherback let out a throaty growl. "Coward," he said.

Kyra shook her head and lowered the book to look into the dragon's fierce eye. "Hold on until you hear the whole story," she said. "You might change your mind."

Leatherback snorted and a wisp of smoke snaked out from his nostrils to dance upon the light breeze that found its way through the rustling aspen leaves around them.

"Where was I?" Kyra asked herself as she looked back to the book. She ran her finger down the page until she located where she had left off. "Ah, yes. Here we go. Lirian shook her head. 'In the Battle of Detean, you fought against the Khattuun, the great lion people from the east. You slew them by the score, and saved the day for all of our tribe. The other tribe leaders and city kings of our alliance each sent thank offerings to our tribe as a testament to your great acts. I would say you do know more about this beast than you admit.'

"Ravenel bowed his head reverently before replying. 'My apologies, milady, but the Khattuun are a great and proud race. They are like lions, and also like men. True it may be that they are fearsome warriors, and among the most feared on the battlefield, but they are much easier to understand than this beast you ask me to slay.'

"'I understand,' Lirian agreed softly. She stood from her ivory throne and motioned for everyone except for Ravenel to exit the room. The large hunter watched as the others filtered out of the room, each murmuring and whispering. After they were all gone and the guards closed the doors, Lirian moved in closer to Ravenel. 'The foul garunda beasts that have attacked our fair city of Kilistyrin, are more dangerous than normal beasts of prey,' she admitted. 'However, they do somewhat resemble the fierce mountain cats that roam along the great mountains in the east, though these creatures are much larger. The primary cause for concern is that their presence is only a prelude to the appearance of a much more sinister creature.'

"'A demon of some sort?' Ravenel guessed." Kyra paused here and nudged Leatherback with her foot. "This is where it gets interesting, so keep listening."

Leatherback didn't say anything, but his blue eye fixed itself on the back of the book as he waited for the story to unfold.

Kyra cleared her throat and resumed reading from the book. "Lirian shook her head. 'A shade,' she said simply."

Leatherback growled again, this time in an angry tone. Kyra didn't bother to pause the story however. Now that she had him hooked, she continued on without stopping.

"Ravenel sucked in a breath and backed away. 'You expect me to slay a shade?' he asked incredulously. 'It would be easier to best a Khattuun with my bare hands,' he declared.

"'I will not lie,' Lirian began. 'I have sent others already, and they have all perished. However, we have enough information to know that there are two garunda in a cave to the east of here. It is my belief that they guard a single shade.'

"'No,' Ravenel said. 'I would need an army, and even then it wouldn't be enough.'

"Lirian shook her head. 'I have sent groups to fight already. They have failed. I believe we stand a better chance if we send one man alone. That way there is less risk of being caught. You are a master with your bow, and you are skilled in stalking and hunting prey of all kinds.'

"'I hunt game. This is not the same,' Ravenel protested.

"Lirian nodded and a frown dragged her ruby lips down. 'Yet, if someone does not defeat the garunda and the shade, then *we* shall become little more than game for a far more sinister force that walks upon our plane.'"

Kyra nudged Leatherback with her foot again. "See, my friend, I told you this would be a good story." She continued, "Ravenel stood silently. He cast a glance to the door behind him, and then looked back to Lirian's desperate eyes. 'A shade cannot be beaten by an arrow,' he said. 'A shade is a Verr'Tai, or blood elf, twisted by Attek's curse into something akin to a vampire, only instead of drinking blood it drains your very soul and life force. Even if I could slay the two garunda, I wouldn't be able to scratch the shade.'

"'I know full well what a shade is,' Lirian chided. 'Only days ago, I watched helplessly as the two garunda stalked into the city and ripped apart men as though they were made of straw. The shade came soon afterward, devouring all who challenged her.'

"'Then you know their kind cannot be beaten,' Ravenel said decisively. 'Our best hope for survival is to move. None can stay here.'

"'They have one weakness that I know of,' Lirian said. 'The rays of the sun burn them, and force them into their holes and burrows.'

"'I am sorry for the misunderstanding,' Ravenel offered as he began moving toward the door. 'It just isn't possible.'

"'We have no one else,' Lirian called out after him. 'As I said before, the warriors we could spare have already gone to the cave, and none have returned. We have only a few men left capable of wielding a sword, and we need them here to defend our citizens from the continued attacks.' Ravenel continued walking to the door. 'We won't leave,' Lirian said. 'This is our home.'

"'Home is where you decide it to be,' Ravenel countered.

"'We are not nomads,' Lirian argued. 'To move north would be to offer ourselves as slaves to the mighty kings and tribes of the north. To go east would be to die by the claw and fang of the Khattuun. We have no ships capable of assisting with a mass exodus, and it would take months to reach the sea. Besides, the garunda and shade would hunt us down as we fled. Tell me, where are we to go?'

"Ravenel stopped in mid-step and looked down to the floor with a great sigh. He could sense the feeling of desperation within Lirian's voice, and he well understood the plight of the city and vassal towns that belonged to the tribe. Within his mind two voices were heard, one urging him to defend those weaker than he, and the other seemed to be shouting for him to run far away from this dark place. He closed his eyes as he sorted out the possible consequences of his actions. In the back of his mind came the nagging notion that none of the nearby tribal lords would be likely to send aid, despite the alliance, and he knew the townsfolk had no place to flee to. Lirian was correct. If he refused to help, then no one else would.

"'There is no one else,' Lirian repeated, as if she was confirming Ravenel's thoughts. 'We are prepared to pay you three fold the usual price for a dragon's bounty.'"

Leatherback snarled. "They hunt dragons?" he hissed. "How much do they pay for one like me?" The anger in his voice was not lost on the young apprentice.

Kyra blushed and quickly turned the page. She had been so wrapped up in the story that she had forgotten to skip that part. She reached out and stroked Leatherback's neck. "Don't think on it, Leatherback. No one will hunt you, I promise."

Leatherback rolled his head to the side on the grass, growling softly. "Continue story," he said after a moment.

Kyra skipped over the part that detailed the payment before continuing. "Ravenel turned back around to face the woman and, despite his fears, within moments he found his head nodding in agreement with her. 'You said you had a map for me to use in finding the cave,' Ravenel said dryly.

"Lirian nodded. She moved to the table beside her throne and picked up a rolled parchment. 'The path is marked for you,' she said. Ravenel took the map. He unrolled it, studied the markings, and then rolled it again and shoved it into his satchel. 'May the gods protect you,' Lirian offered.

"'Perhaps you failed to notice, but the gods abandoned us two centuries ago,' Ravenel said flatly. He then left without another word. As he opened the door to step out into the full, late-morning sunlight, he was greeted by a crowd of people. Some of them he recognized as members of Lirian's court, others were faces he didn't recognize. Most were women, though there were a few older men and some children in the group as well. They all clamored for him, begging him to deliver them from their plight.

"'I am no savior,' Ravenel said under his breath as he pushed through the pressing throng. He left the city as quickly as he could, escaping the pleading and wailing masses as he finally made it beyond the outer walls of the city. He followed the roads that led east, then turned sharply north when he reached the pine forest of Goresthin. He walked along a babbling brook, stopping only for a few moments to drink from the cool, crystalline waters and eat a mouthful of bread and dried apricots that he had packed in his satchel.

"The evening light fell darkly upon the hills before the mountains, barely lighting the way for Ravenel as he carefully climbed up the rocky, dry riverbed that led to the cave. He looked up at the waning light through the trees and sighed. He had hoped to reach the lair before the beasts woke to prowl. Along the trail he found scattered bones and large piles of droppings, the sure tell-tale signs of a predator in the area. He stopped to examine the leg bone of a deer and ran his fingers through the grooves.

"'That's some set of teeth,' he remarked as he set the bone back on the ground. He readied his bow in his left hand and pulled one arrow out of his quiver, sticking it in his teeth for quick retrieval while he pulled another arrow and held it to the string."

"He has no magic," Leatherback commented, a hint of concern in his voice.

Kyra smiled and shushed Leatherback so she could continue reading. "Another twenty minutes of picking his way up the slope over the lichen-covered rocks in the fading light brought him to a large, black hole that led into the side of the mountain like an ever-open mouth waiting to swallow the unwary. Ravenel felt a shiver run down his spine when he heard the wind howl through the cave, but he shrugged it off quickly, knowing that he had work to do. He crouched low next to a waist-high boulder and scanned the area around him before setting his bow down to reach for his satchel.

"First he pulled out a mini crossbow, made similar to the design an elf warrior might use, with vine and leaf patterns etched into the sides. The weight and balance of the crossbow were of such fine craftsmanship that the weapon could be wielded very quickly and with the utmost precision to deliver a powerful, deadly punch to almost any of the lesser beasts in the realm, despite the fact that it was only a fraction of the size of a normal crossbow. Ravenel had even used this same crossbow to slay a frost bear with a single bolt to the head.

"He rigged the mini crossbow to a harness that enabled him to hang it over the back of his left shoulder for easy access, and a bandolier of bolts, filled with various poisons and toxins, crossed over his chest to ensure easy loading of the deadly weapon."

Leatherback sighed woefully. "Poisons will not work on the shade. We know that from the book Cyrus gave you before."

Kyra nodded. "Yes, but this tale has a secret that *Masters of Shadow* did not tell us."

Leatherback purred and a slight grin pulled at the corner of his mouth. "Then read on, and tell me."

Kyra smiled and continued where she had left off. "Then, once the mini crossbow was secure, he reached for the trusty hand-axe that hung from his belt. The blade gleamed as he turned its silvery steel to the side and applied sticky oil to the blade. It was a toxin from the rubosia tenedera flower, a powerful paralyzing agent that he had used on large beasts of prey in the past. Once the oil was in place, Ravenel turned the axe over in his hand and inspected its workmanship. His lips curled upwards in a smile as he read the dwarven runes inscribed along the steel neck."

"Dwarves!" Leatherback said excitedly. Ever since they had finished reading *Ascension*, one of the five books in the *Chronicles of the Dragons of Kendualdern*, Leatherback was always excited when he heard about dwarves.

"Shush, or I'll never finish the story on time," Kyra reprimanded.

"Sorry," Leatherback grunted.

Kyra hid her grin behind the book as she peeked over the top just enough to see the frustration on Leatherback's face. She had never had a little brother, but she had often imagined that a small brother would act much like Leatherback. A squirmy, impatient soul trapped in a body he could not yet fully control, who never knew when to sit and be still. The only problem was, this particular body was the size of a small house, and tipped with claws and fangs, and that was to say nothing of his ability to fly or breathe fire.

"Continue story," Leatherback grumbled.

Kyra's cheeks reddened and she ducked back behind the pages to make sure Leatherback wouldn't catch her grinning at him, then she continued. "As if sensing the impending battle, a howl came from deep within the cave, reminding Ravenel that he had not the luxury of time. He quickly hung his hand-axe back on his belt. Rotating the strap of a satchel slung over his right should that held several daggers and other useful items, he pulled the satchel to rest in his lap and removed two vials of flammable oil. He was quick to put a small strip of cloth in each glass vial and then tuck them gingerly into his belt for future use. Ravenel then checked his tinder kit to ensure his striker was easily accessible. He tucked it into his pocket and then he grabbed his bow and stalked off into the cave.

"Each step inside the cave came slow and deliberate as Ravenel searched the darkness before him, refusing to be caught unawares by the likes of a garunda beast. He smelled the foul, musty stench of mold and blood, a most pungent odor that almost had him gagging. He pushed on, pausing whenever he heard an echoing growl from deeper in the cave.

"Deftly he avoided the piles of bones randomly discarded in different areas of the cave. As he went deeper, he discovered signs of human victims as well. He found a dismembered leg here, a bloody, dented helmet there, and the odd shield or discarded sword. Judging by the remains, he guessed there must have been at least fifty to try their luck against the garunda.

"Minutes later the hairs on the back of his neck stood on end and a shiver formed goose bumps over his arms. Something moved nearby. There were heavy footfalls on the stone floor nearby, a black form slinked by him, and he spotted red eyes gleaming at him in the darkness. He brought out the striker and lit the cloth attached to one of the oil vials. He threw the vial in the direction of the eyes and watched with glee as the glass shattered and spewed flame all around the cave.

"The giant beast opened its feline mouth, emitting a low growl as it stalked into the circle of light. Ravenel's eyes widened when the garunda bared its saber-like fangs in a roar that all but deafened the large archer. The cat was easily at least six hundred pounds, more than any Khattuun he had ever fought, or any mountain cat he had ever heard of. Spikes jutted out from the beast's shoulders, and its skin rippled taut over thick, corded muscles. There was no fur on the demon; it was just a black mass of twisted muscle and fangs.

"Ravenel knew he had to act while the firelight still blinded the beast. He brought the bow up and pulled the arrow back. He loosed the arrow with blinding speed, and the shaft buried deep into the beast's neck. The garunda shuddered and leapt back away from the hero, landing squarely in the burning oil.

"The beast shook its head wildly and screeched a shrill wail as it batted at the flames with its massive paws. Ravenel didn't miss a beat. He loosed the second arrow, piercing the other side of the garunda's neck. Then he stepped in quickly, slicing and striking furiously with his axe across the cat's right side. Lines of green blood appeared on the obsidian body, but it did little to stem the beast's fury. In an instant, the cat reared back on its hind legs as it stood and roared, as a bear might do, then it sent a pulse of magical energy that knocked Ravenel backward through the air, smashing him against the stone wall.

"Ravenel shook his head in an attempt to regain his senses. He was still standing, barely, and he had even managed to keep a strong hold on his bow and axe. The cat leapt through the air, fangs bared and claws out. Ravenel somersaulted to the left, slashing out with his axe and catching the garunda in the right foreleg. The beast howled and crashed into the wall head-first. It turned, growling wickedly and lowering its head with its black ears flat against its skull. It took two steps forward and then started to twitch violently. Ravenel could see the muscles cramping in sharp spasms and knew immediately that the paralyzing toxin was beginning to work on the monster. Ravenel dropped the axe and quickly nocked another arrow. He fired upon the beast one, two, and then three times before the garunda fell to the ground. It yowled and wailed horribly, but it could no longer move. Ravenel grabbed his axe and ran in to finish the beast with a quick chop to the neck.

"Green, acidic blood spurted out from the wound and burned Ravenel's hand. Quickly he scraped the ooze off with the back of one of his knives so as not to spread the viscous goo further on his skin.

"No sooner had he done so than a second garunda appeared in the chamber with him. The cat slowly circled around, hunkering low and ready to spring at any moment. It started to jump to Ravenel's right, but when Ravenel moved to dodge, the garunda switched directions and lunged directly where Ravenel had stepped. Ravenel just barely managed to escape the trap, but he was unable to counter attack before the cat withdrew out of reach.

"'Clever kitty,' Ravenel muttered. He nocked another arrow and took aim for the garunda's chest. The fire from the first vial was starting to die out now, so he fired the arrow quickly, hoping to at least distract the beast long enough to reach and light the second vial. The garunda swatted the arrow out of the air and roared mightily, showing its pink gums and throat. Ravenel grabbed a vial and threw it to the flames. He heard the glass crack, but it wasn't enough to set the oil inside aflame. When Ravenel realized the malfunction, he started for the vial, but the beast lunged in the way, snarling with what seemed to be a wicked grin.

"'Clever indeed,' Ravenel said. His right hand went up for his mini crossbow and he fired at the beast's face. The garunda arched back to dodge, but the bolt sunk deep into the beast's chest. The cat roared in anger and reared up on its hind legs. Ravenel then drew a dagger and threw it at the garunda's exposed underbelly. However, the garunda unleashed a powerful shockwave that knocked the dagger backward, and sent Ravenel flying back again to the opposite wall of the cave.

"Ravenel felt his ribs bend under the pressure as he was crushed between the magical blast and the rock wall of the cave, but he focused enough on the fight to keep from blacking out as the pain rippled through his body. The garunda dropped heavily back down to the ground, but accidentally crushed the vial underfoot. The newly spilt oil caught flame and the cat was enveloped in fire. The garunda flopped onto the stone and howled in agony. The fire grew on the beast as the burning oil clung to its skin.

"The hero set his bow down. His chest and back hurt far too much to draw the string back anymore. He loaded the mini crossbow as quickly as he could and fired repeatedly at the horrid beast. Each bolt slammed into the cat with a sickening crack, sending it twitching and recoiling over the flaming oil. Each jerk of its massive body seemed to take more and more of its remaining energy until finally, after several shots, the beast lay mostly still upon the stone, save for the occasional spasm that often occurs after death.

"Ravenel cautiously walked up to the smoldering beast and, with one swipe of his axe, smote off its head just to be sure that it would not somehow rise from its condition and follow him down the tunnel. This time he was careful to avoid the spray of sizzling blood. He went back to grab his bow, and took a moment to stretch his torso against the aches and stabbing pain that still reverberated through his body. Then, before moving farther into the cave, he dipped his arrow heads into the garunda's blood, hoping it might give him an advantage over the shade he had yet to face."

Kyra broke here and flattened the book on her lap. "Still think he's a coward?" she teased.

"Continue story," Leatherback said quickly.

Kyra picked the book up, quite pleased that she had managed to capture Leatherback's full attention now. She picked up where she had left off.

"Ravenel followed the tunnel for more than half an hour as it wound downward, spiraling deeper into the earth below. He passed by the torn bodies of many more men as he went. The air grew thicker further down, and there arose a somewhat sour odor as he neared the main chamber, but what surprised him most was that there appeared to be a light coming from deeper inside the tunnel.

"Slowly, very slowly, he came around the final bend into the main chamber, and what he saw almost blew him over. There, standing defiantly in the large chamber, was an ancient temple. It was cylindrical in design, rising up as an oversized support column to the cave ceiling above and joining with it thirty feet above his head. The entrance, a single, enormous, black, stone door, was flanked on either side by oversized granite statues of demonic warriors. So astonished was he that his heart almost stopped beating within his chest. Ravenel then noted several large sconces along the outside of the temple, each of them ablaze, sending light flooding through the chamber.

"A low, yet distinct growl alerted him to the presence of yet another garunda. Ravenel slowly turned his head to the left to regard the monster, and he was surprised, happily so, to discover the broken shaft of a large spear protruding from the beast's front leg, along with several arrows embedded deep in her flanks. This beast would not be half as hard to slay.

"The beast continued to growl, but she did not advance, and it was only as she paced sidelong in front of him that Ravenel noticed her oversized belly. This garunda was pregnant. Ravenel thanked the gods for his fortunate timing, for he knew that if the beast had succeeded in giving birth, it would have spelled almost certain disaster for the townsfolk.

"He quickly drew out his mini crossbow, loaded a poisonous bolt, and then let fly for the beast. She tried to dodge the bolt, but she was too wounded to escape. The shaft bit deep into her side, spilling its poison into her blood. Within moments her steps were shaky and her growl was almost inaudible. She roared once, albeit weakly, and then fell onto the stone with her head facing Ravenel. Ravenel then loaded another bolt. He took aim at the beast's head and let loose. The bolt hit home and sent the beast to the fires of Hammenfein. Never one to take a chance against nature, especially the darker forces of nature, Ravenel retrieved one of the sconces from the outside of the temple and set it to the body and let the flames consume the evil beast along with her unborn demons.

"A whoosh of air erupted from the temple then as the large, stone door was flung open with ease. Ravenel spun around to see a tall, pale-faced figure standing in the doorway before him. She wore gray and red robes, with her silver hair in a single plaited braid that sat lazily over her shoulder. A pair of wicked scimitars hung at the figure's sides.

"'You killed them,' the shade sneered as it stepped out from the doorway.

"'I did,' Ravenel replied as he closely studied the new threat. It was almost hard to discern, but he decided that this particular shade was, or had been at one time, a female elf. Her facial features seemed even more prominent now with her faded and gray skin pulled so tightly against her cheek bones. Her teeth seemed almost serpentine-like as she hissed at Ravenel. Her eyes were bereft of all color, leaving only white orbs to look at. Ravenel knew that those white eyes had led to the demise of many people, for the first few to come against this strange and powerful foe had mistakenly thought that the eyes were sightless. This, as Ravenel knew, was not the case. In fact they could see quite well, better than most of the fairer races of the realm even.

"'It was the people of Kilistyrin who disturbed my slumber,' she hissed as she gently floated down over the stone steps to the floor of the chamber, her gray and red cloak flowing out behind her. 'I have slept here longer than those pathetic worms have walked in the sunlight, and now you think you can desecrate my temple without recompense?'

"Ravenel felt his legs go weak. His very energy was being drained from him magically by the shade. His large, muscular frame soon felt weak all around. His mind went cloudy. He reached up to put his hand to his head, but as he moved he brushed against the handle of his dwarf-forged hand-axe. Suddenly he felt a new surge of energy rush through him. He grasped his axe and loosened it from the harness on his belt. He hoisted it in front of him and was amazed to see the old runes come alive, almost burning with a blue glow about them. He knew instantly that the dwarven magic had somehow stopped the assault on his energy."

"Dwarven weapons are the best," Leatherback said with a satisfied hiss.

Kyra smiled and continued. "The shade shrieked as she

realized that she could no longer suck Ravenel's life force from him. 'Your magic won't save you,' she snarled. The shade rushed forward through the air in a blur, eager to devour Ravenel's energy. Down she descended, hard, as she raked a clawed hand out for Ravenel's face. The hero deftly moved his head back, just out of reach, and swiped forward with his hand-axe. The blade connected solidly, swiping off a few of her fingers as it passed.

"The creature howled with a head-splitting pitch that all but shattered Ravenel's eardrums as she leapt into a backwards somersault away from him. To his horror, she grew new fingers almost in the blink of an eye. She then hissed again, even flicking her tongue like a snake as she conjured forth a black fireball and sent it flying toward Ravenel.

"Though he dove aside, the fire grew larger to defeat his dodge. His legs felt the searing heat as the flames ripped through his clothing and licked at his flesh. The smell of burnt hair assaulted his nostrils as he rose to his feet in time to see the shade's mouth moving, conjuring another spell.

"Ravenel quickly put an arrow to his bow and let the arrow fly. The garunda's blood sizzled and crackled as the arrow streaked through the air and sank into the shade's stomach. The horrid creature's eyes went wide and she stared down at the arrow with her white eyes.

"'How could you know?' she whispered harshly.

"Ravenel scrunched his brow for a moment and then realized that the garunda blood prevented the shade from healing. He looked down at his axe and remembered that he had wiped the blood from the blade before putting it back in its harness. He looked to the pregnant garunda, but the flames had already consumed the blood. He dropped the axe and reached for another arrow tipped with garunda blood. He let them all fly, sinking each shaft into the shade's chest.

"With every blow, the shade shrank away, screaming and howling in pain. She tried to send magical assaults, but they only fizzled and died before she could launch them. When Ravenel sent the last arrow, he reached for his mini crossbow and fired. The shade took a hit directly in the forehead, the force of the blow jerking her neck and skull backward as it sank in deep. A slight sizzling sound was made as the shade remarkably pulled the bolt loose from her head. With the exception of a slight burn mark, her skin appeared as if nothing had touched her. She also removed the other arrows and dropped them to the ground.

"'You are better than the others,' she said. 'But you shall die here.'

"Ravenel's jaw hung open in disbelief as he watched her toss aside the bolt that surely would have killed any other creature. He had no other blood-tipped arrows, so he let fly with another bolt, then a second, and a third. The shade simply laughed wickedly at his futile attempts to slay her. Although all of the bolts had hit their marks, nothing seemed to faze this creature.

"Ravenel looked around the chamber, desperately searching for anything that might help him. There was nothing to be found, and soon Ravenel caught sight of another fireball zooming toward him. He did the only thing he could think to do. He ran. He only stopped for a moment to scoop up his axe to protect himself from the shade's life-drain spell."

Leatherback lifted his head and spat a small amount of blue fire out from his mouth. "He needs more garunda blood," he said.

Kyra nodded and continued reading. "Wicked laughter followed him as he sprinted out of the chamber and around the corner of the tunnel. The fireball seared the stone wall as it slammed into it with full force, showering Ravenel in sparks and bits of hot stone. He could hear the laughter coming closer and he knew the shade was stalking him. He sprinted up the winding tunnel, dodging the occasional fireball thrown by the shade. His lungs began to burn from the exertion, but eventually he made it to the small chamber where he had defeated the other two garunda beasts. He dropped down next to the first body and opened it with his axe, allowing the blood to spill over the blade. Quickly he dipped the last of his crossbow bolts into the sizzling ooze and loaded his mini crossbow.

"The laughter stopped. Ravenel huddled low in the darkness and waited as he heard the heavy breathing of the vile shade. His heart pounded within.

"'Can you feel it?' the shade whispered in the darkness. Suddenly a ball of blue fire appeared and bathed the area in magical light. No sooner did Ravenel see the shade than he took aim with his crossbow. The first shot missed, and he had to duck behind a stalagmite to avoid the shade's magical fire. As the fire roared around him, he reloaded the mini crossbow with the last bolt. The blood on the bolt burned his fingers, but he pushed the pain out of his mind.

"In a fury of motion, Ravenel leapt to his feet. He dashed around the corner and ran straight for the shade. He swiped out with his axe for the creature's head, but he missed the mark and barely sliced the creature's left shoulder. The shade hissed and recoiled away, but not quickly enough. With his left hand Ravenel levelled the mini crossbow at the shade and fired. The bolt bit deep into the shade's chest. He could hear bone cracking under the force of the shot. The shade's skin and tissue sizzled and crackled as a small fire ignited on her chest. The shade howled and writhed in agony. Ravenel brought the axe back up and drove it into the shade's neck, severing her head from her shoulders. The shade's eyes rolled back into her head and smoke wafted up from the blistering neck hole.

"Ravenel stepped back from the corpse and watched as a faint, green light emitted from the wounds. Within moments, flames shot out from the shade and the body was soon reduced to ash. His breathing eventually slowed and the ache in his side started to ease up. He replaced his axe, gathered his bow, and made his way to the mouth of the cave. When at last he emerged to the quiet forest, he fell to his knees, overcome with exhaustion.

"He slid back to rest against the mouth of the cave for the night. As he slept, the cool night wind rejuvenated his body and soul. He woke with the first light of the sun and made his way back to Lirian with the good news. He was welcomed with a hero's parade, and given a large ransom for his reward. As for Lirian and her people, they returned to the cave and collapsed the entrance, and were never bothered by garunda or shades again."

Leatherback let out a triumphant roar as Kyra closed the book.

The young apprentice reached out and stroked Leatherback just behind the jaw. "So, all we need to do now is find a garunda beast. If we can find one, we can use its blood to make a poison for the shade. Then, we can kill it."

The dragon let out a throaty growl. "Talk later, priests coming." He flicked out his tongue and his nostrils flared.

Kyra knew better than to argue with him. He was always able to sense them before they arrived. She quickly slid the book back into her bag and pulled out a brown, leather-bound book of folk tales. The last thing she wanted was for the priests to catch on to what she was after. So, from that moment until they came to perform their examination, she read from the book of children's stories.

CHAPTER 5

Feberik walked toward the large door flanked by two large, stone gryphons that seemed eternally frozen in the moment just before flight. He stared at the large, iron ring which hung against the wood of the Headmaster's door. The large man took in a breath before reaching for it. He thought back to what he had done at Caspen Manor, reliving the experience briefly in every smashing detail. Even then he had known he would be held accountable for his actions. It hadn't seemed to matter then.

Now, as he stared at the iron ring, he nodded his head, comfortable with the decision he had made at Caspen Manor, and prepared to take whatever was coming to him. He lifted his left hand and rapped on the door twice while his right hand reached out and pushed the door open.

"Yes, yes, come in, Master Orres," the headmaster called out from inside the chamber.

Orres had not been summoned to the headmaster's office, as would have normally been the case. Instead, he had been instructed to meet Headmaster Herion in a small library down the hall from the office. The room was perhaps only twenty feet deep and fifteen feet wide, with quite a large bit of space dedicated to tall, deep-shelved book cases. A small, arched window of stained glass was the only bit of decoration in the room, and nearly the sole source of light as well. A tall, iron candelabra was situated in the middle of the room, but otherwise the shadows played heavily upon the area.

Headmaster Herion was sitting in a large, overstuffed chair made of off-white cushions, repaired with green patches of cloth sewn into the arms. The old wizard smiled with twinkling blue eyes from behind his gold-rimmed spectacles. His face was dotted with a short, stubbly growth of white hair rather than his usually clean-shaven look. He was wearing a set of flannel pajamas, despite it being light outside and supper still in the process of being prepared.

"I would ask that you pardon my appearance," Headmaster Herion said in his gravelly voice. "I tend to enjoy the more lax schedule in the summer time, and that often means spending an entire day in my pajamas."

Feberik nodded.

"Close the door, will you?" Herion said.

Feberik closed the door and took a couple of steps into the room, clasping his hands behind his back and puffing out his chest as if he were about to be ripped apart by a commanding officer. "You wished to see me?"

Headmaster Herion nodded and brought a glass up to his lips, tilting it high into the air and pulling the very last drop of the burgundy liquid out before setting the glass down upon the small side table next to his chair.

"Have you ever spent a day in your pajamas?" Herion asked.

Feberik balked and frowned. "I'm sorry?"

"Hmm, yes, I bet you are if you have never tried it," Headmaster Herion said as he crossed his left leg over his right. "It is wonderfully liberating, which in turn helps a man think clearly."

Feberik scrunched his brow together and shook his head. "You asked to see me about my pajamas, sir?"

"No, no, of course not," Herion said as he slapped a hand to his knee. "I summoned you to ask about these."

Feberik looked down and watched as Headmaster Herion pulled out a small bundle of opened letters. He unfolded them, and then shuffled a few around that had somehow managed to be turned upside down.

"Do you happen to know a Miss Carlyn Marks?" Herion asked as he held up a letter.

Feberik shook his head. "Can't say that I do, sir."

"Well, it appears that you threw her husband through a window at Caspen Manor a short time ago."

"Sir, he pulled a dirk on me, I had little choice."

Headmaster Herion set the letter aside. "What about a Mrs. Caldwin?"

Feberik shook his head.

"It says here that you tossed her into the hallway."

Feberik shook his head. "I never roughed up a woman. I did help one off of Lord Caspen's lap, but all I did was pull her up and then move her toward the hall. I never threw her."

"I see," Headmaster Herion said as he set the letter down.

At that moment, it sunk in that Herion had called the woman 'Mrs. Caldwin,' and he had to ask for clarification. "Sir, that woman is married?"

"Oh yes, I know her husband well. Master Caldwin is serving in Ten Forts at the moment. I'm sure I have no idea why she would be at Caspen Manor, let alone sitting upon Lord Caspen's lap as you claim."

"Headmaster, you know me. I may be a bit rough, but I never lie."

Herion nodded his head. "No doubt," he said with a short flick of his wrist. "I have several more letters here. Some from nobility, others from the guards or servants of the manor. Feberik, you are not the judge of morality, do you understand?"

Feberik nodded. "I do, but I couldn't let it stand."

"What?" Herion asked. "Are you going to check in on Lord Caspen from time to time and make sure he never has any fun ever again for the rest of his life?"

Feberik cracked a smile he couldn't hide fast enough before Headmaster Herion saw it.

Herion stood up, tossing the rest of the letters onto the side table. He wagged a bony finger at Feberik. "Master Orres, I understand that you have an arrangement to marry Miss Kyra Caspen—"

"Dimwater, sir," Feberik corrected.

"Excuse me?" Herion said as his eyes grew stern.

"Her name is Dimwater, remember sir? She took her mother's name after the tribunal."

Herion sighed and shook his head. "Whatever you want to call her, the point is you can't go around bashing heads together every time they cause an offense. Don't think I don't remember the time you threatened Master Fenn. You have a temper, and you must learn to control it."

"It just didn't seem right," Feberik blurted out. "With all due respect, his wife's body isn't cold yet. He had only just denounced and disowned his daughter. He had no business throwing a drunken party in the first place, let alone cozying up to another man's wife."

"What another man does to ease his pains is none of your affair," Herion said plainly. "It may not sit well with you, but nothing you saw was against the law. Whenever you go out from these halls, you represent not only the Orres family, but Kuldiga Academy."

Feberik shook his head, his temper beginning to get the better of him. "And this school is supposed to stand for honor, or is that only something we tell the students during intake and graduation ceremonies?"

Herion sighed and went back to sit in the chair once more. "Calm down, Feberik, I didn't bring you here to discipline you for humbling a wayward noble. I brought you here because you need to understand that you must control your temper if you are to lead."

Feberik's mouth opened to say something, but then he stopped and left his jaw hanging as he looked to the headmaster. Lead what? What on Terramyr was the old man talking about.

"Truth is, Feberik, that other people have noticed you. You have made an impression upon those in authority. You have also riled some nobles, of course, but nothing will come of that. These letters have no force behind them, but I want you to read them after I dismiss you so you can try to manage your temper in the future." Headmaster Herion pointed back over his head toward the stained-glass window. "What do you see?"

Feberik, now utterly confused, took in a breath and shrugged. "I see a man standing upon a great serpent, running a spear through the serpent's head."

"Feberik, you know that Kuldiga Academy was founded to protect the realm, yes? It was not only to teach the next generation of warriors and wizards who would fight battles for our defense, but it was also created to establish an elite, powerful unit of well-trained individuals capable of accomplishing special tasks for the king. The window behind you symbolizes this unit."

Herion snapped his fingers and the light in the window brightened. The images of the man and the serpent extended out from the window until they were inches from Feberik's face.

"Look at the warrior, Feberik," Herion instructed. He was the first leader of this unit. The serpent is not to be taken literally, however. It represents a group of necromancers. Perhaps you have heard of the Zmea Necromancers?"

"I have," Feberik said with a nod.

Herion snapped his fingers again and the image faded back into the window. "The word 'Zmea' means snake in one of the arcane languages. Therefore, the image depicts the moment of our victory over them."

"What does this have to do with me?" Feberik asked.

"Do you know how the headmaster of Kuldiga Academy is chosen?" Herion asked, switching topics abruptly. Headmaster Herion rose from the chair and walked toward Feberik.

The large warrior shook his head. "I assume by seniority," he said with a shrug.

"Not even close," Herion said with a raspy laugh. "The headmaster is chosen from among those who serve in this special unit. That way, the unit can continue to operate fully, vanquishing evil and stamping out those that would use magic for nefarious purposes. A vote is cast within the cadre of that unit. The name with the most votes become the next headmaster." Headmaster Herion smiled again and placed his hands on Feberik's massive arms. "So what do you say? Want to take a peek at the unit?"

"What would I need to do?" Feberik asked.

"Simple, the unit is commanded by the headmaster, which currently is me. However, I answer directly to King Mathias for everything that is done. If you want a chance to mete out justice, this may be the most fulfilling opportunity that will ever cross your path."

"Can I tell Janik?"

Herion shook his head. "You will take an oath never to divulge your involvement to anyone. More than that, a spell will be put upon you so that you never break that trust, even if tortured by the enemy."

"The enemy?" Feberik echoed.

Herion nodded. "There are dark forces all about, my friend. Shadowfiends, necromancers, demons, dragons. The list goes on. To be sure, some of the other masters help from time to time, but if you want the full taste of action and glory, then you need to shake my hand and accept the offer."

Feberik nodded and looked down to Herion's hand. "If I refuse?"

Herion nodded solemnly. "Then I will wipe your memory of this part of our conversation and you will remember only that I scolded you for your over-zealous indignation at Caspen Manor. The choice is entirely yours. You will not be punished for refusing, but, if you want to help direct the course of Kuldiga Academy, then you should consider joining. I will add that you have no chance of becoming headmaster if you do not join. However, if you do become part of our unit, I have a feeling that in time you will become a top contender for the position."

Feberik took in a breath and thought very carefully. "Is it worth it?" he asked.

Herion smiled and his brilliantly white teeth shone brightly. "Feberik, this is what you were born for. These are special assignments from the king. We root out the most dangerous snake pits in the kingdom, and then we eradicate them. Think carefully before you refuse. I cannot make the offer twice if you say no."

Feberik studied Headmaster Herion's eyes for some time. Everything in his soul was pulling for it. Even despite the doubts in his mind, which were few, he knew what he would choose. The large man reached forward and took Herion's hand. "I'm in," he said.

"Excellent. Go now and take the rest of the night easy. Your induction will occur tomorrow." Headmaster Herion then wove a spell over Feberik and a silvery tingle ran through the man's body. "That's to make sure you don't say anything about it to anyone else. Go now, supper will be ready soon."

Feberik nodded and went for the door.

"Oh, and one more thing," Herion called out.

Feberik spun on his heels to regard the old wizard.

"You really should try spending a day or two in your pajamas, it does wonders for the mind and soul."

*****

Kyra opened the door to the classroom and went inside. The early morning sun beamed in from the east, illuminating several spots on the stone floor with its bright light. Cyrus was seated in his chair behind his desk. He was smoking a pipe today, and looking rather weary as the young apprentice made her way to her desk.

"Figure out the lesson I was trying to teach you?" Cyrus asked, referring to the passage about the wraith.

Kyra nodded. "I think so."

"Good, then tell me what you learned," Cyrus said as he leaned back and puffed three small rings of smoke into the air.

"The text doesn't mention this, but I tried to ask *why* the wraith would attack."

"And?"

"The boy must have had something," Kyra said. "It took

me some time, but I think it wanted his blood."

"His blood?" Cyrus echoed. "Why on Terramyr would it want that? A wraith is not a vampire."

Kyra shook her head. "Maybe it didn't want the actual blood, but maybe there was something about the apprentice that drew the wraith near. I thought of blood because of what happened with me. The first time the wraith attacked me, I had cut myself on a thorn. Now that I know that I have a…" Kyra couldn't say the words out loud. Try as she might, she couldn't shake the shame she felt whenever she thought of what her true father was.

"A vampire," Cyrus said for her.

Kyra nodded. "What I mean is, with that kind of blood, perhaps I attracted the wraith somehow. So, maybe the apprentice cut himself as well, or maybe it was just more obvious, but I would wager that he had something in *his* blood that attracted the wraith."

"Why should vampire blood attract a wraith?" Cyrus pressed, still puffing on his pipe.

Kyra thought for a moment. "I haven't quite figured that all out. I know that a shade is like a vampire, only a shade will absorb energy and magical essence, and doesn't need physical contact in order to extract it. So, I thought either the wraith is naturally drawn to vampire blood, like a moth to a torch, or perhaps the wraith hunts vampires because they struggle against shades."

Cyrus smiled and nodded slightly. "Not bad," he said. "There is still a long way to go, but that is a good start. Now, put that together with the added threat to the wraith. We know there was a powerful master wizard there with the apprentice, so why would the wraith attack so openly?"

Kyra shook her head. "Everything we have read shows that wraiths, though animalistic and fierce, are intelligent creatures. Therefore, it must have wanted something from the boy, or perhaps perceived the apprentice as a greater threat. Otherwise, it wouldn't risk itself like that."

Cyrus nodded again. "I have researched this particular

encounter quite thoroughly. You are on the right track. However, it wasn't the boy's blood, or anything else about the boy himself that attracted the wraith. While that may have played some part in your encounter, the apprentice in this particular encounter had something in his possession that was highly prized by both the wraith, and the wraith's master."

"A shade?" Kyra asked.

"A powerful shade who was known by the name Mitingyra," Cyrus confirmed. "She was hunting a special artifact. The young apprentice had it in his possession, but he did not know the value of he had at the time. The shade sent the wraith to attack him on that particular day, because on the following day the young apprentice was to be enrolled in Calbeton School of Magic and Witchcraft. Had the wraith not attacked when it did, it would then have to try to take the item from the boy amidst more than a dozen experienced wizards, rather than only one."

"What was it looking for?" Kyra asked. "The shade I mean, what did she seek?"

"That is a lesson for another time," Cyrus said quickly as he pulled his pipe from the corner of his mouth and set it down in a red bowl on his desk. "However, I can tell you how she died."

"Yes, please," Kyra said. "How was she killed?" She must have acted overeager, for Cyrus cocked a brow and narrowed one eye on her before he finally told her the story.

"A particularly fine young wizard hunted her down and destroyed her."

Kyra leaned forward, waiting for more details. As the seconds passed and Cyrus didn't say anything else, she frowned. "That's it?" she asked. "I thought you were going to tell me the whole story, or maybe at least let me read about it."

Cyrus smiled and folded his arms. "You can't read about it. In fact, it is only a story that a handful of wizards even are aware of."

"So are you going to tell me?" Kyra asked impatiently.

Cyrus nodded. "Just thought I would have a bit of fun

with you," he said. "Of course I will tell you."

Kyra sighed and shook her head. "That was not funny."

Cyrus shrugged. "I know about the book you took from the library," Cyrus said flatly. "I know you read about Ravenel and the Garunda."

Kyra stiffened. How could he have known? She had hidden the book in her bag. She had only taken it out in the forest, and Cyrus wasn't even aware of where the aspen wood was.

Cyrus held up a hand. "I'm not going to lecture you, Kyra. Icadion knows it wouldn't do any good even if I did. You're too stubborn, and too proud to admit something is beyond your reach. But, do at least listen to this story, all right?"

Kyra nodded.

"As I said, I studied the encounter thoroughly. No one else had ever put it all together. As far as I knew, I was the only wizard that was even aware the wraith had been sent to recover an artifact. I researched through all the materials I could find on the subject. Eventually, I uncovered what the artifact was."

"What was it?" Kyra asked. "Was it a weapon, or a powerful magic spell?"

Cyrus shook his head. "I told you before, that is a lesson for another time. You are not ready for that quite yet. Let's just say that it was something very ancient, dark, and extremely dangerous. As I said before, the young apprentice had no idea what he had found. He thought it was something else entirely. If my calculations were right, this particular item had been missing, and presumed destroyed, for centuries. In any case, once I realized what it was he had found, I knew immediately that we were dealing with something very dangerous. Knowing that most, if not all wraiths serve masters more powerful than they, I dug into what may have been in the area.

"The encounter with the young wizard had been well before my time, but of course a shade can live forever, like a vampire, unless it is killed. The terrifying part was that the artifact was indeed lost during the encounter. Therefore, even though the wraith died, I assumed that its master had returned for the artifact. I began my search at the location of the encounter. I tracked the traces of dark magic and searched the whole of the area by the stream where it happened, but I didn't find the artifact. This would have been roughly eighteen years ago now, about three years before you were born.

"When I failed to find the artifact, I knew the shade had it. So, I researched for another year, hunting down the vile creature. Like you, I read Ravenel and the Garunda." Cyrus stopped then and pulled a metal amulet out from under his clothes. It was a long, rectangular piece of gold with several runes engraved upon it. "So, I had this fashioned at the hands of a dwarf named Al, who is a great blacksmith living in Buktah. He laughed when I told him I was hunting a shade, but he obliged nonetheless."

"It worked?" Kyra asked, her eyes fixated upon the amulet.

Cyrus nodded. "When I finally found the shade, it protected me from her powers. However, I still had to deal with a large and ferocious garunda."

"You've seen one?!" Kyra shouted.

"Seen it? I killed it," Cyrus corrected. "I took its head, and then used its blood to tip arrows in, just like Ravenel did. Of course, I am a wizard, not an archer, so when I found the shade, we battled with magic until I saw my moment, and then I used my magic to throw all of the arrows. Half of them missed, but two landed in her heart and three went into her skull. Just like in the story, the garunda blood prevented her from healing. She burst into flame and I can still hear her screams. They haunt me in the quiet times." Cyrus looked down at the desk then and his lower lip quivered. "It's a sound I doubt I shall ever escape from."

"Did you find it?" Kyra asked after giving the old wizard a couple of moments to ground himself.

He frowned and shook his head. "No," he said. "The shade did not have it."

"So what did you do?"

Cyrus held up a finger. "Before we get to that, let me show you something." Cyrus reached up and pulled at the neck of his tunic. Three large, purple scars ran across his collar bone toward his neck. "The garunda did this, as well as shattered two of my ribs with its psionic blast." The wizard rose from his seat and turned around, conjuring magic with his right hand to lift his hair and show the back of his neck. There were three purple scars there as well. "I was lucky that this attack didn't take my head off." Cyrus turned back around and then lifted his tunic to show a strange series of three round scars in his abdomen, just left of his belly-button. "These I got from the shade. She nearly killed me with her magic."

"You're telling me it's too dangerous to go after the shade that attacked me," Kyra guessed with a nod.

Cyrus grinned. "You probably won't listen, but yes, that is what I am telling you."

"If the shade killed my mother, then I want to go after it."

"If the shade killed your mother, it will have no trouble killing you," Cyrus countered. "I'm not saying let him go, I am only saying that you should wait."

"Wait for what?" Kyra asked.

"Wait until you are stronger. Train for the fight. I can help you, and Icadion knows your dragon can be a source of help as well, but you aren't ready yet. You have to give it time. You understand, don't you?"

Kyra sighed and closed her eyes. Logically she understood the old wizard's words. It made sense. However, she had something that neither Cyrus nor Ravenel did. Kyra had a dragon on her side. Still, she remembered her mother's words of advice. She decided to let Cyrus believe that his advice had sunk in. She nodded her head.

"Will you train me for the shade?" she asked.

"More than that, I will go with you when the time comes to put it down," Cyrus promised.

Kyra nodded and then decided to change the topic, thus making it appear that her mind had released its focus on the shade. "Did you ever find the artifact?"

"I thought I had once," Cyrus admitted. "You know that I accompanied Janik to rescue your mother, yes?"

Kyra nodded.

"I had believed that the vampire that held your mother prisoner had found the relic, but the artifact was not there." Cyrus sighed and his eyes grew distant as he looked up to the window. "I spent some time after that searching for it, but I never did find it." Cyrus shook his head and rubbed his hands over his shoulders. "Come, let me teach you some more effective ward spells."

"I know plenty of wards," Kyra said quickly.

Cyrus flicked his wrist and a blast of air pummeled Kyra, throwing her and the desk back several yards to crash across the floor. "You need more practice," Cyrus said dryly.

Gone was the old wizard reminiscing about glories past.

Now he was the same as always -he crazy old wizard that was anything but predictable.

Kyra pushed up from the floor and dusted herself off.

"Come on now, Kyra," Cyrus said. "The shade will not give you any warning either."

The young sorceress nodded and prepared a ward spell just as another blast of air came at her. Even with her ward, the force of Cyrus' spell had her sliding backward across the stone floor.

"Again," Cyrus called out as she centered herself and prepared for another volley. "We'll work on this until you can deflect my spells. If you have half as much talent as I believe you do, then we should be able to move on tomorrow to a different kind of ward that can dispel illusions. We'll have you ready for the shade in time."

*****

Only an hour after the lesson with Kyra had ended, Cyrus was sitting at a large, stone table in a great chamber dug out from a stone mountain. A warlock approached from a magically sealed doorway on the far side. Cyrus wondered when the suspicious lot would welcome him into their inner sanctum. He had been working with them for some time now, and he was tired of doing their chores.

The warlock sat down and tilted his head to the right. Cyrus noted that this new face was much younger than the representatives of the Order of the All Seeing Eye he had previously met with.

"How does the young sorceress fare?" he asked, fiddling with the sleeves of his black robes until the purple trim around the cuffs was fully displayed properly. A long hood hung loosely over the man's face, partially covering his features. Like all the others Cyrus had seen before, a medallion hung around this warlock's neck in the shape of a gleaming triangle of gold enclosing the image of an open eye. "Has she yet pledged her service and loyalty?"

Cyrus shook his head. "As I said before, the girl is headstrong, and her mother's murder has given her a kind of raging tunnel vision that makes her unwelcoming to any notion other than revenge. However, I do believe I am gaining her trust. She sees me as an ally, especially now that I am sharing her secret regarding the dragon."

"Our order is pleased with the progress."

"Tell me why the girl is so important to you."

The warlock laughed and shook his head. "My brother has already told you all that we shall ever divulge on that matter. She will be a great ally for us."

"Yes, I remember."

The warlock leaned across the table. "If you were to swear fealty to the Order of the All-seeing Eye, I could shed light on some of the visions we have seen of the future."

"I don't need your visions," Cyrus said.

"Then it must be something else that causes you concern," the warlock said. "Is it the fact that the young sorceress has the same name as your late wife?"

Cyrus bristled and his head pulled back. Anger rushed through his veins and it was all he could do to keep from lashing out. "You have no right to mention my wife."

"Just see to it that you do not baby the apprentice out of some misplaced affection or lingering grief. You are, after all, indebted to us."

"Yes, but you know, the information I have gotten from you has never been entirely accurate. First, you tell me that the shade has the dagger. So, I tracked her down and killed her. Then, after that you tell me that Bhaltair the vampire has the dagger. So, I go with Janik to the vampire's lair and the dagger is not there either. Now, you can't even find the dagger. All you can say is that I have to find it before Severin does. Perhaps I would be better off on my own."

"Is that a threat?" the young warlock hissed.

"It is merely an observation," Cyrus replied. "Perhaps your visions are not as powerful as you claim. In that case, I would do well to work the riddle out on my own."

"The dagger is still tied with Caspen Manor," the warlock said. "If you want it, you must look there."

"I have looked there already," Cyrus replied.

"Then the other option is to go after Severin directly," the warlock said.

Cyrus nodded. "I just told the young sorceress about my fight with the shade," he said.

"You told her of the dagger?!" the warlock shouted.

"No," Cyrus said. "I told her only that there was an artifact of great power that I was trying to recover. She doesn't know what it is."

"Then why tell her anything about it?"

"To whet her appetite. She thirsts for revenge, as I said, and has already discovered that a garunda beast's blood can aid in slaying shades. I merely gave her a push in the direction I wanted her to go."

"She will try to hunt the shade," the warlock said.

"If she is successful, then perhaps I can still sneak up on Severin."

"Doubtful," the warlock said. "After your fight with this new shade, I am sure Severin has already been warned of your involvement."

Cyrus nodded. "Perhaps so, but it is still worth a chance. Let the girl and the dragon hunt down the shade, and then I will interrogate the shade to find Severin."

"The Order of the All-Seeing Eye wants the girl alive, if possible, so she can join us."

"And I want the dagger," Cyrus said. "The deal hasn't changed." Cyrus pushed up from the table. "Besides, from what I understand, the order doesn't care much if the girl dies, just so long as she doesn't become your enemy, am I right?"

The warlock sat silent for a moment before nodding. "We prefer her allegiance, but we would accept her death as well."

"Then it is settled," Cyrus said. "Either her pursuit for revenge will help open her mind to joining your group, or the shade or Severin will kill her, thus ending the threat she poses to you. Either way, your desires are fulfilled."

"Very well," the warlock said.

"I must return to the academy. I will keep you informed of our progress."

CHAPTER 6

Kyra sat in the library. She had pulled a small end table and a stool into what she now thought of as *her* part of the library. Even when she wasn't studying about dragons, she brought all the books she wanted to read to the seventh section on the third floor. Hardly anyone else came to that part of the library, and those who did were either lost, or passing through to another part of the library.

Today, Kyra was not reading about dragons, though she did have the next of the Chronicles of Kendualdern out on the table, along with the notes she had been making as she translated the arcane text, just in case she felt in the mood to continue on with that project. The Chronicles had been the last birthday present she had ever received from her mother, and now that she had gone through Ascension front to back a dozen times, she had recently begun work on Dominion. She paused for a moment, running her hand lovingly over the book's cover and remembering the night her mother had caught her in Lord Caspen's study, trying to decipher the titles on this and its companion books. She smirked at herself then, thinking of how strange she was compared to the other apprentices who would be arriving at school in three months. She couldn't imagine anyone else she knew scaling a wall to break into a forbidden reading room to try and translate ancient runes on a book that was locked in a case.

Shaking herself from her thoughts, she turned to the book she had selected. This morning she was busy studying wraiths. From what she could tell, there was hardly anything in the library that mentioned shades, but there were additional volumes about wraiths. Since the wraith she had killed had been working for the shade who had attacked her and Leatherback, hunting her down for its master, she hoped that by learning the habits of wraiths, she might uncover clues about where the shade might be.

If Cyrus had been able to find his answers, then so would she. The young sorcery apprentice already knew that she could use a dwarf charm, and not necessarily a weapon, to ward against the shade's most deadly magic. So, now it was a matter of finding garunda beasts so she could harvest their blood.

Unfortunately, none of the books she had read shed any light on garunda beasts. Though they both seemed to be associated with shades, the passages about wraiths didn't mention the garunda at all. Nor did they say much about where wraiths lived. From everything she could find, it was believed that wraiths lived between the plane of the living and the plane of the dead. It wasn't known how they appeared, or where they went when they disappeared.

She set the last book she had pulled on wraiths to the side and let out an exasperated sigh as she slumped back into her chair, her body sliding down slightly, forcing her head forward. She closed her eyes and tried to think. She had already looked for books on garunda beasts after reading Ravenel and the Garunda. There were no other books in the library that mentioned the animal.

Kyra jerked her head to the side, cracking her neck a bit to relieve the cramp that had crept up on her during her library session, and then she reached out for a nearby book on dragons. If she couldn't find answers today, then at least she could have a bit of fun learning more about dragons.

Suddenly a hand was on her shoulder and she jumped in her chair, uttering a high-pitched squeak and jolting around.

"Easy there, it's just me," Kathair Lepkin said as he backed away a pace.

"Why must you sneak up on me?" Kyra asked.

"Just havin' a bit of fun," he said with a boyish grin. "Sorry, shall I go back out and knock?"

"No, how about you go out and stay out?"

"Ouch," Kathair said as he moved around to look at the books on the table. His blue eyes scanned the titles and he reached out to turn one of the books over.

"It's research," Kyra said.

"Mhm," Kathair mused as he inspected another two books. "Quick question," he said.

"What is it?" Kyra asked impatiently.

"Why are you hunting the garunda?"

Kyra's mouth dropped open. Other than Cyrus and Leatherback, she hadn't told anyone about wanting to find the shade, and only Leatherback knew she was actively hunting the garunda, so how had Kathair guessed her secret? "I don't know what you mean," she said as she collected herself and sat up straight. "These books are about wraiths."

"Yes, but you are hunting garunda," Kathair said. "I bet you are trying to find a connection between the wraiths and the garunda, am I right?"

"Kathair," she began.

"Ooo, you know I hate that name," he said as he scrunched his face into a sour expression.

"Well, *you* know I don't like it when you sneak up on me," Kyra fired back.

"Listen, I'm more than just good with a sword, I have a working brain. It isn't too hard to see what you are doing here."

"It's that obvious?" Kyra asked.

Kathair smiled wide and winked. "Well, that, and you left your book bag open behind you and I can see that you have the story of Ravenel and the Garunda in there."

Kyra breathed out and pushed Kathair away from the table. "Now you are going through my things," she snorted.

Kathair shrugged. "Actually, your bag tipped over, look for yourself."

Kyra turned around and saw that in fact the bag had spilled over, and the book he mentioned was on top. "Still," she said as she collected her things into the bag and propped it against the table leg. "How did you gather that I was hunting garunda if you saw one book about them and all of these books about wraiths and dragons?"

Kathair put a finger to his nose. "I told you, I'm smart."

Kyra shook her head, but couldn't hide the grin emerging on her face.

"Listen," Kathair said as his tone lost its playfulness and became serious. "The truth is, there have been some strange attacks in the countryside. I have overheard the dragon slayers talking about it, but they won't tell me exactly what is happening. All I know, is some dark creatures are prowling around. I don't mean to pry, but given how your mother was murdered, I started looking into it."

"Why?" Kyra asked defensively.

Kathair leaned in and spoke in hushed tones, glancing over his shoulder before speaking. "I meant no offense, just, it seemed odd that these attacks are happening more and more now. I was with the dragon slayers for a couple days after I saw you in the woods. I listened when they thought I was sleeping. It seems that they hadn't heard about these animals, or any attacks, until after your mother was murdered. So, naturally I thought it might all be connected. I started researching it too. I found a connection between wraiths and garunda, and then I found a connection between the garunda and shades." Kathair pointed to Kyra's book bag. "There is another copy of this book," he held up the volume containing Ravenel and the Garunda, "here at the academy, but it's in the headmaster's library."

"What were you doing in the headmaster's library?" Kyra asked, a quick thrill of excitement shooting through her at the thought of another student willing to break into a forbidden location for the sake of a book.

"Never mind that," Kathair said. He reached behind his back and pulled a small book out that had been tucked into the back of his pants. "This is a journal from a wizard. It talks about the connection between wraiths and garunda beasts."

Kyra snatched it out of the boy's hands and opened the

first page. She looked down and saw the name printed upon the page and then looked back up to Kathair with unbelieving eyes. "This isn't *some* wizard's journal. This is Headmaster Herion's journal!"

Kathair shrugged. "Don't get caught with it," he suggested. "Listen, I have to go, but tomorrow morning we are supposed to go and meet with a farmer to the south. I guess he sent a falcon to the school and said his sheep have been attacked every night for the last week. At first he thought it was wolves, but now he wants the school to send a wizard to help him. The attacking animals are leaving the dismembered carcasses on the ground for the carrion birds. It's like whatever is killing the sheep is doing it for fun."

Kyra nodded. "You want me to go with Leatherback tonight," she guessed.

"Not hardly," he said quickly as he backed away. "Apprentices should never get involved with such things." He winked at her. "However, if you and your dragon can keep quiet, maybe you can find what is attacking the sheep."

Kyra sighed through her teeth and shook her head. "If we get caught, then the farmer will announce that there is a dragon."

Kathair's smile faded and he nodded. "It is risky, but I thought I should tell you, just in case it is connected with your mother. If you don't want to go, then I will be going with the dragon slayers. I can report back to you with what I find if you like."

Kyra shook her head. "No, we'll go. Where is the farm?"

*****

Only once the moon was high in the starry sky did Kyra climb up to sit upon Leatherback. The dragon purred, and then went deathly silent as it waited for her instructions. She took in a few steadying breaths, but it did little to slow her racing heart. She reached out with a slightly trembling hand and stroked Leatherback's neck.

"Ready?" Kyra asked in a whisper.

Leatherback nodded his head.

Kyra took in one more breath and then tapped Leatherback twice on his neck. She held on tight to the makeshift harness she had placed upon him as the giant animal lurched backward and arched his back upward. He leapt so high that he cleared the tops of the aspens in the grove by thirty feet before he needed to engage his wings. One mighty flap bowed the treetops toward the ground and shook leaves from the branches as dragon and rider were propelled upward. The wind bit down, cool and crisp on Kyra's face and shoulders. They ascended upward until they broke through a large cloud, hoping to use its cover to avoid being seen.

"South," Kyra said as they levelled out in the air. "We are looking for a farm that is secluded, nestled in some hills to the south of Borshen."

Leatherback growled and started flapping his wings more earnestly. The mist from the clouds below wafted out and upward, curling behind them as they soared through the night sky. Kyra kept her eyes upon the stars above for much of the journey. Her feet were secured in leather stirrups, so she let go of the reins with her hands and held her arms out to her sides. She closed her eyes as the wind rushed all around her, her body lifting and falling gently as Leatherback pumped his wings.

The two flew for over an hour in the darkness. The moon was high at their backs and the clouds were beginning to thin. Leatherback scanned the area below. As they passed over the small town of Borshen, they saw only a few buildings with any amount of light coming from their windows, all the rest were still and quiet.

Ten minutes later, they were soaring over a large field nestled between great, rolling hills. Even from their great height, Kyra could see the sheep sleeping in groups. As they passed over the flock, Kyra saw a small campfire.

"We'll have to be careful," Kyra said. "If the shepherds spot us, we'll be in trouble."

Leatherback purred softly and tilted his head just enough

to look at her and offer a short nod. He understood.

The dragon banked slightly to the left, soaring in a wide arc to return to the hills. They then circled the sky long enough until they found a safe place to land. A thick copse of trees stood atop a hill on the northeast side of the valley overlooking the sheep. It was also downwind from the flock. The dragon gently descended and touched upon the ground as softly as if he were no bigger than a robin. Leatherback then bent low to the ground, huddling up against the trees to help conceal himself.

Kyra stayed in her spot, sitting upon the dragon's back and scanning the area around them. Every once in a while, a sheep would bleat and move a few paces before laying back down in the valley, but no beast came for a long time. The young sorceress was almost worried that it would not show at all. Or, perhaps the beast was coming from downwind also, and would smell Leatherback before it approached. Time crawled by as she kept searching the darkness.

Finally, she saw something appear atop a hill to the north. Leatherback had seen it to, for he lifted his head and turned to taste the air. Kyra couldn't make out detailed features in the soft moonlight, but she could see the animal's silhouette. It sat upon its haunches and turned its head, presumably scanning the valley. Soon, a second animal came and sat beside it.

Kyra's heart jumped. Had she been lucky enough to catch two garunda beasts?

One of the animals moved along the top of the hill, and Kyra got a good look at the creature's profile. Her heart sank. This was no garunda beast. It wasn't even four-legged. It walked upright upon two legs. It had long, curved arms that swung in front of it as it walked, counter-balanced by three tails that swished in the night behind it.

Kyra thought back to the research she had done. She was sure she knew what this creature was. It wasn't a garunda, but it was still a dark, evil monster. She bent low to Leatherback, hoping to remain hidden from the two creatures that were now stalking down the hill toward the valley.

"Are you ready?" Kyra asked.

Leatherback snarled in a quiet, soft voice that she barely heard. "Ready."

Kyra nodded. "We have to hit them fast and with full power. If the fight drags on, then the shepherds will see us."

Leatherback nodded. "We kill fast," he said resolutely.

"Okay," Kyra began, "you fly for the one in front. I'll hit the second one with my magic."

Leatherback's muscles tensed beneath her like a tightly coiled spring with teeth and claws.

"Now!" Kyra whispered.

Leatherback launched into the air, clearing the entire hill they had been hiding upon before using his wings. Two flaps of his massive, leathery wings put Kyra within striking distance. She reached out and sent a bolt of lightning out from her hand. It zipped through the night sky, flashing blue and silvery light across the grass until it struck the bipedal monster in the chest. The creature howled and flailed its arms, which she now saw were really long hooks that could be used to mutilate its prey.

A moment later, Leatherback snarled and jerked downward. Kyra reacted instantly, reaching for the reins and steadying herself. She looked down to see Leatherback rip his foe in half by pulling it with the talons on his forelegs. The creature never even knew what had hit him. The lifeless pieces fell to the ground with a sick, wet *thabump!*

Sheep were up and scattering now, bleating and calling out their alarm.

"Finish it," Kyra called out. "We're out of time."

Leatherback banked hard as Kyra pulled in against him. The mighty dragon was so close to the ground that he half flew, half ran along the hillside toward the second creature. Kyra's magic had stunned it, but not killed it. The monster let out a terrible scream, and then turned to flee, but Leatherback was far too quick. The dragon lashed out with his left foreleg and took the creature's head from its body. The legs stopped, and the body remained motionless, standing in place for a brief second before Leatherback's tail slammed into it, knocking it across the hillside. The dragon then dropped the creature's head and turned to the north, barely clearing the tall hill and escaping into the clouds before Kyra noticed the shepherds cresting over the southern hill with torches.

She smiled and patted Leatherback on the shoulder. "That was good," she said.

"No garunda," Leatherback said.

Kyra nodded. "True, but we took care of things that the shepherds never would have been able to beat on their own. We may have even saved their lives tonight."

Leatherback purred softly and flew back toward the aspen wood.

When they arrived and settled into the cool glade, Kyra was surprised to see Njar sitting upon the large rock that had become his habitual perch. His furry form was only slightly visible in the darkness, but she knew it was him. The satyr slid off of the rock and approached them.

"You went out hunting?" he asked pointedly.

Kyra nodded. "Of a sort," she replied evenly. She slid down from Leatherback and pet the dragon once more on the side of his neck. Leatherback turned his neck around so he could nuzzle her with the top of his snout. Even with his soft, gentle sign of affection, the dragon managed to nearly topple Kyra onto her face. She stumbled forward two steps and Njar shot his hands out to steady her.

"What were you hunting?" Njar probed.

"Some shepherds to the south had reported that their flocks were being killed. We went to help."

Njar shook his head. "Let the shepherds deal with wolves. If they were to see you, Leatherback would be condemned to death, and you would have to flee as well. You have already been blessed to receive lenience from those in authority, but don't underestimate how thin their tolerance is. If the public at large were to discover that a dragon lived in the Middle Kingdom, they would call for his blood.

Leatherback snarled and spat a small orb of blue fire into the air. "I hear you," Leatherback said.

Njar nodded. "I don't say this to upset either of you. I say it as a sincere warning."

Kyra finally put all the signs together and recalled the name of the beasts that they had seen. She blurted it out, partly because she was happy that she finally remembered what they were, and partly to show Njar that they were doing something important. "They were wylkins," she said. "Two of them, in fact."

Njar stepped back from Kyra and glanced from her to Leatherback. "Wylkins you say?"

Kyra nodded. "I remember now. I had read about them before, but I couldn't remember their name when I saw them. They had three tails, walked on two legs, had large, scimitar like hooks for arms, and they had spikes along their shoulders and backs."

"You killed them?" Njar pressed.

"I hit one with a lightning bolt, but it only stunned him, so Leatherback finished him off along with the other."

"Did you use fire?" Njar asked as he turned to Leatherback.

The dragon shook his massive head. "No, I used claws."

Njar nodded. "That is good. A dragon's flame could be seen for a long way, and there is nothing else quite like it. I won't say that what you did was smart, but I am impressed that you found and killed two wylkins."

Kyra smiled smugly. "It was nothing."

Njar shook his head. "But tell me this, what were you after?"

Kyra's smile faded. Did Njar know about the garunda beasts also? Surely he hadn't heard her read the story out loud to Leatherback, so how could he know? Perhaps he had seen a vision in those magical pools he had shown her before. That must be it; he had looked into the future.

"I was hunting garunda beasts," she said honestly.

Njar nodded and reached up to stroke his beard thoughtfully. "You are going to hunt the shade that attacked you, aren't you?"

Kyra folded her arms. "Why does everyone seem so surprised by this? He killed my mother."

"I am a satyr," Njar said. "I do not understand vengeance. I seek balance. If you tell me that you are hunting this creature out of anger, then I would caution you to alter your path. Remember, you must help Leatherback stave off Nagar's Blight. The more you remove him from this glade, the more the power of the curse will affect him."

Kyra hung her head low and nodded. She hadn't thought of that. She had been so focused on the garunda that her only thought was of getting closer to the shade. "I understand, she said."

Njar produced a staff in his hand and held it out. "I noticed you had misplaced your staff. Remember, it was made with the same magic as that which flows in this glade. If you must hunt outside, then take it with you at all times. It does not offer the full protection of the glade, but it will help Leatherback. I'll make a harness for it attached to the side of your saddle so you can carry it easier."

Kyra nodded. "I am sorry," she said. She took the staff. "I promise I will keep it with us."

"One more thing," Njar said. "If you were to tell me that you seek to kill the shade in order to protect and restore the natural balance in this realm, then I would grant my blessing upon your quest."

Kyra looked up at him, wondering whether he might be willing to help her in a more active capacity. "What do you mean, exactly?"

Njar sighed and shrugged. "I may know a thing or two that could help."

Kyra shook her head. "I can't lie to you. I would do it partly to rid the Middle Kingdom of the shade and his evil powers, and to stop the creatures which obey him, but mostly I am hunting him to avenge my mother."

Njar stepped in and placed a heavy hand on Kyra's shoulder. "Would you hunt him even if your activities threatened to kill Leatherback? Remember, those priests will see the taint in him. I will see the taint in him. If it appears to grow at all, we will use all of our powers to destroy him."

Leatherback snarled fiercely, but Kyra held out her hand. The dragon's eyes glowed angrily and the fire burned in his throat.

Njar pressed his questions. "If you had to choose between protecting Leatherback, and slaying the shade, which would you choose?"

Kyra sighed and looked longingly to her angry friend. She would be torn if she could not find and kill the shade, but she could not risk losing her best friend. "If it came to that choice, then Leatherback and I would fly north, and we would forget about the shade," she said.

Njar patted her shoulder. "Then I will lend what help I can. Go back and sleep tonight. Return tomorrow, and after the priests leave, I will show you something."

"What?" Kyra asked.

Njar turned and walked away. An orb of light opened up, and Kyra could see Viverandon through the portal. The satyr stopped and turned back. "I know of strange creatures attacking throughout the Middle Kingdom. They are dark, evil beings, so it is hard for me to completely discern what they are, but perhaps we can find the garunda together. I will show you what I know tomorrow."

*****

Linny shook off the early morning chills that had grabbed hold of her on the short walk she had taken from the carriage to the entrance to the school. The sun had not quite peeked over the horizon, and the weak light that was seeping into the area did little to chase away the yawns that beset the young girl as a result of her bumpy ride to Kuldiga Academy. She shuffled her feet nervously as the man in front of her limped terribly, nearly dragging his left leg with each step. It was painful to watch him walk, and the young girl could only wonder what had caused such a deformity in his leg and his bent wrist.

When they finally stopped in front of an open door, the man with the crooked hand knocked on the doorway and an old voice instructed them to enter.

Linny passed through the doorway to see an elderly man sitting in a chair reading a book while dressed in what appeared to be his pajamas. The man looked up and smiled from behind a pair of gold-rimmed glasses.

"Janik, what has you up here so early this morning?"

The man with the crooked hand bowed his head and then replied, "Headmaster, this is Linny Ravia. She has come for the remainder of summer term in preparation for her first year here at the academy."

The headmaster closed his book and stood on his feet, pouting out his lower lip and clasping his hands behind his back as he approached them. "It's a bit late to begin summer term," he said. "You are already a couple of weeks behind. There will be much to catch up on."

Linny nodded. "I will do my best, sir," she said in a mousy voice.

The headmaster smiled. "Well, I suppose we can make it work. What school will you be in?"

Linny didn't understand the question. She was here at *this* school. Where else would she intend to go?

Janik answered for her. "I have her papers," he said. "She is studying sorcery."

The headmaster frowned. "Hmm." He reached out and took the papers in hand, shuffling through them and giving them only a cursory once-over. "Well, all of the sorcery masters are away at the moment on assignment. You'll have to give me some time to scrounge up a suitable instructor."

Linny nodded.

The headmaster tossed the papers onto the chair behind him and then turned back with a smile. "My administrator is on leave for the summer as well, but I will have him process your paperwork properly upon his return. Until then, let's have you bunk with the other first-years that are here for summer term."

Janik cleared his throat. "Beg your pardon, Headmaster, but we don't have any other first-years here. We are renovating their dorms this summer, as you instructed."

"Ah yes, quite right," the headmaster said with a nod. "Very well then, I have an idea. Janik, take her up to bunk with Kyra Dimwater."

"With Kyra, sir?" Janik echoed.

The headmaster nodded. "Sure," he said. "She is the only other apprentice sorceress here at the moment. Besides, she is only going in to her second year, so she is close enough to young..." The headmaster stopped and looked to the young girl. "What was your name again, dear?"

"Linny, sir," she said.

"Right! As I was saying, Kyra will be close enough to young Linny's age. Once the renovations are done, and the other incoming first-years arrive, we can move her back into her proper age group."

"As you wish," Janik said with a slight nod. "Come on, Linny, let's go."

CHAPTER 7

Kyra was had only been able to get a few hours of rest by the time she had made it back to Kuldiga Academy and before someone knocked on her door. She stretched and yawned, trying to shake the sleepiness from her body. Another knock came at the door.

"I'm coming," Kyra said wearily.

The door cracked open just a bit.

"Kyra, are you dressed?"

Kyra smiled when she recognized the voice. It was Janik, a once powerful warrior who had saved her mother from the vampire, along with Cyrus. Now, he was reduced to a janitor within Kuldiga Academy, but he never appeared to her to mind. His face was always smiling when she saw him. More than that, he had become a welcome buffer from Feberik.

"I'm dressed, come in," she said.

The door swung open and Janik limped into the room. He waved with his good arm while his gnarled left wrist hung stiff at his side. His green eyes seemed to sparkle as he entered the room. "I have a special announcement," Janik said.

Kyra smiled and then she noticed something behind the large man. At first she couldn't tell what it was, but soon she saw it was a head of hair. Kyra leaned to the side on her bed, trying to get a better look.

"This is Linny Ravia," Janik said. "She has come to the academy early and Headmaster Herion has decided to bunk her with you."

Kyra balked. "Don't the new students usually live with their peers?" Kyra asked.

Janik nodded. "We are renovating the dorms for the first-year girls. If you two don't get on together nicely, we can move her back after the start of the year, but until then, Headmaster Herion thought it best for you to show her the ropes. Maybe even help her with some of her studies a bit."

A young girl stepped out from behind Janik as the man turned and gently pushed her forward.

"Don't be shy now," Janik said.

Kyra smiled at the sandy-haired girl. Linny had gorgeous blue eyes, a narrow nose, and freckles across her face. Her hair was tied up with a pair of green silk bows that matched her dress.

"Hello," Linny said nervously.

Kyra couldn't help but realize that this was going to make visiting Leatherback quite difficult. Still, there was something about the girl that she felt drawn to, though she had no idea what that might be.

Janik turned back to the hallway and waved. A pair of large men shuffled into the room and set a large trunk down, then turned and left. Janik then nodded to Kyra and smiled.

"Perhaps you two can get to know each other. Breakfast will be ready shortly."

Kyra smiled to him and nodded. Linny wrung her hands and bit her lower lip, her eyes shifting to look at her trunk. Janik limped out of the room and closed the door behind himself.

"What are you going to study?" Kyra asked.

Linny offered a half-smile. "Magic, I think," she said in a mousy voice.

"You think?" Kyra echoed. "Don't you know?"

Linny shrugged. "Not really. I heard that I have magic in my blood, but I have never tried anything before. I don't know anything about it, really."

Kyra thought her statement odd, after all, having magical ability was something as natural to her as breathing, and she couldn't remember a time when she had been unable to do simple spells. How is it that a noble family had known of magical abilities in their daughter, and not helped her to develop the gift? Even the least talented of the students she had been in classes with before being assigned to Cyrus had come to school knowing a few basics. Perhaps that is why she had been sent to school early for the summer term— to help prepare her for the beginning of regular classes in the fall.

Instead of dwelling on this too much, she thought to ask about Linny's family. "Where are you from?" Kyra asked.

"Nortwyn Abbey," Linny said. "It's a small town in the east."

Kyra nodded. "And your father and mother live there, then?"

Linny winced.

"Sorry," Kyra offered. "This is probably your first time away from your family, I suppose."

Linny nodded. "Yes, it is," she said.

Kyra noticed the tears in the young girl's eyes, but tried her best to redirect the subject.

"Would you like me to show you a spell?" she asked as she patted the bed beside where she sat.

Linny didn't move. She fidgeted with her fingers and bit her lip once more.

"I won't bite," Kyra said with a genuine smile. "Come on, I can show you something." Kyra waved her hand in the air in front of her and then turned her palm upward. She snapped her fingers and whispered the words to summon a small spark of blue flame. It hovered and danced above her hand, then she blew on it gently and sent it into the air. It grew into a round orb of fire, roughly the size of a small tangerine, and then it disappeared. Kyra watched Linny's eyes grow wide and a smile creep upon the girl's face.

"Come on," Kyra said. "Let's have you try it."

Linny took a step, and then hesitated for a moment before finally skipping over to the bed and jumping up onto it. "I don't know the spell," Linny confessed.

Kyra leaned in and whispered the words into Linny's ear. "Got it?" Kyra asked.

Linny nodded.

"All right, now, it isn't enough just to speak the words. You also have to focus on the spell, and picture the flame in your mind. Can you do that?"

Linny nodded again.

She held her hand out and closed her eyes, squinting them shut. "Plami yavlai," she said in a whisper. She opened her eyes, a bright smile on her face and an excited giggle issuing out from her. Linny's excitement died down when she saw nothing in her hand.

"Don't worry, it takes a bit of practice. Try again," Kyra coaxed.

Linny closed her eyes again and repeated the words to the spell. Again nothing happened. Three times more she tried, and with each disappointment her frown grew longer.

Kyra then hopped off the bed and walked toward the large, black trunk. "Some students use wands," she said. "Do you have a wand?"

"I don't know," Linny replied.

Kyra shook her head. "You should know if you have a wand," she said.

Linny shot off the bed. "Oh yes, I do have a wand. Sorry, I didn't hear you right the first time." Linny bounded over to the trunk and opened it, while Kyra studied her carefully. Linny didn't act like any of the other girls Kyra had met here last year. There was no air of arrogance about her. She didn't move in stiff, "proper" movements like all the other young women at the academy subscribed to. She was different. The clothes fit. The ornate trunk was like any other. Even the ornate wand Linny pulled out appeared to be similar to what any other apprentice at the school would have, but none of them would behave like Linny, or talk like her for that matter. Even the shyest of girls had always talked down to Kyra before.

Linny waved her wand, which was made of ebony and had four opals set into the handle. "Here it is!"

Kyra nodded approvingly. "A wand helps to enhance

your focus. So, this time try to perform the same spell, but don't focus the image into your hand. Instead, imagine the flame leaping off the end of the wand."

Linny nodded. She turned and pointed her wand at the stone wall. "Plami yavlai," she said. Nothing happened.

"It's all right, just focus on the tip of your wand," Kyra encouraged her.

Linny nodded. She took in a deep breath and stared at the wand. "Plami yavlai!" A blue spark jumped from the end of the wand, circled around the air for a second, and then vanished. Linny's eyes went wide as eggs and she turned around, jumping up and down. "I did it! I did magic!"

Kyra smiled. "See, you'll be just fine here," she said. "Shall we go get breakfast?"

Linny shook her head and practiced the spell again. Her smile disappeared once more when there was not even so much as a hint of a spark. She shook her wand. "Come on," she said. "Plami yavlai!"

Kyra stepped in and gently took the wand. "It's all right, you can't force it. Come, let's go have something to eat, then we can try again." Kyra placed the wand back into the trunk and closed the lid. "I can help you unpack later as well, if you like."

Linny sighed and nodded. "I never thought I could do that," Linny said under her breath as she stared at the spot where the spark had floated.

"You know, I bet they have ham steak and eggs today. Do you like ham steak?"

Linny nodded.

"Come on, then, let's go." Kyra slipped her hand in through Linny's elbow, something Kyra's mother used to do sometimes when she was sad, and pulled her out into the corridor.

*****

Cyrus was sitting in the classroom when Janik found him.

The curtains were drawn over the windows and only a few candles illuminated the room. Janik closed the door and cleared his throat. Cyrus looked up from a book and leaned back in his chair.

"What is it?" Cyrus asked. "I am expecting Kyra to come for classes soon, so we need to be brief."

"She hasn't yet gone down for breakfast. We have time," Janik countered. The lame man limped into the room, dragging his twisted leg with each step. "We have a slight problem," Janik said.

"Oh?" Cyrus said as he closed his book and slid it to the side of his desk.

Janik nodded and pulled a chair up to the opposite side of the desk. "Kyra has a roommate," Janik said. He looked around as if searching for eavesdroppers in the room.

Cyrus flicked his wrist and the candles burned brighter, illuminating Janik's face fully so the old wizard could see the sour expression. "Why should that be a concern?" Cyrus asked.

"This isn't just any girl," Janik started. He fidgeted in his chair and wiggled his lower jaw side to side as he pulled in a breath through his flared and crinkled nose. "My father, rest his soul, was not always an honorable man," Janik said.

"Most aren't," Cyrus replied. The wizard leaned back in his chair and folded his arms impatiently.

"I'll just come right out with it, then." Janik blinked at the desk, unable to make eye contact with Cyrus. "My father sired a child with another woman."

"It happens," Cyrus said flatly.

Janik nodded. "I saw her once. My father had left a portion of his estate to her, and to the child's mother. I was the executor of the will. I went to meet with the mother and child…"

"But you never gave them what your father desired?"

Janik shook his head. "My mother was still alive at the time. I couldn't dishonor her, or bring open shame upon the family."

"And now you believe the roommate to be your half-sister, is that it?" Cyrus asked.

Janik nodded. "I don't just believe it, I know it. She has false papers, and has been admitted to the academy. Headmaster Herion has instructed me to put her in Kyra's room. I dropped her off only a few minutes ago. I spent some time in my office, I needed a drink to calm my nerves, and then I came here."

Cyrus nodded. "Yes, well, that might be something hard for you to deal with on a personal level, but I fail to see why this is a problem for me, or why it should matter that she lives with Kyra."

Janik shook his head. "What if they figure it out?" Janik asked. "If the girl knows I am her... her..."

"Half-brother," Cyrus put in.

Janik nodded. "If she tells Kyra, then Kyra will not trust me. I told Kyra that there were no daughters in our family."

"And that is the truth," Cyrus said. "Most nobles don't recognize illegitimate children. She'll either understand this point, or she will hate you for your callous attitude toward an innocent child," Cyrus said bluntly. "Either way, it shouldn't matter for our purposes. If anything, that might push her closer to me. I wouldn't worry about it."

"What about Feberik?" Janik asked.

Cyrus shrugged. "Does he know?"

Janik shook his head. "I am the only one who knew my father's secret."

Cyrus sighed and rubbed a hand over his face before bringing it down to tug on his beard. "So you are nervous because of what he did at Caspen Manor?" Cyrus guessed.

Janik nodded. "I have given him the potion each night, but something like this will always rile him up beyond reason. I fear it might also make him too strong for the magic."

Cyrus grinned. "You know, I would have liked to watch your brother at Caspen Manor. That whole incident sounded like a lot of fun."

Janik arched a brow. "I'm serious, what if Feberik turns against me because of this? If I can't keep him under the spell of the potions you give me, then we will lose him."

Cyrus nodded. "Have you asked the girl whether she knows you?"

Janik shook his head and frowned. "No. If I ask her that, and she knows nothing, then I will only cause her to suspect something."

The old wizard sighed again and began tapping on the desk with his forefinger. "My suggestion is to wait and let things play out however they may. If she knows who her father was, then it will come out in the open. Or, perhaps it won't. If she has false papers to be here, then she might fear outing herself and getting expelled. Best case scenario is she doesn't know, and won't be a threat."

"She came to study magic," Janik said after a moment.

"Why do you warriors always say things like that as if the person is possessed? Not all magicians and wizards are bad."

Janik chortled. "Well, considering you are the wizard I deal with the most, can you blame me?"

Cyrus smiled and flicked a brow up for a moment. "Fair point. However, the mere fact that she is studying magic is nothing to worry about."

Janik sat silently, shifting his gaze to the floor and sighing loudly.

"I can hear you breathing," Cyrus said. "I don't like it."

Janik looked up and snorted. "Yes well, if you hadn't rescued me in that vampire's lair, I guess you wouldn't have to listen to me breathe."

Cyrus's features grew hard and he shook his head and waved Janik away. "Go. I have studies of my own to attend to before Kyra comes. Keep this matter to yourself. It will all work out in the end."

Janik left in a huff, mumbling something about imbecilic, senile wizards and their schemes as he exited the room and pulled the door shut behind him.

Cyrus sat at the desk, pondering this new information.

He went to a statue of a large crow that sat in the corner of the room. He waved his hand and a small piece of parchment appeared in front of the statue. As he thought the words, they appeared upon the parchment in glowing, green ink.

Dear Hairen,

I have thought about your proposal much since our last conversation. I believe that working with you may be more beneficial than my current arrangement with the warlocks of the Order of the All-Seeing Eye. Additionally, I may have found a new recruit for your coven. Give me some time, and I will inform you of my progress.

Sincerely,

Cyrus

*****

Kyra and Linny had only just finished their plates when Kathair walked into the room. He was smiling wide and approaching fast.

"Hi Kyra, can I talk with you for a moment?" Kathair asked.

Kyra looked to Linny and excused herself. She stood from the table and they walked a few yards away for privacy.

"I've made another break through on my project. I think you will want to come with me," Kathair said.

"Why? What are you grinning for?" Kyra asked.

Kathair leaned in close. "The school received a falcon today. It described how the monsters in the south were killed. The dragon slayers aren't too happy, but I overhead the headmaster saying he was going to call a special meeting. Come with me, and we can listen in."

"Listen in?" Kyra echoed. "I don't think we can just walk into his office and sit down."

Kathair shook his head. "Of course not, but I do have a few tricks up my sleeve. I mean, how do you think I got that book for you?"

"Well, I was going to help Linny unpack her things."

"Kyra, we don't have much time, come on," Kathair urged.

Kyra nodded. "All right. Give me a moment." She walked back to Linny. "Are you able to find your way back to the room? I have something I need to do."

"Sure," Linny said with a hollow smile.

Kyra felt conflicted about leaving her, but Kathair was already walking by, having heard Linny's answer.

"Great, I'll have her back to you soon. Nice to meet you." He shot Kyra an expectant look and then continued walking toward the exit.

Kyra felt pulled in two directions. She wanted desperately to hear what Kathair was so excited about, but she hadn't missed the fact that Linny was having a hard time. There was a large part of her that wanted to stay with her and help.

"It's all right," Linny said. "I can find my way back. I'll see you soon," she said. Linny made the choice easier for Kyra by getting up and walking in the opposite direction.

Kyra walked briskly to catch up with Kathair. He was nearly to the courtyard by the time she caught up with him. She was about to suggest they not go into the open courtyard, for Feberik might see them, but Kathair turned down the corridor to the left before Kyra ever brought it up.

"Come on, hurry up," Kathair said. He quickened his pace and Kyra nearly had to jog to keep up.

"What's so important?" Kyra asked.

Kathair held a finger to his mouth and shook his head. He stopped suddenly at a large door and tested the handle. It turned easily in his hand. He poked his head through and then opened the door wider.

"Through here," he said quickly.

Kathair led her through a laundry room full of large vats of steaming water and linens hanging on lines. They snaked around the large tubs and then stopped at a grate that was about three feet long and two feet wide. Kathair bent down and pulled the grate up as if it was made of sticks.

"What are you doing?" Kyra asked.

"Come on, in you go," he said.

Kyra shook her head. "No."

Kathair sighed and set the grate aside. Then he dropped down into the hole. His feet hit the bottom before his head dropped below floor level. "Stay if you like, but I promise you are going to want to see this." He held his hand up for her.

She looked at his blue eyes, sparkling above his impish grin. Finally she nodded and jumped down beside him, making a point of not taking his hand for help. Kathair then grabbed the grate and pulled it into place.

"What if someone locks it or something?" Kyra asked, gesturing to the grate as they ducked.

Kathair shook his head. "Won't happen, and if it does, then I know another way out. Come on, we have to hurry before they start."

"Before who starts what?" Kyra asked.

Kathair was already hunched low and waddling through the tunnel.

Kyra sighed and followed him.

The light stretched for quite some way into the tunnel. Whenever it appeared to dim significantly, there would be another drain from above that would allow in more light to help them see by. Kyra noticed that none of the other drains were nearly large enough to crawl through. They were all the normal kind that appeared to be just a few inches across, nothing like the one from the laundry room.

They made their way through a series of turns and twists, and then they emerged from the tunnel to stand in a room that was ten feet across and about fifteen feet long. Kathair moved to his left and struck a match, lighting a candle.

Kyra's eyes widened as she saw not only a table and chairs, but a small bookshelf, a pair of swords crossed behind a shield hanging upon a wall, and a rug made of some sort of animal hide, though it was far too large to be a bear or anything else she was aware of in the area.

"Welcome to my sanctuary," Kathair said.

"I thought you said there was going to be a meeting?"

Kyra said.

Kathair nodded and moved to the bookshelf. "Right this way," he said. He gripped the left side of the bookshelf and pivoted the thing out to the side in an arc, revealing a small doorway that led to a wooden ladder. The young swordsman motioned for her to go first. "Ladies first," he said with a bow.

"I'm in a dress," Kyra pointed out.

"Oh, right!" Kathair said as he blushed. "I'll lead the way then." He moved through the doorway and made his way up the ladder. Kyra followed him, a little hesitant to start climbing. The ladder went up at least two stories, and there was no way for her to know where it led.

He was nearly at the top before she finally decided to go after him. She went up the ladder and then had to crawl into a small space at the top that led into another tunnel. There were cracks in the wall, spaces where the mortar had fallen out, that let in enough light to see by.

Kathair turned to her and put his finger to his lips. "Nothing more than a whisper," he cautioned.

Kyra nodded, noting how much he looked like a rogue with the small band of light striping across his eyes. He led her around, crawling slowly through the dim tunnel until they came to a dead end. Kyra looked up and saw that Kathair was now in a crouching sit, staring through a small gap between the large stones in the wall. He pointed at the crack and motioned for her to come close and take a look.

Kyra scooted beside him and then leaned forward until she nearly touched the stone. Through the crack she saw a rectangular room, with sconces along the far wall and a long table in the center. Wooden, high-backed chairs were situated along the table. A few people were already sitting there, their backs turned to the wall behind which Kathair and Kyra hid.

A door on the right, bearing a large engraving of an eagle, opened, and in walked Headmaster Herion. The old wizard was dressed in a black tunic and green trousers. He moved into the room and then turned to motion to someone else.

Kyra felt her heart nearly stop when Feberik walked

through the open doorway. So far, she had avoided him for most of the summer. The very thought of their arranged marriage made her feel ill, and she had to compel herself to stay in place and not scurry back down the ladder and run away.

"I believe you all know Master Orres," Headmaster Herion said in his gravelly voice. "We have taken care of his initiation already, though I believe a few of you were absent for that." Headmaster Herion turned to look at someone sitting in the chair nearest them.

A tall man in black robes stood and nodded. "Welcome, Feberik," the man said as he held his hand out cordially.

"What, no insult today?" Feberik replied in his booming voice as he took the proffered hand. The man in the black robes shook his head, mumbling something about dull swordsmen, and Kyra got enough of a glimpse of his profile to know at once who it was. The man was Master Fenn, Lady Priscilla's husband.

For a moment, it felt like snakes were crawling through Kyra's stomach. She hadn't seen Master Fenn for a long time either, and seeing him now brought back the memory of throwing Lady Priscilla into a wall. Kyra closed her eyes and tried to steady her nerves. Fortunately, there was little silence, for Headmaster Herion broke it quickly.

"Have a seat, Master Fenn," Herion said. He then turned to Feberik and gestured to a chair further down the table. "You may sit next to Lady Arkyn."

Feberik nodded, the reddish-blonde streaks in his otherwise dark hair catching the light just right. He walked around the table and Kyra held her breath as he stepped closer to where she was hiding. She wasn't able to exhale until the large man pulled out his chair and sat down.

Headmaster Herion then moved to the head of the table. "I have called you all here to witness a mission. I sent Master Baird and Lady Stirling north, across the sea to one of the islands. I am not going to name the location, and if any of you recognize it, be sure to keep it to yourselves."

Headmaster Herion waved his hand and a large, purple ball of crystal descended from the ceiling. It glowed dully and sent tendrils of golden light out to steady itself as it neared the top of the table. Herion whispered a command and the ball began to glow brighter.

"In the interest of full disclosure, I should warn you all that this may not end well. You have all heard the reports of strange beasts attacking the countryside lately, have you not?"

A few of the individuals nodded.

Master Fenn pointed down the table toward Feberik. "You mean the events that started occurring after the death of Feberik's fiancé's mother?"

Feberik rose out of his chair and pointed right back at Master Fenn. "You'll do well to keep your mouth shut, or I'll close it permanently."

Headmaster Herion snapped his fingers and two bolts of yellow light shot out from the purple ball. One struck Master Fenn and the other hit Feberik. Kyra jumped when she heard the loud *kapop* that accompanied each strike.

Master Fenn dusted his arm off in the spot where the bolt had landed upon him. "All I am saying is that we should not be harboring someone like her here."

Feberik stormed around from his chair and Kyra could barely breathe. His blue eyes were alight with crazy fury and his face grew red.

Headmaster Herion slammed his fist on the table and the purple ball began to crackle and come alive with a stormy mess of golden bolts. "Sit down!" Herion ordered. He then turned to Master Fenn and pointed at him. "You keep your mouth quiet. Kyra is no different from any of the other students here."

"Except for the fact that she is born of a vampire," Fenn shot back.

Kyra blushed and looked away from the crack in the wall. She couldn't take it anymore. She turned to leave, but a gentle hand on her shoulder stopped her. She turned to see Kathair looking at her empathetically.

"Sorry," he said. "I wasn't trying to embarrass you. Stay, they will get onto another topic, and I think you will want to see it all."

Kyra nodded sorrowfully and went back to the crack, and then she looked to Kathair. She felt as though he needed an explanation. "I didn't know I was a vampire's daughter," she said.

Kathair looked to her and his brow drew in tightly as he shrugged. "What difference does it make?" he asked sincerely. "You are who you are, and I like you. That's good enough for me."

Kyra sat there and smiled. Kathair turned back to the crack and continued watching.

"Just," Kathair began out of the side of his mouth, "don't chomp on my neck or anything all right? I don't think we could be around each other anymore if you started drinking my blood and all."

From anyone else, that might have cut her, but coming from Kathair, with his playful tone, it turned the negative experience into a funny moment. She stifled a laugh and backhanded him in the ribs. He jumped and then shushed her, putting on a mock-serious face and pointing toward the crack in the wall.

Kyra looked back to the room. Headmaster Herion had regained control of the room, and the ball was glowing brighter now. The sconces flickered around the chamber.

"As I was saying," Herion began. "There have been many attacks lately. They point to something sinister operating in the area. This is no shadowfiend, for they normally operate alone and don't let minions and monsters roam free for fear of being discovered. This points to something else."

"You said that the girl had been attacked by a shade, so it makes sense that we should see monsters operating in the area," Lady Arkyn said in a youthful voice.

Herion nodded. "That may be true, but I believe it to be more than that," he said. "I believe the shade acts on behalf of another."

"Who?" Master Fenn asked. "What could possibly control a shade?"

"In this case," Herion said with a frown, "I believe it is a vampire."

"A vampire?" Fenn asked skeptically. "But shades don't work with vampires."

Herion patted the air. "That is all too true. Normally they are territorial rivals at best. However, in this case, I believe we are dealing with a powerful and ancient vampire who somehow has gained control over a shade, as well as many other beasts. I was able to find a lead, and that is where Master Baird and Lady Stirling are headed at the moment. I thought it best we observe their mission and see what we might learn."

A hush fell over the chamber. The sconces flickered and then their flames died. The purple ball of crystal grew five times its size, until it was large enough that it appeared capable of swallowing Feberik.

Kyra watched in amazement as the innermost part of the orb became clear and a scene opened up inside.

Kyra watched through the orb, which opened up the scene behind a shorter man with dark hair and a green cloak who was facing a taller, thin woman. They were both standing upon a large ship that bobbed gently in the water. Kyra could only assume that they were Master Baird and Lady Stirling. Lady Stirling wore a dust cloak, concealing all but the end of a slender leather case under her left arm, and a series of daggers tucked into a specially fashioned belt that hung across her chest. She drew her black hood over her golden-haired head and the two quickly turned to disembark from the ship. Wherever they were, the fog covered the docks thickly and hung in the air. Rain was pouring down too. It looked gray, cold, and miserable. They didn't speak to anyone they saw on the docks. Instead, they went straight to the first tavern they saw.

"Figures they would head for the tavern," Master Fenn called out.

Headmaster Herion shot the man a look that made Kyra gulp and clench her mouth tightly shut.

She then turned back to the images in the orb and watched as Master Baird opened the door and the two walked into the tavern.

"Sure is a wet one," declared a short, plump barkeep as Master Baird and Lady Stirling approached the bar. Baird slapped a pair of coins on the table.

"Indeed it is a wet day," Master Baird replied as he removed his rain-soaked cloak and hung it on a stool next to him.

"This rain is most unusual for this time of year. I've seen only four or five such days in all my years here."

"An ill omen," Lady Stirling replied.

Master Baird turned and scanned the room. From what Kyra could see through the orb, a few patrons were inside, occupying themselves with various card or dice games and a tavern maid was busily hopping from one table to another filling and refilling mugs of ale. Apparently satisfied, Baird turned and nodded to Lady Stirling. She laid a long, leather case on the bar in front of her.

"What'll it be?" the barkeep asked, hardly glancing at the leather case.

"We have not come for drink," Master Baird replied.

"A room then, surely you will not want to be out and about in this weather," he offered. "The Green Door Inn is proud to offer the finest rooms at the lowest prices, and they're clean too," he said with a wink.

"We are looking for someone," Master Baird and Lady Stirling replied in unison.

The barkeep stopped and gaped at them both for a second. It seemed to Kyra that he wasn't sure what to make of the pair.

"What kind of business are you about?" the barkeep said with a grin and cleaned a smudge from his spectacles.

Master Baird shook his head sourly. "We have come on official business."

Lady Stirling opened one end of the leather case to reveal the hilt of a sword. She pulled it out part way and Kathair nudged Kyra.

"That sword is Stormfang, I would recognize it anywhere."

"Stormfang?" Kyra asked.

Kathair nodded. "It's an important weapon. It belongs to the school."

They both looked back to the orb eagerly.

"Ah, now that is something quite different. I apologize; you see I didn't recognize you. We don't get many of your kind out here."

Lady Stirling slid the sword back into the case and closed it again. "Surely you understand now?" she asked.

The barkeep nodded. "I know the sword. Master Heimdal with his mighty sword, Stormfang, crushed the shadowfiends and established Kuldiga Academy over the ruins of their fortress. I know the legend."

"It is more than a legend," Master Baird replied. "It is fact."

"Of course, sir, as you say," the barkeep said with a reverent nod. "Look, King Mathias doesn't actually govern this island, but, I can help you out so long as you promise to take your business outside of my inn. The last time one of your lot showed up out here, the blacksmith's shop was burned down along with three houses. I can't afford that kind of loss."

Lady Stirling nodded. "We don't believe the person we seek is in town, but we have heard he comes in to town from time to time."

"The man's name is Vincent," Master Baird began, "and we have it on good authority that he is here on this isle. Is that so?"

"Vincent," the barkeep repeated and scrunched up his eyebrows as if he was concentrating real hard. "That name doesn't sound familiar."

"He isn't the sort of man that's likely to interact with others much. Probably hardly even noticed by most folk here, I imagine," Master Baird said. "Try to think of a man who comes in maybe once a week or every other week, keeps to himself, and just buys supplies or perhaps mills about the docks for a bit before leaving town."

The barkeep snapped his fingers and set the mug down. "Aye, there is a man like that who comes into town, but it's only once a month or so. A strange sort of man he is; always keeps to himself and never says much to anyone, except to buy supplies like you say. Spends most of his time at his little cabin in the forest he does. I've wondered what would make a man live all alone like that as if he was hiding from something. I guess with the two of you here, that might be exactly what he is doing."

"Out of curiosity, ever see him during the daytime?" Lady Stirling asked.

The barkeep shook his head. "Not usually. He comes later in the evening, and usually heads out after dark. Why, you think he is a vampire or something?" The barkeep let out a belly laugh, but once he noticed that neither Baird nor Stirling joined in his laughter, he stopped and his face grew long. "By the gods, you don't think he is, do you? I mean, we would know, wouldn't we?"

"Tell us where to find his cabin," Baird said.

"And here are a few extra coins for your silence."

"Just take the main road west until you come to the forest, and then head southward into the hills. You can't miss it, but I wouldn't go today if I were you. There isn't enough light to get there and back today."

"That's alright, we'll find out way," Baird said.

"You could at least warm yourself by the fire before you go," the barkeep offered.

"No," Master Baird said as he waved his hand. "It is not a cold rain outside. We'll be fine." He pushed the coins to the barkeep.

The two left the tavern and traveled out from the town and southward along the main road for quite some time. Kyra had to shift her position as her feet were starting to tingle and go numb. None of the others in the special chamber said a word as they watched the purple orb intently. Even Master Fenn was quiet.

After a while, the rain finally let up and the sun dared to peek out from behind the leaden clouds.

Baird and Stirling stopped to shake the water from their cloaks in an effort to dry off a bit. Then, Lady Stirling waved her hand and whispered a word Kyra didn't understand. A strange, yellow fire washed over the two of them and their clothes were entirely dry, but unharmed by the magical flames. They then walked up a hill and then down around a small outcropping of trees. No sooner had they rounded the bend than a pair of highwaymen approached from the nearby copse of trees. Master Baird and Lady Stirling stopped in place and turned to face the men.

"If you come to rob or slay me, you will find that I am more than equal to your challenge," Baird warned.

"Ah, blast them with a sleeping spell and be done with it," Master Fenn called out.

Headmaster Herion held his hand up, calling for silence.

The two highwaymen looked to each other and laughed.

"How about it, a bit of sport before supper?" one of them said to the other.

"Don't mind if I do," said the other. The both of them drew swords.

Master Baird turned to Lady Stirling who opened the leather case to retrieve Stormfang. He then turned to the two bandits. "Well, let's get this over with, I have a meeting that I am late for."

The two bandits looked to each other and then laughed.

The highwaymen rushed forward, swords at the ready. Master Baird spun under the first strike and brought Stormfang up into the man's ribs. A second later, Lady Stirling sent a stream of fire from her hand that burned through the second bandit's chest. Both of the dead cutpurses fell to the ground at the same time.

"Brutish," Master Fenn called out. "They could have

spared them."

"Better to let the highwaymen seal their own fates and receive their just reward," Feberik said loudly.

Kyra, despite her displeasure upon hearing her fiancé speak, couldn't help but agree with him.

She turned back to the orb and watched as Baird and Stirling continued on their way. As the sun began to set in the west, a fierce, biting wind nipped at the two. They drew their cloaks in tightly and bent forward into the wind. They drew their hoods up over their heads and continued on.

Soon, they found what they were looking for.

"Just as the barkeep said," Master Baird said to Lady Stirling.

Lady Stirling turned and smiled at him.

Kyra saw through the orb a cozy log cabin on the top of a nearby hill. In the gray light of dusk she noted a bit of smoke flowing from the chimney. It didn't look like a vampire's lair, and was certainly nothing at all similar to the place her mother had been held prisoner. It was the sort of home one would expect to see out in the middle of a field with a pair of kids playing around the house while parents worked in a family garden.

"He looks to be home," Master Baird said as he pointed to the chimney.

"Be on your guard," Lady Stirling warned.

Master Baird motioned for her to come close. He held the sword between them, blade pointed to the ground and his head bowed reverently. "Icadion, All-father, watch over us now. Give us the ability to act quickly and the strength to overcome any obstacle." Then Baird fastened Stormfang to his belt.

"Not sure why you pray," Lady Stirling said. "Icadion no longer hears the prayers of Terramyr. He left long ago; that's why it's up to us to chase away these kinds of demons."

Master Baird shook his head and then motioned to the house with his chin. "Do we knock, or just go in?"

Lady Stirling shrugged. "If he is in there, then better we surprise him."

"But if it isn't him, then what?" Baird asked. "We can't just barge into every cabin out in the woods now can we?"

Master Baird and Lady Stirling walked up to the door and tried it. The door didn't budge.

Lady Stirling waved her hand and whispered a spell, but again the door was sealed.

"I can break it," Master Baird offered.

Lady Stirling shook her head. "Let's knock and claim to be weary travelers caught after dark. The sun is almost gone. It might work."

Master Baird nodded and rapped on the wooden door with his gloved fist. "Hello, is anybody home? We are looking for shelter, and maybe some food for the night."

As Kyra watched them, she could hear something on the other side of a door that sounded like a plate being dropped on the floor. Footsteps thumped on the floor until they came to the door. A series of bolts and locks slid aside, grinding against metal slots and brackets. The door itself cracked just a bit and a short little woman with beady eyes peered out.

"Who are you?" the woman demanded in a raspy voice.

"My name is Baird, and we have been caught out in the rain and now it is dark. Could we impose upon you for the evening? We have money to pay for your hospitality" Master Baird pulled out a small coin purse and opened it toward the woman.

"I suppose I can offer some soup. I only have one bed though, so you will have to sleep upon the floor." The woman nodded as she opened the cabin door wide enough to reveal herself and a good view into the cabin. Master Baird and Lady Stirling eyed the woman carefully.

From her vantage point behind the wall, Kyra watched too. The woman appeared to be well into her sixties, stooped over with age, and carried a sizeable hump on her back. Her face was lined with wrinkles and her hair had long ago turned gray. Her body was thin, frail looking, and barely occupied more than half the doorway's width as she stood. Not an imposing foe by any measure, and certainly not the vampire

Master Baird and Lady Stirling were searching for.

"Come in," the woman said. The two travelers followed her in through the doorway.

"The soup is here," the woman announced as she moved to a pot hanging over a fire. Just then, the door slammed shut behind them and the bolts slid back into the locked position.

Master Baird and Lady Stirling turned, but no one was near the door. They wheeled back around to see the woman sneering at them. Instead of the hunched, old woman, she was now tall and beautiful, with a perfect spine and youthful looking skin. She smiled wickedly and a pair of fangs shone out from her mouth.

Kyra gasped as the strange woman attacked, but Master Baird struck out with Stormfang and Lady Stirling sent a column of fire into the woman's face. The woman shrieked and screamed, then fell to the ground. She writhed and twitched as the flames continued to consume her head. Master Baird stepped in and severed her head with Stormfang, then he plunged the weapon into the woman's heart.

Kathair leaned in close to Kyra and whispered, "Stormfang is an enchanted blade. It is able to kill vampires and their ilk."

Kyra looked at him with wide eyes. "Can it kill a shade?" she asked.

Kathair shrugged. "Not sure. Maybe we can look into that possibility when Master Baird and Lady Stirling return."

Kyra turned her eyes back to the orb. Master Baird and Lady Stirling were now sprinkling some sort of powder on the body, and great, blue flames jumped up and turned the corpse to ash. Stirling collected a vial of the ash and then the two of them began searching the cabin.

After several minutes, they moved to the hearth and pulled the pot out from the fireplace. Lady Stirling waved her hand and said the words of a spell Kyra didn't know. Suddenly the back wall of the fireplace glowed green.

"I'll dispel the trap," Stirling said.

Baird nodded and stepped back.

Lady Stirling bent down and wove her hands in the air for several moments. Line by line, the glowing design faded away until the chimney wall looked normal. Then she extinguished the fire and pressed the wall inward, opening it to a secret passage that led downward.

Slowly they maneuvered themselves into the small tunnel and carefully descended the slope inside. There was an eerie glow in the tunnel, but there were no fires or torches. Soon they came to a cliff. They carefully lowered themselves over the side and searched for footholds. They ended up needing to go down a single ladder that was apparently cut into the stone with footholds carved from the rock. Kyra watched with baited breath until the two reached the cave floor.

In the eerie light, Kyra could see bats hanging from the cave ceiling. Large spiders crawled along the walls and water dripped from a few of the stalactites. Master Baird and Lady Stirling walked forward, mindful of the sheer drop to their right that descended into a crevice that appeared to go on forever until it was swallowed by darkness. To their left were a couple of smaller caves branching out into the belly of the mountain.

"Let's follow the main tunnel," Lady Stirling said.

"We should have sent more people with them," Master Fenn commented from his chair as everyone watched the scene unfold in the orb.

Suddenly, the tunnel opened to a large chamber filled with bones, as if a great beast had discarded its meals for hundreds of years. The two crept into the opening and searched the area. There was no sign of any movement.

To the right, the floor inclined up to a small landing of stone, upon which stood a man with silver hair that hung down to the middle of his back. He wore a leather vest over a silk shirt tucked into wool trousers that were in turn tucked into mid-length leather boots. The man seemed to be standing in front of a desk or pedestal of some sort and reading something.

Lady Stirling lifted her hand and looked to Master Baird.

The man held Stormfang at the ready and nodded to her.

The sorceress sent a blast of blue flame at the vampire's back. The fire struck its target and then the man faded away.

"It was an illusion, you fools!" Master Fenn shouted as he rose in his chair. "He'll come from the side while you aren't looking!"

To Kyra's horror, that is exactly what happened. A mass of darkness leapt at Master Baird. The man spun around with Stormfang, but was struck down before he could wield the weapon effectively.

Lady Stirling shouted some sort of curse and sent a crimson shockwave out from her. The vampire was knocked backward through the air enough for her to get to Master Baird.

She helped the man to his feet, but he was only barely conscious. His left arm had been severed just above the elbow, and he was losing a lot of blood.

"I love the scent of blood," the vampire said in a surprisingly low voice.

Lady Stirling summoned an orb of light to pierce the darkness. The silver-haired vampire was standing near the far wall, smiling at her. He snapped his fingers and the darkness closed in on her. The magical orb winked out of existence and the ambient light in the cave dimmed so that the vampire was hidden once more.

"You are not the first to come for me," the vampire said.

Lady Stirling fired a bolt of fire through the air at the voice, but it hit nothing.

The vampire laughed at her. "You shall die as all the rest," he hissed.

Master Baird handed Lady Stirling the magical sword and then fell to the ground.

Lady Stirling summoned another orb of light. She saw the vampire walking toward her confidently. She fired another column of fire, but the vampire dashed to the side with the speed of a lightning bolt. He then opened his mouth and a flood of bats flew out to assault Lady Stirling. She erected a wall of fire to ward them off. The bats collided with the flames, bouncing out and shrieking shrilly as they died.

Kyra held a hand over her mouth and gasped. No one inside the secret chamber heard her, for they were all shouting as well.

The vampire appeared behind Lady Stirling. He stabbed her with a short sword and lifted her writhing body into the air. The sorceress flailed about, trying hopelessly to cast spells at the vampire. The creature reached up with wickedly long claws on his left hand and gripped Lady Stirling's neck.

"I think I will take that sword from you," he said.

Kyra only barely heard the beginning of a scream and then the orb went dark and shrank to its original size. Everyone in the room was silent after that. The sconces erupted with light once more. Headmaster Herion held his head bent toward the table. Master Fenn slammed his fist on the table and wheeled on the old man as if to say something. Instead, he shook his finger and then stormed out of the room.

"Come, we should go," Kathair whispered.

He nudged Kyra through the tunnel and they didn't stop until they reached the chairs down in the small chamber and he closed the secret passage behind the bookshelf.

"That was terrible," Kyra said.

Kathair nodded. "I didn't think it was going to be like that," he replied. "I heard them say they needed to talk about a clue they had about the strange beasts. I thought maybe they might have had a lead on the shade, or a garunda or something."

"It's all right," Kyra said. "But, I think I am going to go back to my room now."

"Sure," Kathair said.

Kyra turned to leave, but then noticed a book on the small table and paused. "Is this how you were able to find the headmaster's journal?" she asked.

Kathair shrugged and offered his impish grin. "Well, you heard them right, this academy was built on the ruins of a shadowfiend fortress. There are lots of little nooks and crannies."

She smiled and nodded. "Thanks," she said.

Kathair shrugged. "Of course," he said. "I do what I can to help."

Kathair remained in the secret room while the young sorceress left. Kyra made the long journey back to the laundry room, then stopped by her classroom to apologize to Cyrus for keeping him waiting, but the wizard was nowhere to be seen. She then went directly to her room.

CHAPTER 8

Kyra opened the door to her room and walked in. In the wake of what she had just seen, she had almost forgotten that she now had a roommate. Her hand went up and she almost opened the portal to the aspen wood, but stopped short when she saw Linny on her bed, curled up and facing the wall.

"Are you all right?" Kyra asked.

Linny looked over her shoulder with puffy eyes. She nodded and then put her head back down on her pillow.

Kyra noticed that Linny hadn't unpacked anything at all. She was just lying on the bed. She moved over to Linny and sat on the edge of the girl's bed. She reached out and put a hand on Linny's shoulder.

"Is there something I can do for you?" Kyra asked.

Linny shook her head. "No, I just miss my mum," Linny said.

Kyra nodded empathetically. If anyone knew what it was to miss their mother, Kyra was that someone. The young sorceress patted Linny's shoulder. "Come on, it'll be all right. You'll see. We'll have so much fun, and you will have enough homework that Winter Festival will be here before you know it. Then you can go home for a couple of weeks and see your family. Don't worry, it'll be all right."

Linny shook her head. She scooted away from Kyra and sat up, back against the wall, and leaned into the corner. "No," she said quietly. "My mum is dead. I won't ever see her again."

Kyra blinked and her mouth parted slightly. Had Linny's mother been killed by creatures of dark magic as well? A part of Kyra wanted to interrogate the young girl, but fortunately, the part of her that was like her mother took over and instead of grilling the fragile girl in her grief, Kyra reached out and enveloped her in a hug. Linny gave in and bent her head down upon Kyra's shoulder, crying softly and wetting Kyra's dress with her tears.

They held each other for several minutes until Linny sniffled her last sob and pulled away to wipe her face. She looked at Kyra and tried to smile, though in reality it was hardly more than a small pull of the left corner of her mouth.

"Come to class with me today," Kyra suggested.

"But, I was told that all the sorcery masters were on assignment for the summer. The headmaster told me to stay out of trouble until he could find someone to take me on," Linny replied.

Kyra nodded. "I have a private instructor who gives me a few sessions a week. Maybe you can get a jump on things by coming with me. In any case, it will help take your mind off of things."

Linny nodded. Her eyes shifted to a point on the bed and her focus turned distant. "She died of consumption," Linny said. "I tried to help her, but…"

Kyra reached out and took Linny's hands. "It isn't your fault," she said emphatically. "Come on, let's get dressed."

Linny looked down and realized that her top had been soaked in tears. She nodded dully and the two moved to change into fresh clothes.

"Where did you go?" Linny asked, pulling a large bit of cobweb off of Kyra's back.

Kyra turned and regarded Linny carefully. The younger girl looked up to Kyra and there was something there that formed between them, a bond of some sort that made Kyra feel responsible for Linny. She decided that it was appropriate to tell Linny a bit about her own mother. Not everything, of course, but enough so Linny would know she could trust her. Kyra would have given anything to have someone to talk to that she fully trusted back when she first heard about her mother. Now, seeing someone else going through the same type of loss, Kyra knew she had to help.

"Linny," Kyra began softly, "I know how you feel. You see, my mother died last year, during my first term here at Kuldiga Academy."

Linny's eyes went wide.

"I'm not saying I am a great font of wisdom for how to recover, but I can be there for you anytime you want to talk. Okay?"

Linny nodded. "Was your mother sick?" Linny asked.

Kyra shook her head. "My mother was murdered," Kyra said. "Kathair, the boy you saw come for me in the dining hall, he was taking me to a meeting where someone had a clue about my mother's murder."

"They never solved it?" Linny asked.

Kyra shook her head. "No, but it's important that you never tell anyone I am looking into it, all right? The headmaster can be kind at times, but he is concerned first and foremost with the school. If he were to find out a student was trying to find a murderer, he would likely expel that student."

Linny nodded. "I understand," she said. "If I were you, I would want to do the same thing." Linny held out her hand and extended only her pinky finger. "I hereby swear that your secret is safe with me."

Kyra smiled and wrapped her pinky around Linny's. "Thank you," she said.

The two changed clothes and then Linny followed Kyra through the halls and into the classroom where Cyrus was waiting, standing near a window and staring out.

"I heard there was a pair of wylkins killed last night," Cyrus said as he slowly turned around.

Kyra blushed and dipped her head until Cyrus realized that she was not alone. Thankfully, the old wizard recovered gracefully.

"I thought I might explain what a wylkin beast is, that way you can see how terrible a monster they are," he said as he gestured to the desks. "I see you have brought a guest. Might I ask her name?"

Kyra nodded and smiled. "This is Linny Ravia. She is my new roommate. I thought I might bring her to classes over the summer if that is all right with you."

Cyrus smiled and walked to his desk. "The more the merrier, I suppose." He looked to Linny and nodded warmly as he gestured to a seat once more. Kyra and Linny took seats next to each other. "Linny, in this class I teach how to defend against dark creatures. We have already covered imps and a host of others. Now, I want to discuss wylkins, seeing as how two of them have been terrorizing shepherds to the south for a few days now."

"What's a wylkin?" Linny asked.

Cyrus smiled. He turned to Kyra. "Have you explained to her that I deal in live demonstrations?"

Kyra froze with fear. Would Cyrus actually bring a wylkin into the classroom? She had been so quick to jump to the conclusion that Linny needed a distraction that she had forgotten to think about whether it was appropriate to bring a girl who could barely conjure a spark to any of Cyrus' lectures. She slowly shook her head.

Cyrus waved the notion off. "No matter, in this case, I cannot perform a live demonstration. A wylkin is a dark creature. A servant of the halls of Hammenfein, in fact. They are despicable creatures that can be quite troublesome."

"But you said they are dead," Linny interjected. "How did they die?"

Kyra felt her stomach churn. Fortunately, Cyrus played into the question well, both answering it directly, and concealing Kyra's involvement.

Cyrus smiled wide. "An accomplished sorceress was able to defeat them."

Linny nodded. Kyra bit her tongue, hoping that Linny wouldn't press for the sorceress' name. To Kyra's great relief, Linny seemed to be satisfied with the answer given.

"Now then," Cyrus began, "I will conjure up the image of a wylkin. This will not be real, therefore it cannot harm either of you. Please try and refrain from screaming, if you can."

Cyrus waved his hand and his desk slid back against the wall. Then, he whispered a few words and pointed his index finger to the space on the floor where the desk had been sitting.

A white light appeared, and then it grew. As it developed, the light took shape and became green. Two feet appeared upon the floor, green and tipped with talons on the long toes. The scaly shins then formed, growing upward to the round, strong knees and then to the massive thighs. The pelvic area and waist developed next, and then sprouted three tails out the back. The tails swayed gently back and forth, with barbed points on the ends. The torso was lean, but extremely muscular. From the waist up, the torso widened to the chest and shoulders. The light then expanded out from the shoulders to show strange, thin upper arms. At the point where the elbow joints formed, there grew long, sabre-like hooks.

Linny gasped and held a hand to her mouth.

Kyra squirmed in her seat. Seeing the wylkin in full detail, she couldn't help but realize how foolish her attack might have been. Surely, had Leatherback not been around, she would have died.

Out from the shoulders, sets of spikes emerged from the skin. Some were short, others taller and thinner. All of them looked absolutely horrid. The neck formed next, and then the jaw, filled with sharp fangs. The rest of the face appeared nearly humanoid, except for the fact that there was no nose, per se. It was little more than a pair of gaping holes divided by a line of bone, as if she were looking at an uncovered skull. The eyes were narrowly set, shaped like almonds. The brow had a series of bony bumps and protrusions growing out from under the green skin, and a ridge of spikes grew along the middle of the skull.

Cyrus waved his hand and turned the projection of the beast to the side. From this viewpoint, Kyra could see that the spikes grew in a line from the top of the head down to the tails. Smaller, wider spikes that looked like miniature pyramids flanked the row of longer spikes along the spine.

"That's disgusting," Linny said.

Kyra was surprised by how calm Linny was upon seeing the beast.

"Disgusting? Perhaps," Cyrus said. "However, there are creatures yet that would make this one appear as friendly as a kitten."

Kyra scoffed and Cyrus turned to her.

"I have faced wylkins before," Cyrus said. "So I know what it takes to kill one. In general, they need to be pierced through the heart or decapitated. Some have an uncanny ability to regenerate limbs or heal minor wounds. Other wylkins have a natural defense against magic, and can seemingly shrug off what would be a fatal spell for a human. Their long hooks can cut a horse's head clean off; they are that sharp and powerful. Their fangs are obvious weapons, of course, but their tails are just as deadly. The barbs on the ends have been known to rip hunks of meat off of their prey. Worse yet, some wylkins have the ability to wield magical spells of their own."

"Where do they come from?" Linny asked.

Cyrus grinned and shrugged. "Some say they were originally a beast that plagued the night and were hunted nearly to extinction many thousands of years ago. Others claim they are the literal spawn of Hammenfein, the embodiment of wandering spirits that escape from the plane of the dead."

"No one can escape the plane of the dead," Kyra said.

Cyrus held up a finger and shook his head. "No, there are creatures that can traverse the plane of the dead. There are also rumors of men who have gone into Hammenfein and escaped. I won't bore you with the details, but it is possible. Believe me, I have researched it well."

"So you believe that is where wylkins come from?" Kyra pressed.

"No," said Cyrus with a shake of his head. "I believe they are creatures summoned by powerful masters. However, I also believe that they are crafty devils in their own right. Perhaps these particular wylkins that were killed last night came from the underdark. There are creatures down there the likes of which would wreak such havoc and chaos upon the Middle Kingdom so as to burn it to stubble in a matter of seconds."

"The underdark?" Linny asked.

Cyrus nodded. "Tunnels that burrow deep into the core of Terramyr herself," he replied. "It is known by other names as well, of course. Some call it sub-Terra, and others more familiar with its intricacies name it Iverglendar, the land of the shadow."

"If there are such terrible monsters down there, then why don't they come up?" Linny inquired.

Cyrus nodded and smiled. "Some try to, like the wylkins, from time to time. Others cannot, for they cannot abide the light of the sun. Still, most of them are kept in check by other forces. Some of those forces are friendly to those of us that dwell upon the surface, and so they spend their lives in an effort to guard our homes in an ever raging war against the demons of Iverglendar. Another major factor is the reality that the monsters themselves are highly territorial, and fight amongst themselves."

"Will they ever emerge in force?" Kyra asked.

Cyrus shrugged. "I have studied the material on this matter as much as any other wizard I am aware of. All I can say is that they have not yet been able to do that. However, should that day come, it will be a very red day indeed, and many will suffer and die." The old wizard let his words hang in the air for a few moments and then he dismissed the image of the wylkin with a wave of his hand.

"Kyra, I had been intending to help you recognize the presence of dark magic, but this is an advanced lesson, and not one I can give to neophytes who have not been properly prepared."

Kyra glanced to Linny. The younger girl blushed and prepared to leave.

Cyrus cleared his throat and regained the girls' attention. "Therefore," he began, "I thought it might be more appropriate if you could practice lower level wards with Linny. Let's see if we can't catch her up a bit, and perhaps give her a jump on her upcoming classes. Once Linny has an instructor assigned, I will continue with the lessons we had scheduled," Cyrus looked to Kyra and nodded, "does that sound fair?"

Kyra nodded back and smiled. "Thank you," she offered. An idea came to her then and she got up and approached Cyrus. "May I take her to practice in the kitchen?"

Cyrus turned and looked at her curiously. "In the kitchen?" he repeated. "Whatever for? Are the potatoes going to rise up and attack?"

Kyra smiled and whispered softly. "She is quite new to magic. So, I thought it best to start her out slowly. I was going to perhaps throw dough balls at her and have her try to ward those off. That way, if she misses, she doesn't get hurt."

"Sounds a bit messy to me, and somewhat unorthodox…" Cyrus stroked his beard and thought for a moment.

"It's how my mother taught me lesser wards when I was young," Kyra put in.

An understanding of Kyra dawned on Cyrus and a warm smile crossed his lips. He gave a nod of permission, and then motioned for her to go.

"Thank you," Kyra said as she turned and motioned for Linny to follow her.

The two raced down the halls, both excited for the unconventional lesson ahead of them.

They only stopped when they reached the kitchen. Kyra peered in as she slightly pressed the door open. There were a few cooks milling about preparing lunch. Two were fussing over a large, steaming pot. Another was chopping onions and occasionally wiping his eyes and sniffling. A fourth was mixing something in a large metal bowl. After a few minutes, the cook put the bowl down and set the wooden spoon out to the side. Kyra saw bits of bread dough clinging to the spoon.

"That's what we want," Kyra said.

Linny tapped on Kyra's shoulder and edged forward. "Allow me," she said as she hunkered down and slipped in through the doorway. She crawled on all fours, stopping behind a large table where the cook cutting the onions suddenly gave in to a fit of sneezes and had to walk away from the table. Linny looked back to Kyra and offered a wink, then she shot off through the kitchen like a mouse, quiet and fast.

She yanked the bowl of dough down and scurried back to the doorway.

The two of them were running back through the halls long before any of the cooks knew the dough was missing. They ran all the way back to their room. Kyra took the bowl of dough in hand and smiled. There was still the pang of sadness that accompanied the memory of her mother throwing bits of dough at her, but it was lessened by Linny's presence.

She took a small amount, rolled it into a ball and then turned to Linny.

"What do I do?" Linny asked.

Kyra pointed to the clothing trunk. "First, get your wand out. We know you need a little bit of help."

Linny nodded. "Right!" She moved to the trunk and retrieved her wand.

Kyra then decided it was best to demonstrate the technique. "Here, you take this ball and throw it at me when I tell you." Linny took the dough and cocked her arm back, waiting for the command. Kyra steadied herself and turned to face Linny fully. She then tried to recall the rhyme her mother had taught her to remember the words of the spell. "All right, the word you want to remember for this spell is 'damwiu,' got it?"

"Dom-wee-ooo," Linny repeated slowly, enunciating each syllable.

"This is another reason my mother used dough to teach me. The word is spelled D-A-M-W-I-U, and you can remember it by saying the phrase, 'dough at me, ward I use,' it's a pneumonic device."

"Dough at me, ward I use," Linny said. "Damwiu." She nodded. "I say it out loud?"

"Or you can focus on the word," Kyra replied. "Throw it."

Linny launched the dough. A second later it splatted against an invisible wall in front of Kyra. The dough flattened and then began to peel off, rolling off backward and then plopping on the floor.

"Like that," Kyra said. "Now, ready your wand."

Kyra took a bit of dough and lobbed it in an underhand toss.

"DAMWIU!" Linny shouted as she flicked her wand. The dough plopped onto her shoulder. Linny grimaced and brushed the dough away with her hand. "Again," she said determinedly. Kyra tossed another ball of dough. This one smacked Linny in the cheek.

Kyra giggled softly and Linny gave a toothy grin. The younger girl then grabbed the gob of dough and hurled it back. Kyra had not been paying attention, so it struck her in the forehead. Kyra's mouth fell open and then curled upward into a large smile.

"That's it," she said, "no more playing nicely." Kyra grabbed a huge handful and slowly moved it into position to throw, all the while Linny was shaking her head and waving her wand. Kyra heaved the glob into the air. Linny shrieked and pointed her wand at it while she scrunched her face and turned away.

To Kyra's amazement, a blue bolt of fire leapt out from the wand and struck the dough, splattering the ball into smaller gobs that fell all around the room, showering both of the girls in the process.

Linny looked as shocked as Kyra.

"What was that?" Kyra asked.

Linny shrugged. "I don't know, I just thought of the flame we were trying to cast earlier and... I guess it worked."

Kyra nodded approvingly. "Excellent!" she said. "Come, let's keep trying the wards. I bet you will get it quickly enough. Kyra shaped five small balls out of the dough, laying each one on her bed until she was ready to start throwing. The first two smacked Linny in the arms. The third bounced off of something that looked like a blue shield upon impact and the two girls shrieked with delight.

"You got it!" Kyra shouted.

"I did it!" Linny squealed at the same time.

Kyra threw the last two dough balls. One bounced away and the last one got through before the ward went up. They continued until all of the dough was spent and there was a thorough mess in the room, then they sat upon their beds, laughing and trying to pull all of the bits of dough up from the walls, floor, and their clothes so they could place them back in the bowl.

"Isn't there a spell for cleaning this mess up?" Linny asked.

Kyra shook her head. "My mother never taught me that one," she said, still laughing. "We usually just made messes."

It took them a couple of hours to clean all of the dough and place it into the bowl. By that time, lunch had been prepared and the two went down to eat. As they slurped their soup in silence, they couldn't help but blush or giggle any time someone asked for bread and the cooks had to apologize that there was none, which then led into a tirade by said cook as she returned to the kitchen, fussing all the way about the missing bread. After lunch, Linny got up and said she was finally going to unpack.

She thanked Kyra for listening to her, and for showing her some more magic, then she left.

Kyra watched her go, this time confident that the younger girl was not going to break down into tears and curl up on the bed. Kyra left and walked outside.

She glanced over her back a few times, ensuring the priests hadn't somehow seen her. None of them had been at lunch that day, so she wasn't sure where they were. Once she made it to the rocky nest where she had first found Leatherback's egg, she opened her portal and stepped through to the aspen wood.

She found the dragon sitting and listening to Njar play his panpipes. The satyr merely waved with his free hand and continued playing while Leatherback purred and swayed his tail in the air behind him. Kyra moved in to her usual spot and petted Leatherback just behind the jaw as she slid down and leaned back into the large animal.

The panpipe music was melodic and sweet. Kyra couldn't help but nearly be carried away into sleep as she closed her eyes and simply enjoyed the moment. She let go of all thoughts and allowed the music to penetrate her soul.

When it was finished, Njar slipped down from the boulder he sat upon and moved to sit cross-legged in front of Kyra. Leatherback arched his neck around and placed his head off to the side of them both, still purring with his eyes closed.

"I must admit," Njar said, "I am more than a little surprised by our friend here. He seems to be strong enough to resist the taint so far. None of it has permeated his being, and more than that, he has the sweet disposition of his mother."

"You said you would show me about the beasts today," Kyra reminded Njar.

The satyr nodded. "Yes, but after the priests have finished with their examinations," he replied. Njar looked to the sun and nodded. "I should go. I will return later today." The satyr rose to his feet and opened his portal to Viverandon. He waved farewell and then stepped through. The magical doorway closed behind him, leaving no trace of him in the aspen wood.

"Priests come," Leatherback said as his eyes opened lazily.

Kyra waited, trying to put on a confident face, but her heart was pounding in her chest. She knew they would know what she had done. They would read it somehow, in her aura, like they always did. There was no secret that was safe from their magic.

It wasn't long before the three priests entered the grove, the youngest one holding aside a large bush that had grown over their usual path into the grove as the older two priests entered.

Kyra thought it strange that they had never offered their names to her. No, it was more than strange. It was hypocritical, she realized. They could read her inner most thoughts and feelings, but she was not even allowed to know their names. Not even Headmaster Herion had told her.

That was why she had made up her own names for them. First there was Dumbly, he was the taller of the two priest who were clearly older than their third companion. Dumbly was so named because he never seemed to speak. Occasionally he would clear his throat or make other noises, but he hadn't spoken more than two or three words since Kyra had met him in the Headmaster's office. The other older priest, who was a bit shorter than Dumbly, was named Glumly. He always appeared to be frowning, even when he was delivering good news about Leatherback's state. The younger priest, who appeared to be in charge, still seemed friendly enough, but it wasn't the same kind of warmth she had felt from him before. So, as she had seen a large wart on the back of his hand, she dubbed him Warty.

The three priests approached, hands tucked into their sleeves in front of their waists and their gray eyes scanning about.

"We are here to see him," Warty said with a smile.

Leatherback puffed some smoke from his nostrils.

Kyra nodded and got up to her feet. She moved away, as she had always been instructed to do before.

Glumly walked by her and placed his hands on Leatherback's side. Dumbly did likewise. Warty, however, stayed with Kyra. He turned to face her and smiled.

"What have you been up to lately?" he asked.

Kyra sighed, and tried to concentrate on the two priests who were examining Leatherback. The dragon did not purr or close his eyes. He watched the priests warily, and that unnerved her.

Warty glanced to Dumbly and Glumly and then said, "They won't hurt him. I promise. They are only ensuring the taint is not present."

"I read a book once," Kyra said quickly. "It said that you worshipped dragons, so how is it you now lord over him as if he is a threat? He has done nothing wrong. He has never hurt anyone."

Warty smiled wider and nodded. "Well, perhaps no one human," he countered. "I heard about the wylkins. We all agree that the two of you were responsible."

Kyra grew silent.

"Your aura tells me that I am right," Warty said.

"We helped a shepherd save his flocks," Kyra said after a while. "Leatherback never touched any of the sheep, and we don't need your lectures any more than we need praise from the shepherds."

"Quite right," Warty said with a nod. "I understand your motives. You seek not only to hunt your mother's murderer, but also to prove that you are not merely the daughter of a vampire."

Kyra's face flushed with anger.

Warty put a hand on Kyra's shoulder and the young sorceress pulled away sharply.

Upon seeing that, Leatherback stood up, pushing both Dumbly and Glumly away a few feet. The dragon snarled and looked down upon Warty with fierce eyes.

"Easy," Warty said as he put his hand in the air. "I was only talking with her."

"You make me uncomfortable," Kyra said honestly.

Warty gestured for Glumly and Dumbly to step away. Then he backed away from Kyra a couple of steps. "I must apologize, for that was actually my intention," Warty said with a bow of his head. "For weeks we have examined him," he said, indicating Leatherback. "We have seen nothing in him that showed us the taint was present, but we can see a streak of ferocity in his aura that we have been trying to probe. It is true, we do worship dragons, but not all dragons. We worship only the Ancients. All other dragons are highly revered and respected, but they are less predictable, and capable of violence and destruction as much as benevolence and wisdom. Forgive us, but I had to know what actions might provoke a violent response from him."

Warty then turned and bowed his head to Leatherback. "I

now see that your ferocity is placed within your loyalty to Kyra. This is what we had been hoping to see. This helps us understand that your strength is not on the cusp of turning into feral anger."

"What are you talking about?" Kyra asked. She folded her arms across her chest and glared at Warty.

The priest turned and smiled. "I am afraid we have not been entirely honest with you. You see, we can easily discern your aura at a glance. We could examine you even from a distance. However, dragons are more complicated. We cannot decipher their auras as clearly. We can see parts of it, but not all of it. In the past, some dragons have even been able to fool a few of our priests, which resulted in disaster. This is why we come so often, and must physically touch Leatherback for our examinations. This is why it also unnerves him as much as it does. I imagine that though our examinations are not painful for him, they might feel something like a worm or a snake working its way through his veins. Still, even with our combined efforts, we couldn't see the extent of his ferocity. So, today we tried a new tactic. I am happy to say that if his anger has only ever been provoked upon him seeing you uncomfortable, or possibly under a perceived threat, then he is more than likely not a threat to others, so long as the taint never touches him that is."

"I don't want you to do that anymore," Kyra said. "You can check for the taint, but don't try to provoke him again."

Warty smiled. "No, Kyra, we will not need to do that again. I have seen enough of him now to know his character. What you have here is a special bond." Warty then turned to Leatherback once more. "Tell me one thing, if you love her so much, then why place her in danger by hunting wylkins?"

Leatherback snorted and a ball of fire shot out into the air a few feet before turning to a cloud of smoke. "Something hunts her. I protect her. I fight like Gorliad did. I protect my family."

Warty nodded. He turned back to Kyra. "And why do you not just fly north, beyond the curse's grasp?"

Leatherback answered for her. "Kyra still in danger. I am not strong enough to fly her with me that far. Now we fight. When I am bigger, we will leave."

Kyra nodded and met the priest's gray eyes. "Hopefully he will be ready soon, but until then, we will hunt down the creatures that have threatened me."

Warty nodded. "We will reduce our examinations. From now on, I believe once a week is enough."

Glumly cut in. "I should think that we ought to check him the same as we do now."

Warty shook his head. "No, we do not need to." He then smiled and bowed his head once more to Leatherback. He turned to Glumly and Dumbly. "Let's head back now." The other two priests began walking to the edge of the grove. Warty stepped in closer to Kyra. He didn't fail to notice Leatherback tense. "Kyra, your bond here is something more than special. I should like to send a letter to our prelate. We have been keeping him apprised of the situation here, of course, but I want to ask him to send someone else here."

Kyra shook her head. "I don't want others to know where Leatherback is. What if the dragon slayers should see the message?"

Warty shook his head. "We priests do not command a wide array of spells, but along with our gift of true sight, we have the ability to write with magical runes. The paper will seem blank to anyone who should intercept it. Furthermore, the message itself will ask only that the individual meet us at the academy. I shall not divulge Leatherback's location."

"Who is it you want?"

Warty let out a soft sigh. "I will send for the Keeper of Secrets. It is a special officer within our order. I believe he may want to speak with you."

"With me? What for?"

Warty pointed to Leatherback. "Whether it is by chance or design, you have stumbled upon the first dragon to be untainted by Nagar's Blight in the last several hundred years. More than that, you have bonded with him and formed the most unlikely of alliances. The Keeper of Secrets would come to speak with you, for there is a prophecy about a dragon's champion that is to rise, and save this land from Nagar's Blight. I do not have the right to say it, but I wonder whether you might be that champion."

Kyra's eyes widened and she looked to Leatherback.

"What do you say, may I have your permission to send for the Keeper of Secrets?" Warty asked.

Kyra shrugged and continued to watch Leatherback.

The dragon grinned and nodded. "Send for Keeper. Kyra is a mighty champion."

CHAPTER 9

After the priests had left the aspen wood, Kyra could tell that Leatherback was still a bit unnerved by how the entire examination had gone. She had a remedy though, as she usually did on examination day. She motioned for the dragon to lie down and then slipped a small book out of her bag.

"I brought another short story," Kyra said. "I could read it if you like."

Leatherback snorted, refusing to answer verbally.

Kyra moved in and sat in her spot, leaning back against the dragon's neck. "I'm going to start reading. If you don't like it, then we can go and swim."

Leatherback closed his eyes and took in a deep breath.

Kyra patted his neck and then opened the book of children's stories. "Once there was an old man. He was poor, and had very little to eat. His shack had holes in the roof and cracks in the walls. His clothes were torn and dirty. Yet, despite his poverty, he was a happy man. He loved to whistle as he repaired his leaky roof or mended his clothes. He also sang while he worked in his garden pulling weeds and planting seeds.

"One night, late in the summer, a terrible thing happened. The air was so cold that ice and frost descended on the old man's garden and killed all of his fruits and vegetables. The old man was very sad when he woke and saw his garden destroyed. Worse yet, he had only a small amount of food left in his shack.

"He tried to save something from his garden, but it was no use. Everything was ruined. The old man decided to travel to the city to hopefully find some work so he could buy enough food to get through the winter. He packed the last loaf of bread left in his cupboard, a bag of nuts, and the last of the pickled beans he had prepared the previous fall for him to eat on his journey.

"As he walked through the green forest, he met a man sitting next to a broken carriage. The man was obviously tired.

"'Do you need any help?' the old man asked.

"'The wheel broke,' the tired man replied. 'My brother went for help yesterday, and should be back soon.' The tired man's stomach grumbled. 'Do you have any food?' he asked.

"'I have a little,' the old farmer replied. 'I suppose I can share some.' The old man opened his container of beans and gave it to the tired man.

"'Thank you,' the tired man said with a mouthful of beans. The old man smiled and walked onward. It wasn't long before he saw a squirrel, crying on the side of the trail.

"'What's wrong little fella?' the old man asked.

"'A group of birds found my secret spot and stole all of my nuts. Now I have no food for my family for winter.'"

Leatherback snorted. "Squirrels don't talk."

Kyra jabbed him softly with her elbow. "Well, they do in this story, so hush."

Leatherback grinned slightly, and Kyra knew that he was enjoying himself, despite the show he was putting on to the contrary. She began reading again from where she had left off. "The old man frowned. This was very sad news indeed. He couldn't bear to watch the squirrel cry. 'Do you have a big family?' the old man asked the squirrel.

"'There are thirteen of us altogether; six sons, five daughters and me and Mrs. Squirrel,' Mr. Squirrel replied in a squeaky voice.

"'Wow that is a big family!' The old man reached into his sack and pulled out his bag of nuts. 'Would this be enough for them?'

"The squirrel squealed and danced around joyfully. 'Oh yes, yes, yes! Thank you!' The squirrel took the bag of nuts and scurried off into the forest. The old man started whistling and walked along the road. After a while he stopped to rest on a large rock by a brook. He pulled out his bread and took a bite. As he chewed, a little fly landed on his nose.

"'Excuse me sir, might I share your bread?' the fly asked."

Leatherback chortled and shook his massive head, jarring Kyra a bit as his neck moved. "No fly can speak, they are too small!"

"Shush!" Kyra said adamantly.

Leatherback blew through his mouth, letting his lips flap together to display his displeasure.

Kyra cleared her throat and read some more. "The old man wrinkled his brow and frowned. 'I'm afraid this is all the food I have left.'

"'I promise sir, if you let me eat first, there will be enough left for you,' the fly said.

"The old man scratched his head. 'Well, I suppose you are right.' He set the bread down on the large rock for the fly and went to the brook to get a drink of water and wash his face. When the old man returned, the bread was gone. The fly lay on its back, patting its tummy and smiling.

"'Thank you, sir,' the fly said.

"The old man slumped to the rock and started to cry. 'You ate every last crumb! Whatever shall I do now?' The old man shook his head. 'I thought you promised there would be enough left for me. Now I have no food.'

"'Yes, I know,' said the fly. 'I saw you give your beans to the man with the broken wagon. I also watched you give your nuts to the squirrel. Then, even though it was the last thing you had left, you gave me your bread.' The fly buzzed over to land on the old man's knee.

"'What shall I do?' the old man asked again.

"'Take me to the city, and I will get you enough food for the winter.'

"'How can you do that?' the old man asked.

"'I am no ordinary fly.' The fly buzzed its wings furiously, producing a fine yellow dust. 'You have been very kind to others, and now I shall repay your golden heart.'

"The old man's mouth fell open as the fly first doubled, then tripled in size. Soon it was as large as the old man's fist. The yellow dust formed a cloud around the insect for a few minutes. 'Remember,' said the fly, 'a man is judged by his heart. As you have a heart of gold, so shall your reward be.' The yellow cloud dispersed, revealing a large, golden fly.

"The old man picked up the solid statuette and smiled wide. He took it to the city and sold it for enough money that he never worried about food again. He even bought a new house and clean clothes. But, he never forgot what the fly had said. For the rest of his days he continued to share what he had with others in need." Kyra closed the book and looked to Leatherback. "Well, did you like it?" she asked.

Leatherback grinned. "Good story," he said, "even if flies and squirrels can't talk."

"Well, I thought it was a nice moral. Be nice to others, and someday the niceness will return to you." She patted him on the neck and was about to say something else, but then a flash of light erupted in the grove and Njar stepped through from his portal.

The satyr held a grim expression on his face and walked toward Kyra with a determined gait. "Kyra, you are in grave danger," he said.

Leatherback began to stand. "Where is danger?" he thundered.

Njar shook his head. "Not yet, but they are coming for you."

"Who is coming for me?" Kyra asked.

Njar summoned his staff and struck the ground. A golden wave of light went out in all directions, encircling the entire grove like a great bubble of magic. "This will help ensure no other prying ears can hear us."

"Njar, what is wrong?"

"I have seen visions in the Pools of Fate. The shade comes for you, but he is not the only one."

Kyra nodded. "Yes, I know of the vampire," she said. "I

found out from Kathair."

Njar nodded. "This vampire is no simple foe. He is a great master of the arcane dark arts. If I had a thousand years, I do not believe you would be ready to face him, for he has had several thousand to perfect his abilities. He now also wields Stormfang, a powerful weapon once wielded by the founder of Kuldiga Academy."

"Yes, I know," Kyra said. "I saw all of this. Headmaster Herion had a special orb, and I watched this."

Njar shook his head. "I will not even speak the vampire's name," he said. "Were I to do so, he might find us even now, and come for us."

"Let him come," Leatherback said with a defiant roar.

Njar shook his head and pointed his spear at Leatherback. "This vampire has killed more than a score of the dragon folk in his day. He is not one to be trifled with. No, you must run."

"Where can we go?" Kyra asked.

Njar shrugged. "I do not know, but maybe it is time to try and fly to the north."

"Why not go to Viverandon?" Kyra asked. "Surely the vampire won't find us if we hide with you."

Njar shook his head. "This vampire seeks something," Njar said. "Perhaps if you give it to him, then he will let you go north."

"What does he want?"

Njar sighed. "I saw a dagger in the Pools of Fate. I saw another vampire who once held the weapon. I then saw your mother kill that vampire with it. I believe this new vampire, the one who sent the shade to your house, seeks the dagger."

"Then he must already have it," Kyra said. "The shade killed my mother and her office was torn asunder. If she had the dagger before, then it is gone now."

Njar shook his head. "No, I disagree. I have seen dark creatures in the Pools of Fate. They are circling closer to your home once more. Others are coming closer to the academy. It appears as though they are looking for you, and for the dagger."

"Did you see where the dagger is now?" Kyra asked.

Njar shook his head. "I saw your mother slay the vampire in the woods near your home. After that, I could no longer see the dagger. But, I did see that using the dagger awoke the second vampire. That is why he sent the shade to your home."

"Then I should return to my home," Kyra said. "If they are going back for it again, then I have to warn my…" Kyra stopped in mid-sentence. The word 'father' caught in her throat, and would not come out. "I should go."

"I will go," Njar said. "There is no reason to put yourself in peril this time. I suspect that the shade may be setting a trap."

Kyra then remembered something from her encounter with the shade. "Actually, I think the shade asked me where the dagger was when we fought before. The dagger must be back at my home."

Leatherback stepped forward. "I can take you," the dragon offered to Njar.

Njar shook his head. "No, I will go alone. You will stay here. Kyra, I want you to return to the academy. The headmaster there would be able to protect you if anything came to the school. Go, now."

"You said that you would help me find the garunda," Kyra reminded him.

Njar nodded. "I suspect more than garunda are heading for your home as we speak. There is no debate on this. I go, and you will stay."

Njar disappeared through a flash of light and was gone.

Leatherback reached down and nuzzled Kyra with his snout. "Go," he said softly.

Kyra nodded, but she didn't open a portal to Kuldiga Academy. She created one that went to the woods near Caspen Manor. She stepped forward and into the portal, but something snatched her and pulled her back. She felt long, hard teeth grab the back of her clothes and lift her up.

Kyra looked down to her portal and tried to squirm away. "Let me go!" she cried.

Just then, something stepped through the portal. It was a man, with only a loincloth covering him and black tattoos that stretched across nearly every inch of visible skin. He looked up and pulled a wicked knife.

Leatherback stomped on the man, crushing him, and then flicked his body through the portal.

Kyra then waved a hand and closed the portal, realizing that leaving it open was not smart. "Sorry," she said softly.

Leatherback set her down on the ground. "Njar will fight. This time, you stay with me, or go to your room."

Kyra nodded. She knew that had she gone through the portal, she likely would not have seen the strange assassin in time. She turned and hugged Leatherback's foreleg. The great beast craned his neck down and around her to reciprocate the gesture.

*****

Njar stepped through the portal and found himself atop the manor's roof. He scanned the area quickly. He could feel the shift of magical energies creeping through the forest around the manor. The hairs on the back of his neck stood and he turned to see a man covered in black tattoos climbing atop the roof near a chimney.

"Blacktongues," Njar hissed. He hated the dark band of assassins. He rushed toward the foe, leveled his staff, and pummeled the man in the face before he could rise to his feet. The Blacktongue flipped end over end until he slammed upon the ground in a crumpled heap.

Two more Blacktongues were down in the woods near where the first one fell.

Njar narrowed his golden eyes and leapt into action. He jumped from the roof, summoning a cushion of air to rise from the ground and soften his landing. As he descended, he blasted two bolts of lightning out from his staff, pulverizing the Blacktongues. He then sped through the forest, following the scent of dark magic that lingered in the air.

From what he had seen in the Pools of Fate, he expected the more deadly creatures to be lurking in the woods to the north. The fact that he had killed three Blacktongues was a good sign, but he had seen four in his visions.

Njar rounded a large mound and a fallen oak tree and then stopped short, staring at a crushed Blacktongue's body. It was bloody and mangled, as if a large animal had gotten to him. Njar shook his head and moved on. There was no time to waste.

As he moved, the air grew thicker and darker. The trees cast shadows over the forest and a strange chill hung in the air. Njar stepped into a small clearing and waited. This is where he had seen them appear. He readied his staff and turned his head to each side, his goat-like ears twitching this way and that to pick up the slightest of sounds.

He held his left hand out and studied the energy coming from the ground. A thin layer of green mist glowed as he used his magic. Flowers bloomed in the field and the grasses grew taller, but it was not to last. A river of black mist poured in from the north.

"They have come," Njar said. He quickly cast a ward spell around himself. A great orb of gold appeared, encircling and protecting the satyr.

A moment later, the black mist widened and through it came a hideous shape like a ghost. It had bony fingers and ragged robes that hung loosely around its body. A dark hood covered its head and face, but Njar knew what it was.

The wraith shrieked and stalked around the golden orb, studying it and testing for weaknesses with its foul fingers.

Njar turned his staff on the creature and sent out a shockwave. The wraith flew backward, but was not banished. Instead, the river of black mist flowed around the clearing like a massive python, squeezing the green energies into the center around the golden orb.

The satyr turned and saw two more wraiths enter the clearing. Worse than that, a shadowy figure stood on the north end of the clearing, hidden just beyond the line of trees.

"Where is the girl?" the figure hissed. "She was supposed to come."

Njar snarled, "Sorry to disrupt your plans."

The figure raised his hands and the three wraiths began to scream. The black mist rose up like a great dome, covering the clearing and blotting out the sun. The only visible light came from the green energy swirling around him, and Njar's golden orb.

The figure stepped more fully into the dome of darkness so that Njar could see him. He was a pale figure. He looked exactly as Njar had expected. His body was like that of an elf, with pointed ears and gaunt features. He was exceptionally tall, however, standing nearly eight feet. He was slender, but Njar knew that the shade was imbued with unnatural strength both physically and magically. He wore dark colored clothes with a flowing over-cloak. His hair was long and silver in color, which only accentuated his prominent cheekbones that protruded out from his gaunt face. A pair of fangs became visible as he sneered at Njar and spoke.

"Why risk yourself to save her?" the shade asked. "What can you hope to accomplish?"

Njar didn't answer. He let the shade speak while he silently calculated the time he needed to finish conjuring the right spells to escape from the trap and weaken the shade.

"My master seeks the dagger," the shade said impatiently. "Where is it?"

Njar knew he needed a bit more time before his energy would be ready for what he had planned, so he engaged the shade with his own question. "If I give you the dagger, will you leave her alone?"

The shade tossed his head back and laughed. The evil mist closed in on the orb. The green energy was entirely swallowed in the darkness, except for that which remained untouched within Njar's orb of protection.

"No," the shade said with a shake of his head. "My master also demands that I bring him the girl."

"For what end?" Njar asked. "She is but a child."

The shade shook his head. "No, she is more than that. She is Bhaltair's daughter. My master should like to take her for his own designs." The shade stalked forward and drew a long, sharp nail across the outside of the golden orb. The spell screeched and hissed as the nail created a sizzling line that threatened to crack the spell open.

"Then there is nothing I can help you with," Njar said.

The wraiths screamed loudly and the darkness pulsed inward like a great current. The orb was struck like a gong and a terrible shockwave flowed through to Njar, shaking him and causing him terrible pain.

"Your orb will not protect you," the shade hissed. "Give me what I want, and I shall make your death quick. Tell me where the girl is, and the dagger."

Njar felt the green energy from below hook into his hooves and strengthen his legs. The spell had finally worked. Terramyr herself was sending the satyr energy to banish the creatures. He soaked the energy up through his legs, letting it course through his entire being like a warm fire in his veins. He smiled at the shade.

"I think I would rather send you back to Hammenfein," the satyr said. He raised his staff and struck the ground with the butt of his staff, then he stabbed out with the top of his staff and smashed the inside of the golden shell. A blindingly hot flash of light erupted from within the orb. It was a fire of green and white that grew around the satyr within a fraction of a second. The orb expanded, cracked, and then burst open. Rays of searing light pierced the darkness, tearing holes in the dome around him. One of the beams ripped through a wraith, dissolving the creature into a pile of screaming ash on the ground. Njar leapt out toward the Shade, his staff alight with white and green flames.

The shade hissed and leapt back, receiving only a grazing swipe across his left shoulder. The wound smoked and bubbled, refusing to heal. The shade roared in anger and prepared a counter spell, but at that moment Njar's spell erupted again and a roiling wave of light rolled out until it destroyed the dome of darkness. The sunlight poured in as the trees around the clearing were blown to the ground and caught fire. The other two wraiths were disintegrated in the spell as well.

The shade screamed in pain as the sunlight burned his exposed skin. He leapt back into the woods and snarled at Njar, heaving for breath.

"I'll be back," the shade warned before disappearing into a shadow.

Njar looked around. His chest was moving quickly, pulling in as much air as he could. His body leaned heavily upon his staff for support. He hadn't been entirely sure the spell would work, but he was pleased to see that he had accomplished his goal. The Blacktongues and the wraiths were destroyed. The shade had at least been injured.

Njar could now feel the energies in the forest return to their natural, balanced state as the shade's presence was no longer upon the woods. The satyr turned to walk, but a terrible pain stung his leg. He looked down to see a terrible gash running across his furry thigh. Blood ran down in five different rivulets across his fur, and his muscle was barely able to function at all. He could feel his energy leaving him quickly. He glanced back to the shadow where the shade had escaped and tried to remember what had happened.

He hadn't felt it when it occurred, but he had seen a silvery flash when he leapt at the shade. It occurred to him now that he must have seen the shade swinging a sword, or perhaps wielding some sort of spell.

Whatever it was, he needed to get home. He tried to cast a portal to Viverandon, but nothing happened. He hadn't the energy left to cast a spell to travel that far. Njar slipped down to his knees. His breath was slowing, becoming hard to pull in with each inhalation. He then thought to open a portal to the aspen wood. It was much closer than Viverandon and wouldn't require as much energy.

He waved his hand and the flash of light rent the air in front of him. Through the portal, he could see Leatherback's blue eye staring back at him. He reached out for the dragon, and then fell over onto his face.

A great pair of talons reached through the portal and slipped under Njar's armpits, then they dragged the satyr through the portal just moments before it closed.

*****

Leatherback startled when a portal opened to the grove. Kyra had already returned to her room, and he did not expect her to return. At first, when he saw the woods through the portal, he thought perhaps another strange warrior would emerge, but he soon saw the truth of it. Njar was kneeling upon the ground, injured badly and weak. The satyr reached out his hand.

The dragon reached out to grab Njar, but not before the satyr fell over. He barely managed to pull him through before the portal closed. Njar moaned and winced as Leatherback set him down upon the grass. The dragon turned Njar onto his back and looked down into the wound. The flesh around the gash was beginning to turn black, and strange green ooze was forming at the edges.

Njar held up his hand toward Leatherback. "Your head," Njar said weakly.

Leatherback bent down and touched his head to Njar's hand.

A flash of light shot into Leatherback's mind and he saw himself flying up and over the trees, out to the northwest across a large sea, and then landing upon an island where a large tree stood. Then he saw the tree open a doorway to a new area and the vision stopped. The dragon felt cold as the light pulled back into Njar's hand. He knew what he had to do. He scooped the satyr up gently in his clutches and launched into the air with a mighty roar. He beat his wings harder than he had ever done before. He flew the same route he had seen in his vision, except the vision had been much, much faster. In reality, Leatherback flew through the night. They traveled hundreds of miles in that time, and didn't land upon the island with the large tree until the first rays of dawn broke over the horizon.

They went deep into the forest and stopped at a grand oak tree. To say it was large would not begin to describe the gargantuan tree. The speckles and patches in its bark alone were bigger than the base of most oak tree trunks. The lowest branch looked to be six feet in diameter. By all accounts, the tree should not have been able to stand. A single leaf on the tree was half the size of a man.

Leatherback moved toward the tree and nudged Njar with his nose.

The satyr woke and smiled faintly when he saw the tree.

"This is Nonac, the gate to Viverandon," Njar said weakly. "Go close to it." The satyr played a tune on his pipes and then pressed his hand to the tree. The tree groaned and lifted itself from the ground, exposing massive roots and pulling dirt up. The taproot was actually two giant roots entwined together. Slowly, they untwisted and opened up to what appeared to be nothing more than the forest beyond.

Njar pointed to the opening. Leatherback had to crouch and squeeze through, but he was able to make it, though it was a tight fit.

Once beyond the tree, Leatherback turned around to watch Nonac resettle into the ground, but he saw no large oak tree. There were only pine trees behind him. He stopped and turned slowly, taking in the new scene around him. He stood in a vast meadow of wildflowers of every color. Butterflies and bees made their way from blossom to blossom and the sun hung high in the center of the sky.

Njar held his hand out and a strange, green mist rose up to his hand. The satyr breathed easier and then slid out from Leatherback's clutches.

"Thank you, my friend," Njar said as he tried to stand. He leaned heavily on his staff and winced in pain.

Leatherback looked beyond the meadow to see a line of pine trees. There was nothing else.

Njar pointed to the far side of the meadow. "We must go there. Help me, would you?" Njar asked.

Leatherback bent down and let Njar ride upon his back. As they reached the other side, Njar played his flute and a pair of pine trees lifted and pulled their boughs back to open the way through.

Beyond the wall of trees stood a small city. There were houses, walkways, and fruit trees all around. The houses stood in a very strange arrangement, unlike anything Leatherback had seen while flying over human cities. Some were close to the trees they had just passed, others far off, but there were never more than two or three in a single grouping. Some even stood in the middle of walkways, as if someone had built the house atop where a road should be. The apple trees and other fruit bearing trees stood in a similarly chaotic arrangement. There was no perfectly lined orchard. There were scattered groups of trees, or single trees standing wherever a seed fell and took root it seemed.

The grass was up to Leatherback's ankles, and felt cool and soft as he walked, adding to the city's warm charm. Leatherback grinned at a pair of satyr children who played near a house and stopped to look at him with mouths agape.

"No one here will harm you," Njar said. "They all know I have been working with you."

Leatherback continued to smile, undaunted by the gawking satyrs he passed as they made their way through the meandering town and out the other side toward a brook. The water coursed over and around large, smooth stones crashing and splashing gently between two banks of verdant grass dotted with red poppies and golden dandelions.

The satyr tapped on Leatherback and the dragon stopped walking. Njar put his pipes up to his lips. He blew three notes gently, holding the third for a few seconds before pulling the pipes away from his mouth.

The air shimmered and waved before them, like a heatwave rising from the ground. Then, a large stone tower formed in front of them. Gray, smooth stones came into view along with a door of dark ebony wood at the base of the tower. Ivy and morning glory crept up the stonework, adding life to the otherwise cold and foreboding structure.

The door opened, but there was no sign of light from within the tower.

"Take me to the door," Njar said.

Leatherback did as he was told and then leaned down to allow Njar to slide off. The satyr hobbled in through the doorway and then turned to Leatherback.

"I need rest. When I am able, I will take you back to the grove."

Leatherback looked behind him and then back to the satyr. "I could fly back," the dragon said.

Njar cocked his head to the side. "You should rest too," he said. "You have already made a long journey."

Leatherback shook his head, but then the satyr pulled the panpipes up to his mouth and blew four notes. It was as if the music brought exhaustion upon the dragon. He felt his muscles go lax and he slowly slumped down to the ground and his eyes closed at the same time the ebony door of the tower was shut.

CHAPTER 10

Kyra didn't sleep more than a couple of fitful hours as she tossed and turned all night long. She couldn't open a portal to the grove either, for it would likely wake Linny. She thought about leaving the school grounds, but for some reason, Janik and Feberik were sitting in the hallway a short distance from her room.

They had arrived only a few minutes after Kyra had returned to her room after teleporting to the rock nest and jogging back to the academy. They had checked on her, and then told her not to leave the room, closed the door, and moved to take up positions in the hallway.

Even Janik wouldn't tell her what was going on, and Cyrus was nowhere to be seen.

She was still awake, lying in bed, when the first rays of the sun broke through her window. She slipped her feet to the floor and looked outside. The day was born with a gray, drizzly rain that slowly fell upon the school. Kyra looked toward the woods and wondered what had become of Njar.

The young sorceress went to her door and opened it. Not only were Feberik and Janik still in the hallway, they had been joined by Headmaster Herion. The old wizard was speaking to the other two, but dismissed them upon seeing Kyra open the door.

Feberik looked her way and offered her a smile, which she did not return. The large man frowned and hung his head as he turned to leave. Janik didn't look at her as he turned to follow his brother.

Headmaster Herion, on the other hand, made his way for

her room. His face was as serious as she had ever seen it before. His walk seemed invigorated by a sense of duty as well, for he strode toward her with determined, strong steps that echoed in the hallway.

"Go inside," he called out.

Kyra didn't move out of the way in time, and the old wizard turned her about with a hand on her shoulder and began directing her toward her bed as he entered the room somewhat forcefully.

Her mind began to race. Had he figured out that she and Kathair had seen the secret meeting? Did he know it was her who killed the wylkins? Or maybe the priests had told him something that had him upset. A firm hand pushed her onto her bed and then Headmaster Herion walked toward Linny. He shook her shoulder until she woke, and then instructed her to go to breakfast.

The young girl glanced to the headmaster, and then to Kyra. She almost shook her head as if to defy him, but the wizard pulled her up and gave her a slight shove toward the door.

"Move along," Herion said roughly.

Kyra nodded to Linny to show she would be all right without her. Linny nodded back and then closed the door behind her.

Headmaster Herion fumed as he paced back and forth in front of her.

Kyra opened her mouth to try to head off the tongue-lashing she was surely about to receive. "Headmaster, if I could say something—"

Herion spun on her and held a finger out in front of his face, eyes wide and crazed looking. "You may not!" he shouted. "Do you have any idea what you have done?"

Kyra shook her head.

Headmaster Herion put his hand into his pocket and pulled out a parchment. He tossed it into Kyra's lap and then pointed at it. "Open it!"

Kyra did as she was told and unfolded the letter.

"Go on, read it!" Herion said, fuming again as he began pacing anew.

Kyra looked down and read the words.

Esteemed Headmaster Herion,

It is with the greatest respect that I must inform you of an infiltration of dark magic and monsters in the Middle Kingdom. With a burdened heart, I am compelled to report to you that the Pools of Fate have made it known to me that there shall be an attack on Caspen Manor tonight. I should like to ask for your assistance in protecting Kyra, as she is a dear friend of mine and I should not like to see any harm befall her.

If possible, please send a few of your masters to Caspen Manor. I may need some help protecting the people there.

Yours in magic,
Njar

Kyra frowned and read the letter again. This is what the headmaster was furious about? She looked up to the man and shrugged. "This is a warning letter. He was trying to help."

"Trying to help!" Herion shouted. "Do you have any idea who Njar is?"

Kyra nodded. "I know he leads a tribe of satyrs in Viverandon. He is a wizard, like you."

Herion shook his head. "He is nothing like me, dear girl!" Herion spat. He snapped his fingers and a chair materialized in the room in front of where Kyra sat. "Have you never heard that satyrs are tricksters and fiends?" he asked. "Have you never read anything about those terrible creatures?"

Kyra scowled at the headmaster and shook her head. "He has been nothing but kind to me."

"How did you meet him?" Headmaster Herion asked.

Kyra closed her mouth. She was not about to betray Njar. It was he who maintained the aspen wood to help Leatherback.

Headmaster Herion sat in the chair and leaned in close. "Does he know about your dragon?"

Again, Kyra said nothing.

"All right, be silent if you must, but you will listen." Herion leaned back in his chair and folded his thin arms across his chest. "Njar is not who you think he is. I don't care if he has been nice to you or not. He is a traitor, and an enemy of the Middle Kingdom."

Kyra drew her brow in together and shook her head. "You're wrong," she said.

Herion shook his head slowly. "No, I am not. Did you know he once led an army against the Middle Kingdom? It was before King Mathias' time on the throne, but it's true. Njar led an army of four hundred satyrs against us. They had called a meeting to discuss balance in the Middle Kingdom, and the effects of Nagar's Blight since the Battle of Hamath Valley. So, King Jarek, Mathias' father, took a host of officers out to Kelboa, an island in the sea to the north west of here. Njar arrived by ship, accompanied by three of his so-called councilors. They went into the meeting place, a manor that no longer stands, and started the talks. By all accounts from the survivors, the king led a peaceful summit there, but Njar had betrayed him. Instead of coming to discuss a way to rid our lands of the curse, portals opened up in the manor and the satyr army came rushing in. They killed all but three men. A wizard named Dremathor, who was close to the king, escaped in the fury and was able to take down more than a quarter of the satyr army. He has never been heard from since, and it is widely believed that he later died from the wounds he suffered there. The other two survivors were a pair of young wizards. One you know as Cyrus, the same man who rescued your mother."

Kyra's eyes shot wide. Cyrus had never mentioned anything like that before, but then again, Kyra had never told him of Njar before either.

"Before you start to come up with more excuses, I should tell you that I was the third wizard," Headmaster Herion said.

"I was much younger then, but I was there and I remember it like it was yesterday. I can still smell the stench of blood and charred flesh." Herion stood up and shook a fist at her. "I held my dying king in my arms and watched helplessly as his life ebbed out of him. Njar and thirty of his soldiers were able to escape death, but they had dealt our kingdom a major blow that day. One the likes of which I shall never forget."

Kyra shook her head. "No, this must be a mistake. Njar wouldn't do that. He is peaceful, and only fights if he must. There has to be something else."

"I was there," Headmaster Herion said. "You were not. If you don't believe me, then you should talk with Cyrus."

Kyra held her hands up and looked away. She needed time to think it through. This didn't sound anything like the satyr she knew.

"You should know something else," Herion said. "After I received this letter before dusk, I sent the priests out to find your dragon. He is gone."

Kyra frowned and shook her head. Tears welled up in her eyes. "No, that can't be right. He never leaves that area."

Herion slapped his hands together. "If you have just handed a dragon to Njar, then we are all in a lot of trouble."

Kyra stood up. "You're wrong," she said. "Njar is the one who helped me and Leatherback. He brought us to the aspen wood that shields Leatherback from Nagar's Blight. His efforts must be working, because even the priests from Valtuu Temple say there is no taint to be found in Leatherback."

"Kyra, you are dangerously close to expulsion!" Herion shouted.

"Then expel me!" Kyra yelled back, not giving an inch of ground. "You think I like living here and seeing Feberik? Go ahead and send me away. My father has already denounced me after my mother's murder, so why should I care if you want to send me away too?" Kyra's hands balled into fists and her eyes would have melted the wizard like wax had she had that kind of power.

Herion was about to say something else when the door

burst open. He and Kyra looked to the doorway and saw Lady Arkyn, a beautiful blonde-haired half-elf.

"I have the report," she said.

"Out with it then," Herion said.

Arkyn nodded. "There are four human casualties at Caspen Manor, all of them are Blacktongues."

"Blacktongues?" Herion echoed. "I thought them extinct."

Arkyn shook her head. "There is more. I found a small clearing with scorch marks all around and trees that had been splintered and burned. In the clearing, I found three ash piles. I collected samples." Lady Arkyn moved her hand to a small leather pouch and produced three glass vials filled with gray ash.

Headmaster Herion took the glass vials and turned them over as he held them up in the sunlight. He whistled through his teeth as they sparkled and shimmered a strange, greasy purple color.

"They are the remains of wraiths," Lady Arkyn said.

Herion nodded his agreement. "That they are." He gave the vials back to her. "What of the servants, and Lord Caspen?"

Lady Arkyn shrugged. "None of them saw anything. One of the servants heard an explosion and later saw smoke rising from the forest, but no one saw any sign of an attack until I arrived and found the Blacktongue bodies."

Kyra then asked, "Do Blacktongues wear tattoos across their bodies?"

Lady Arkyn nodded.

Kyra folded her arms and looked back to Headmaster Herion. "I opened a portal to the woods outside my old home. I would have walked through, against Njar's orders for me to return here, but Leatherback pulled me away. As I was held in the air, a Blacktongue came through the portal and looked as though he wanted to kill me. Leatherback stomped on him and tossed him back through the portal. Now tell me, does that sound like Njar was trying to hurt us?"

"Njar?" Lady Arkyn asked. She turned to the headmaster. "You didn't mention he was involved."

Herion waved Arkyn off. "Did you see any sign of him?"

Lady Arkyn shook her head. "None," she said.

"Speak of this to no one," Herion told Lady Arkyn. She nodded her head and exited the room, closing the door after her.

"Njar isn't our enemy," Kyra said.

Herion shook his head and sighed. "Then where is Leatherback?"

Kyra shrugged. "Let me go to the grove. I will look for him."

"Out of the question," Herion replied. "I can't send you out there alone."

"Then the priests will go with me," Kyra said. "They trust me. They know I am not lying."

"I don't think you're lying either," Herion clarified. "I am only worried that you have been deceived."

"Very well," Kyra began, "then you can come with me too."

"What?" Herion squawked. "Go traipsing about looking for a dragon that officially I have to pretend doesn't exist or else the king will have my head? No, thank you!"

"You, me, and the priests. If we all go together, then you will see the truth of it."

Herion opened his mouth to speak, but the door opened again.

"Oh for the love of the Ancients, what is it now?!" Herion shouted as he wheeled on the intruder.

To their surprise, Cyrus stood in the doorway. He bowed his head.

"I do apologize, but perhaps I could offer my assistance," he said. "I will accompany Kyra to the grove."

Herion narrowed his eyes on Cyrus. "Who told you about this?"

Cyrus snorted. "Does it matter?" he asked. "What matters is we have an old enemy that is meddling in our affairs. I will accompany Kyra, and then I will repay the satyr for what he did to our king those many years ago."

"No!" Kyra said. "You cannot do this."

Herion stroked his chin, then he nodded. "Very well," he said.

Cyrus then held up a finger. "However," he began, "I might wonder why an enemy would send us a fair warning."

"What?" Herion replied.

Cyrus shrugged and looked to Kyra. He winked at her and then pointed to the letter. "You say he warned us of the attack. I just heard Lady Arkyn's report of the event at Caspen Manor. I should say that I am of the opinion Njar is on our side in this fight."

"What on Terramyr would make you say that?" Herion asked.

"A shade is a powerful enemy. Njar knows this. He knows that if he lets it fester, a shade's nest can grow to uncontrollable power. I say, let me go and talk with the satyr. Let me see what kind of scheme he is playing at. If I feel like he is the same trickster from before, then I will kill him. However, if he is an ally, even a temporary ally of convenience, then I say we let him be."

Herion bristled. "I can't believe you are saying this. It's an outrage!"

Cyrus smirked. "I thought Feberik was the one with the temper around here?"

Herion shook a finger at Cyrus. "Why should I go along with this?"

Kyra wanted to explain that Njar was helping her locate the garunda beasts that would lead her to the shade, but she dared not say that for fear the two wizards would lock her up for her own protection. She just stood there and watched the two old men argue until finally Cyrus held up his hand and said something that Herion had not been prepared to hear.

"I know why the satyrs attacked us," Cyrus said.

Herion folded his arms and puffed air loudly to show his disbelief.

Cyrus was undeterred. "There were necromancers and warlocks among the king's court," Cyrus said.

"Hogwash!" Herion shouted. "Kuldiga Academy exists to hunt such foul creatures down. None would ever get so close as to be among the king's court."

Cyrus shook his head. "There were three that I am aware of. Two of them died in the attack, and one shadowfiend escaped." Cyrus stepped in close to Headmaster Herion, his brow stern and his eyes alight with fury. "Herion, I know we haven't walked the same path since that day. In fact, we never met again until I came to work here, but you know of my reputation. I hunt the darker creatures of magic. If anyone knows a shadowfiend, it's me."

"Then tell me, who was the shadowfiend that escaped?" Herion asked.

"His name is Dremathor," Cyrus said flatly. "Of course that is not his true name, but it is the name we knew him by."

"Dremathor is dead," Herion countered.

Cyrus shrugged. "Perhaps, but I would doubt that very much. Just because someone has not been heard from in a long time does not mean they are dead."

"When did you learn about this?" Herion asked.

"I went to his home, after the attack. The items I found therein left little to the imagination. I am telling you, he was a shadowfiend."

"You are saying the satyrs lured us there in order to kill the necromancers, warlocks, and shadowfiends that had embedded themselves within the king's court?" Herion shook his head. "I have heard some whoppers in my day, but this one tops them all."

Cyrus sighed and shook his head. "Will you allow me to go with Kyra and investigate the matter?"

Herion thought for a moment, and then nodded his head. "All right. You may go, but you had better be right about this."

Cyrus nodded.

Herion stormed out of the room without another word and slammed the door.

Cyrus turned and moved his finger in the air, the lock slid into place on the door to allow them some privacy. "A bit emotional, that one," Cyrus commented.

Kyra burst into a fit of laughter and then sat on the bed. "Is everything you said true?" she asked.

Cyrus shrugged. "I can't be certain, but that is what I've put together in the time since that attack. Besides, if Njar warned us about the assault on Caspen Manor, I see no reason to distrust him now. Even if he only desires self-preservation, it appears that the satyr is on our side."

Kyra nodded. "I believe he only wants to help." Her mind then turned to the things Njar had told her about before sending her to the academy. "Cyrus, the artifact you mentioned before, the one that the wraith attacked that boy for and the thing you thought my vampire father had, was it a dagger?"

Cyrus' eyes shot wide and he looked at Kyra suspiciously. "Why do you ask?"

Kyra narrowed her eyes on the old wizard, as if puzzling it out in her own mind before telling him the rest. After a moment, confident that she was on to something, she proceeded to tell him what Njar had seen in the Pools of Fate. "Njar saw a dagger. He said he could see it in my mother's possession, and then she used it to kill Bhaltair, my vampire father. After that, Njar said he lost track of the dagger, but the attack on Bhaltair is what awoke the shade and other creatures in the area. He thinks the dagger is at my house, and that's why they attacked it."

Cyrus nodded thoughtfully. "Then we have no time to lose. You go and wait for your dragon in the grove. I will go to Caspen Manor and search the place for the dagger. If it is there, I will find it, and destroy it."

"Why destroy it?"

Cyrus stopped for a moment and looked her in the eyes. He nodded and finally opened his mouth. "You remember how I spoke of the creatures in Iverglendar, the underdark, right?"

Kyra nodded.

"This dagger can summon creatures from there, or possibly even from Hammenfein itself. It's a very powerful relic, and it needs to be destroyed. If we get rid of it, the shade might even be forced to leave."

"You can destroy it?"

Cyrus nodded. "To tell you the truth, the last time I fought a wylkin, it was in Bhaltair's lair. He must have had the dagger in order to create a slave out of that terrible creature. Now that I realize your mother took it when we rescued her, it makes sense. Now, I just have to find where she put it, and then I can end this madness. You'll be safe, and then you can focus on getting Leatherback out of here before the curse overtakes him."

Kyra looked at the old wizard curiously. How did he know about that? She hadn't mentioned to him that she was thinking of flying to the north. So how could he have known?

Cyrus smiled. "Don't look at me like that. Leatherback isn't just a friend to you, he's family, am I right?"

Kyra nodded.

Cyrus patted her on the back. "We'd all do anything to rescue our families." He stood up and motioned to the floor. "Come on, we should go. You wait for Leatherback at the grove. I'll go to your old house."

"Are you sure it will be safe?" Kyra glanced at the door. "Headmaster Herion seemed pretty convinced that Njar was out to hurt us."

Cyrus winked. "I think I would rather trust your instincts on this one. You have dealt with him the most recently. You would know by now if he wasn't what he seemed. Let's not give heed to doubts from an old man that has harbored hate for decades."

Kyra nodded. She opened her portal and stepped through.

Cyrus waited until the portal closed and then he let out a wicked laugh. "Now I shall have the dagger, and soon I shall use it to slay those piddling warlocks and keep it for myself. Then, no one shall be able to stop me."

The old wizard opened a portal to the woods outside of Caspen Manor and stepped through.

He exited the portal amidst a copse of twisted elm trees.

He could still smell the musty odor of the magic that had exploded nearby. It held a sulfuric tinge to it that was unmistakable to the wizard. Lady Arkyn had left that detail out of her report, but that was not entirely unexpected as she was not as experienced in magic as he was.

The wizard stalked his way out of the woods and stopped as he approached the east side of the manor. He was not entirely unfamiliar with the home. He had been here before. He had even searched for the dagger here as well, but he had never found it. Now that he had reliable information that led him to believe it was still here, he was determined to find it.

He floated up to the window that belonged to the late Lady Zana's office. A wave of his hand was all it took to open it, then he sailed through as easily as a summer breeze. He set down lightly upon the floor and was intrigued to see that the office was still in shambles, exactly as it had been after the night of the murder. The desk was overturned and books were everywhere. Bookshelves were tossed across the floor and bits of paper and glass were strewn all over the room.

Cyrus went to work searching for the dagger. He checked every book, every drawer or space in the overturned desk, and every inch of the office. When he found nothing, he pulled a vial of crushed red crystal from his pocket and shook some out into his left palm. He threw the crystal into the air and watched it fall. If dark magic was present in the room, the crystals should have floated toward it, but they fell straight to the floor.

Cyrus sighed and went to the door.

He pressed his cheek to the wood and heard music coming from somewhere in the manor. He tried the knob, but it was locked. Cyrus pointed to the keyhole and the pins slipped up into place with tiny little *clicks*. The door opened easily after that, and he stepped into the hallway.

Now that he was out of the office, he could clearly hear fiddlers and boisterous laughing coming from down in the lower levels.

It appeared that Feberik's recent visit had had little lasting effect on Lord Caspen. Not that it bothered Cyrus of course, but he always found it interesting to learn about peoples' vices. He couldn't help but wonder if Caspen had been this kind of man all along, or if it was a weakness brought to the open by the shock of losing a wife and then learning that Kyra was not even the nobleman's daughter.

Whatever the reason, Cyrus was grateful for the cover that the party downstairs afforded him. He was able to easily walk through the halls until he found the late Lady Zana's room. Unfortunately, the search there went the same as in her office. He checked every jewel box, drawer, and every bit of space in the large wardrobe. He even lifted the mattress and looked under the bed. At last, he pulled out some more of the crushed red crystal. He tossed it in the air and grimaced when it fell straight down again.

There was no other place to look. He sighed and sat on the bed.

A thought came to him as he pondered where else he might look. Perhaps Kyra's mother had hidden the object in Kyra's bedroom. Cyrus got up to his feet and left the room, closing the door quietly and locking it after himself. He then padded softly down the hall and opened each door he came to. The first was a water closet. The second was a storage room of sorts, with old blankets stuffed inside. The third was a small room with a spinning wheel and various colors of fabrics and threads collecting dust upon a series of wooden shelves that covered the wall.

The next room was entirely empty. Cyrus almost closed the door, but something nagged at him. He slipped inside and closed the door. The sunlight from the window was more than enough to illuminate the chamber. The wood floor was bare. There was no furniture, and nothing upon the walls. The window didn't' even have any curtains.

Cyrus then looked to the corner and saw scratches in the wood floor. He moved to the area and noted that there were four scratches, each originating in points that could have easily have been where corner posts for a bed had once been.

The old wizard knew that he was now standing in what had once been Kyra's bed chamber. Even he had a hard time not feeling some amount of empathy for her as he realized that Lord Caspen had literally removed any reminder of her existence. How odd it was that the mother's office and room would be left untouched, while the daughter's room would be entirely cleared.

Cyrus shook his head. He doubted whether he would ever understand Lord Caspen.

He exited the room and stepped into the hallway. As he closed the door, someone else opened a door at the far end of the hall. Cyrus looked up to see a servant, or at least that is what he assumed the man to be judging by his drab clothes and unkempt hair.

The servant pointed to Cyrus. "What are you doing up here? The party is downstairs."

Cyrus couldn't afford to be seen. On the other hand, he couldn't cause any sort of hysteria by killing the man either. Kyra knew where he was. If he used magic to kill the man, she would know it was him, and then there would be no keeping her trust. Though he planned to double-cross the warlocks of the Order of the All-seeing Eye, he had no intention to harm Kyra if he didn't have to.

He quickly cast a spell that froze the man in place. Cyrus then quickly moved to the man and pulled him into the room he had just exited from. Luckily, it was a large room with a sizeable liquor cabinet. Cyrus smiled at his good fortune and grabbed a bottle of whiskey. He drank some himself, and then poured some down the servant's throat, using a spell so that the liquid would slide down without choking the man. Cyrus then magicked the man into a nearby chair and rendered him unconscious.

The old wizard weaved a spell of forgetting on the servant, erasing his memories for the day, and then placed the half-empty bottle of whiskey in the man's hands. Cyrus then went to the window and looked down. The woods were a short distance away, but there were a pair of workers down there loading empty crates into a horse-drawn cart.

Cyrus decided it was simplest just to open a portal from inside the room and return to Kuldiga Academy. Better to return empty handed than to be caught red handed in Caspen Manor.

CHAPTER 11

Kyra waited in the grove for Njar for the entire day. He never showed. Worse than that, Leatherback never appeared either. Kyra sat in the grass in the middle of the aspen wood until the sun began its descent toward the western horizon, then she slowly began walking back toward Kuldiga Academy.

She didn't use her portal this time, preferring instead to think as she walked. Headmaster Herion's words echoed in her ears a thousand times over, giving room for the seeds of doubt to grow in her mind. She thought back to everything Njar had done for her, and for Leatherback. She couldn't believe that it would be just to gain her trust and take Leatherback away from her. What purpose could that serve?

After a while, she came to the pool she and Leatherback had made in the mountain stream. She leaned over the high walls of earth and dipped her hand in the cool waters. She laughed as she thought about the flying mud and the mess they had made of this place.

Kyra decided that it was time to let go of all of the stress. She stripped down to her undergarments and then jumped into the pool. As the water caressed her body, she pushed everything out of her mind, giving herself the freedom to simply enjoy the moment she was in. She swam across the pool, then dove down into the water and swam back across without coming up for air until she reached the opposite bank. As she popped out of the water, she ran her hand over her face, wiping the water away and pulling her hair to the back of her head.

She swam the breadth of the pool twice more, and then

she emerged from the water and laid upon a large, flat rock until she was dry enough to put her clothes back on. Then, she opened a small portal and jumped farther into the woods, beyond the rock nest and closer to Kuldiga Academy.

She made it back to her room a half hour before supper. Linny was inside, sitting cross-legged upon her bed and staring at a piece of paper in front of her.

"What's that?" Kyra asked.

"My new class assignment," Linny replied. "I was assigned to a Master Obren, have you heard of him?"

Kyra shook her head. "No," she said. "How many days a week will you have to meet?"

Linny shrugged and tilted her head to the side. "I guess all of them. It says that we have a lot of lessons to catch up on, and that I will be spending every day of the week with Master Obren. It's a good thing I already have my textbook."

Kyra nodded her head. "I can always help if you have homework," she offered.

Linny smiled. "Thanks."

Kyra smiled back and moved to lie upon her bed, flinging herself backward and landing haphazardly on the mattress.

"Are you all right?" Linny asked.

"I'm okay," Kyra said. She wasn't about to share her secret about Leatherback with anyone else at this point.

Linny slid off her bed and flattened out the front of her skirt. "I'm going to go down for supper. I start my new class tomorrow, so I want to be back to bed early."

Kyra nodded. "I'll catch up soon," she said as she threw her left arm up over her eyes. She heard Linny walk out of the room and close the door. Kyra was now back to thinking about Njar and Leatherback. She wished she knew where they were. If they were in Viverandon, then how could she reach them? Njar had shown her the pools of fate once, but she would not be able to create a portal to get that far away from Kuldiga Academy. It may as well have been across the world for how hard it would be to find.

Footsteps approached her door and then stopped. A

knock sounded against the wood. Two taps and then the latch clicked open.

"Kyra?" Kathair's voice called out. "Linny told me you were back."

Kyra peeked out from under her elbow and nodded. "I'm here," she said flatly.

Kathair entered the room and then closed the door. "Seeing you now, I take it you haven't seen Leatherback today?"

Kyra shook her head and pushed up to a sitting position. "No, and I don't know when, or even *if* he'll turn up."

"Bah," Kathair said with a wave of his hand. "For all the time you spent with him before he hatched and afterward, you may as well consider yourself his mother. He'll be back before you know it."

Kyra didn't respond.

Kathair held up a rolled parchment and smiled. "Besides, I think I have a lead on that garunda we need."

"We?" Kyra echoed skeptically.

Kathair nodded. "You didn't think I would let you face the shade alone, now did you?"

Kyra shook her head. "Kathair, honestly..."

Kathair shook his head. "Hey, I stopped sneaking up on you, I even knocked just now," he said as he pointed to the door. "The least you can do is call me Lepkin."

Kyra smiled. "All right, Lepkin, but I don't think you should come with me. It isn't exactly the same as sword practice."

Kathair nodded. "I know that, but we're friends. Your fights are mine too. Now come on over here and take a look at this." Kathair unrolled the parchment to reveal a poorly drawn map.

"You make this yourself?" Kyra asked.

Kathair grinned. "I never said I was an artist, but it gets the job done. Look here." He pointed to a square on the parchment that had the label 'Caspen Manor' written next to it. "This is your old house, where the recent attack took place.

Over here," he said as he pointed to a mess of circles drawn squished together, "is where you found the egg. Remember the wraith that attacked you there? Well, I think this might be the best range to search in for the garunda."

"You mean the miles and miles between the two points?" Kyra asked with a shake of her head.

"Well, yeah, but I already did the research. I wouldn't come to you if I didn't have a more specific area to search." He pointed to a pair of squares that were nearly in the middle between the first to points. "This is Midton, a fairly good sized city. I overheard that there have been strange attacks during the nights there. Not every night, but a lot of them. I also did some research and discovered that there are a couple of foothills nearby the town. In those foothills is an old, abandoned silver mine. It's the perfect location for a garunda."

"If the garunda is there, then so is the shade," Kyra reminded him.

Kathair shook his head. "From what I have read, shades can't abide by silver. Something about it irritates them, weakens them, or harms them, depending on the book you are reading. I think this might be a stray garunda."

"A stray?" Kyra questioned. "And where would you get the idea that there can be stray garunda beasts roaming the countryside?"

Kathair smiled wide and produced a book from the back of his trousers. "I may have borrowed one more journal from Headmaster Herion's office."

"You are going to get caught if you keep snooping around like that," Kyra said.

Kathair shook his head. "Nah, I always put them back when I am done. Anyway, this journal has a passage on garunda beasts in it. It says that it isn't uncommon for the animals to stray away from their master at times. And, listen to this," Kathair said excitedly as he flipped to a page that had a small ribbon pressed into it for a place marker. The young man cleared his throat. "Garunda beasts who stray from their masters are often wont to hide in silver mines, where they can rest easy knowing that their masters will be averse to following them inside due to the adverse effects they would suffer." Kathair turned the book around and handed it to Kyra. "You see, it's perfect. I located a garunda beast that is alone, and has no shade to help protect it. With any luck, we can kill it, take its blood, and then we can hunt the shade."

Kyra smiled wide. She would prefer that Leatherback go with them, but she couldn't pass up this chance. The only question was how to get there.

"Are we going by horse, or am I going to try and teleport us there blindly?"

"Can't you send us both there?" Kathair asked, his smile fading somewhat.

Kyra shrugged. "I haven't tried to take another person with me before. I'm not sure it would work. Also, I have to have been at the place once so I can visualize it, and even then I can only cover medium distances."

"You've never been to Midton?" Kathair asked.

Kyra shook her head.

Kathair frowned, pouting out his lower lip and drawing his brow into a tight knot above his nose. "We could go by horse then," he said. "It's only a few hours' ride from here. The sun hasn't gone down yet. If we hurry, we can make it by nightfall."

"Do you have a horse?" Kyra asked.

Kathair grinned that boyish, impish grin of his and his blue eyes sparkled with delight. "Follow me," he said.

The two of them wound their way out into the courtyard and snuck along till they reached the stables. A pair of large horses nickered as the two of them approached. One of the horses Kyra recognized.

"This is Feberik's horse," she said as Kathair was busy grabbing the saddle.

"Yep," he said as he tossed the saddle up and onto the horse. Then he bent down and began fastening the straps.

"I don't want to take his horse," Kyra said.

"Why not?" Kathair asked. "If it can carry his giant

backside, it should easily be able to get us to where we need to go."

Kyra stifled a laugh. "No, it isn't that, it's just I don't want to ride *his* horse. Let's take this other one." She pointed to the large paint in the next stall over.

Kathair shook his head. "Can't take that one."

"Why not?" Kyra asked. "Whose horse is it?"

Kathair shrugged and yanked on the saddle, testing it before he leapt up onto Feberik's horse. "I dunno, but you see those beads woven into the mane?"

Kyra looked around and saw three red beads woven into the horse's hair. "Yes," she said.

"That is a special kind of horse. I don't remember the name of the breed, but they are raised at Cedreau Manor. The beads signify that the horse has an owner, and the special thing about Cedreau horses is that they are loyal to one rider for their lifetime. If you try to ride it, it will throw you off, I guarantee it. Seeing as how there are no other horses, that leaves us with Feberik's horse." Kathair held his hand down to Kyra. She finally relented, sighing and cursing her luck as she moved around to mount the horse.

Kathair looked around the courtyard once more, and then he kicked the horse into a quick trot out through the open gates. As soon as they were clear of the academy, he kicked it up into a full gallop. They rode for a little more than two hours, galloping over a well-built road that took them directly to Midton. The two of them spent the journey in silence, with only the sound of the pounding hooves *clip-clopping* in the air.

As Kathair had guessed, the two arrived just as the sun was beginning to touch the western horizon. The bright pinks and oranges lit up the sky as though it were alight with magical flames. A cool wind blew in from the east, carrying with it the scent of cattle fields that they had passed on their way into Midton.

They didn't bother stopping in the town itself, but rather continued on out the other side, headed for the old silver mine. They reached the tunnel just as the first, long shadows of night began to stretch their fingers across the foothills.

A strange sound came from within the tunnel, something like a roar and a growl mixed into one.

The two dismounted from Feberik's horse and stretched their legs. Kathair drew a longsword and a mini-crossbow. Kyra was armed only with her magic.

"It's going to be dark in there," Kyra pointed out.

Kathair nodded. "Well, we can either use light, or we can wait at the entrance and see if the beast comes out."

Kyra took in a breath and thought for a moment. If they made a torch, it was likely that it wouldn't give enough light to see the beast before it pounced on them. On the other hand, if they used a magical light, it might alert the beast to their presence long before they ever got close enough to attack it.

"I wish Leatherback were here," Kyra said.

Kathair nodded. "I won't pretend that it wouldn't make me feel better also, but he isn't. So, what do you want to do?"

"Maybe let's wait for it. If we sit on top of the entrance and pounce on it when it comes out, then we might have a better chance of catching it by surprise."

"Sounds good. It has to come out some time for food, right?"

Kyra nodded. "You sure there is only one?" she asked, nerves causing her voice to crack.

Kathair nodded emphatically. "Reports from Midton always claim to see one large, black beast that attacks animal or man after dark."

The two of them scrambled atop the entrance and sat there quietly, waiting for the monster to emerge. A screen of silvery clouds rolled in front of the bright moon, dimming what little light they had to work with.

Off in the nearby distance, Feberik's horse whinnied nervously and pawed at the ground.

The two of them waited for well over an hour before they heard anything.

Then, a low growl emanated from the tunnel. It grew louder and louder until they could hear heavy footsteps on the ground. The horse whinnied again and turned to run, its hooves echoing in the night. A black mass of fur and claws came shooting out of the tunnel, snarling as it ran for the horse. Kathair jumped down, but missed the quick beast.

Kyra jumped to her feet and summoned a fireball, but it too missed the speedy demon as it rushed the now frantically galloping horse. A moment later the beast lunged, and the horse was tackled to the ground, screaming and shrieking as the snarling beast ripped into its flesh.

Kathair ran forward a few steps, and then took aim with his mini-crossbow. He fired, and the bolt struck the beast in the left side. It snarled and turned on him, baring its yellow fangs that shone wet with blood in the moonlight. It pawed the ground and took two steps on all fours toward Kathair. The young man lifted his sword to the ready position and called out to the beast.

"Come on then, let's have us a dance, shall we?"

At that moment, the clouds moved away from the moon, uncovering its full brightness.

Kyra's heart stopped in her chest and her mouth dropped in horror as she grasped for the words to scream.

The beast rose up to stand upon its back legs. Its torso was wide and muscular, and black fur covered its entire body. Its snout was filled with fangs and its front legs ended in razor sharp claws. It howled into the night air, sending chills down Kyra's spine.

Then the werewolf charged.

Kyra, still frozen with fear, watched as the beast sprinted for Kathair.

The young man seemed undaunted by his mistake, and ran forward, shouting and yelling. An instant before the two collided, the werewolf leapt forward and Kathair ducked out to the left, swinging his sword up into the creature's side as he spun safely away.

The werewolf snarled and landed upon all fours again. It spun around nimbly and Kyra watched its hulking shoulder blades rise and fall as it stalked toward Kathair. The young man grinned and held his sword up, ready for another swing.

Kyra finally regained her senses and summoned another ball of fire. She sent it hurtling toward the werewolf, who was caught unawares in the rear. The fire blasted its fur from its body and scorched its rump. It howled and its back legs collapsed under itself. Kathair rushed in and slashed at the werewolf's neck. The beast recoiled from the attack and the blade managed only to graze the werewolf's skin. It stood on its hind legs and swung out with its left hand, but Kathair was quick to leap away several feet.

Kyra sent another ball of fire, this time aiming for the werewolf's head.

The beast ducked under it and came running toward her with alarming speed. It tore up the ground with its furious claws as it closed the distance between them.

Kathair called out for her to run, and tried to pursue the beast, but he was nowhere near as fast a runner as the werewolf.

The monster leapt into the air, claws out in front and fangs close behind.

Kyra summoned a powerful ward and put her hands up in front of her. The beast slammed into a blue orb, scrambling to get atop it and claw at it ferociously. It slammed down with its arms and even bit at the orb, but nothing was getting through.

Still, with each assault on the orb, Kyra could feel the strain of maintaining her spell. Soon a crack formed in the orb and the beast moved to concentrate on that point. A small piece of the orb was ripped away, making a sound like shattering glass. The werewolf howled in delight and then stretched his arm down to swipe at Kyra. The young sorceress ducked low and tried to reinforce the orb.

Just then she heard a feral yell and looked up to see Kathair. He had managed to climb up the side of the hill and was now leaping through the air toward the werewolf. The beast tried to retract its arm and move away, but Kathair was faster. His blade chopped down and severed the werewolf's arm just inches below the shoulder.

The werewolf cried out and tumbled down to the ground below the hill and writhed in pain. Lepkin bounced off the side of the orb and stumbled down the hill as well. The monster rose up, eyes filled with bloodthirsty rage and it turned on Kathair. It raised its good arm to strike at the young man, who had not yet recovered from his fall.

Kyra shouted out in anger and directed her fury at the werewolf. The orb disappeared and in its place a column of fire swirled out from her hands. The whirling flames shot out like lightning, blasting the monster and lifting it high into the air. The werewolf spun around and around, caught in a fiery tornado of death. It howled one last time and then turned to ash that fell softly to the ground.

The young sorceress then scrambled down to check on Kathair. The young man was lying upon his back and grinning wildly.

"So, I guess that was *not* a garunda beast then?" he said with that devilish grin.

Kyra thumped him in the chest and puffed air angrily as she walked toward the pile of ash on the ground.

Kathair laughed a couple of times and then hurried to follow after her, placing his sword back into its sheath. "Also, next time we should take Leatherback," he added.

Kyra glared at him and pulled a glass vial, which had been meant to collect garunda blood, out of a satchel on her belt and scooped up some of the ash.

"What are you doing?" Kathair asked.

Kyra shook her head. "With Feberik's horse dead, we will need proof that we did something worthwhile," she replied.

Kathair's smile disappeared. "Nu-uh, I'm not telling Feberik *anything* about his horse."

Kyra corked the vial and stood up. "You would let him think it just disappeared?"

Kathair nodded. "Yep," he said. "I'll even let him think a monster killed it, but he doesn't need to know that I was the one who brought it out here."

"Let me get this straight, you will laugh off fighting a

werewolf, but you don't want to tell Feberik that you stole his horse, is that what I am hearing?"

Kathair scratched the back of his head. "Maybe we can buy him a new one here and he won't notice..."

Kyra shook her head and began laughing. "You're ridiculous," she commented.

Kathair shrugged. "Call me whatever you like, but I am not telling Feberik, and that's final. Now, can you teleport us back to Kuldiga Academy, or do we have to walk?"

CHAPTER 12

Kathair spent most of the next morning sitting in the chair next to the bookshelf that concealed the ladder leading to the crawlspace beside Headmaster Herion's secret meeting room. He was busy gnawing on a pear and hoping that Kyra kept to her word and had not ratted him out about Feberik's horse. Kathair assumed that Feberik would figure it out eventually, but he hoped to be back in the field with the dragon slayers by the time that occurred.

Either way, he had absolutely no plans for leaving the safety of his hidden room today. Dengar and the others were preparing to conduct a routine patrol out to the north, and had given him the option of staying, so there would be no expectations for him to be seen on campus by anyone at all.

He had even been sure to swipe enough food from the kitchen that he could comfortably stay hidden for at least another day if he had to.

After two pears were chewed down to their seeds and stems, Kathair grabbed Headmaster Herion's journal and tucked it into the back of his trousers. He thought it wise to at least return the book sooner rather than later. If he was going to be hung for stealing a horse, perhaps he could avoid adding being burned alive by an angry wizard.

It was peculiar, really, how much he had changed since coming to Kuldiga Academy. Kathair had always explored before, and been in plenty of trouble with the elves for getting into places that he should never have set foot into, but he hadn't really ever been a thief before. He had always looked and thought about how to get things from the places he explored or snuck into, but he had never actually done it. He didn't have to think long before coming up with the answer as to why he was doing it now, though. Even a fool could see he was doing it to impress Kyra. It was working too, but now as he made his way into a small tunnel that he could barely crawl through, and which smelled of mold and stale water, he had to wonder if it was worth it.

After all, Kyra was betrothed to Feberik, and Feberik had made it perfectly clear that he would be more than willing to crush Kathair like a bug if he caught him hanging around Kyra.

Kathair lifted his shirt collar up over his nose and crawled through the dank tunnel. Maybe it wasn't the smartest thing to do, but he liked Kyra, and they were friends. If he could help her solve the riddle of her mother's murder, and bring the culprit to justice, then that is what he wanted to do. Had he ever known his own mother, he would assume he would appreciate someone helping him in similar circumstances.

After about two hundred yards on his hands and knees, Kathair was finally able to stand up. A small, rectangular chamber allowed him to choose between three additional tunnels - two more that had drained into the chamber at some point in the past, and one that flowed outward, or at least he assumed it did, for it sloped downward and was set lower than the others, like a drain. He had never actually followed it though. He had always been just wary enough that someone might unleash water from somewhere and sweep him away that he never dared chance it.

He didn't choose any of the tunnels, however. Instead, he turned around and found his chosen handholds in the jutting rocks above him. He climbed up the wall of the chamber and then squeezed into a space that went straight up. It was narrow enough that once he was out of the chamber, he could push his back against the wall behind him and scoot upward with his hands and knees. It was essentially like crawling again, only this time if he slipped, he would end up with a lot more than just a face full of moldy water.

Up he went, about thirty feet or so, before he found the

ledge he was looking for. He reached out with his right hand and pulled himself into a chute that ran horizontally. It gave him a chance to rest his knees a bit. He wormed his way through for about twenty feet and then the chute turned upward again. This time, it was wide enough that he used one hand and one foot on either side, using a kind of half jump to propel himself vertically for another twenty feet. At the top, the chute opened up into a large, square area with beams of wood running parallel to each other across it and smaller poles crossing underneath the beams. The poles held wooden panels in place in the ceiling above Headmaster Herion's office.

It had been an accidental discovery the first time, but once Kathair had found it, he had often returned to this spot. Just lying on the beams above the wooden panels was close enough for him to hear any discussion in the office. Some of the conversations had been horribly boring, but many had been quite informative. Why, in his time in the space above the ceiling, Kathair had learned more about the Middle Kingdom than he had in all of his years before, and that included when he had studied with the elves of Tualdern.

He snaked out onto the nearest beam, careful to move slowly and silently. He didn't hear any talking from below, but there was no way to be sure the room was empty until he removed a ceiling panel. For all he knew, Headmaster Herion might be sitting in the office reading, as he was often wont to do.

Fortunately, as Kathair reached down to pull up his favorite panel which rested above a sturdy bookshelf that reached up all the way to the ceiling and had an actual ladder that he could drop down to, he found the office to be empty.

He maneuvered himself through the open panel and lowered himself down. He was hanging by his hands at arm's length, just about to drop, when he heard the lock on the door click open and the latch began to turn. Quickly, Kathair pulled himself up, slid over the top of the ceiling, and placed the panel back into position.

He could hear footsteps entering the room. There was a

cough then, followed by a sigh. A few moments later, another set of footsteps entered the room.

"Ah, Master Fenn, come in," Headmaster Herion said.

"You wanted to see me?" Master Fenn asked.

"Yes, I wanted to ask you something," Herion replied. "Close the door."

Kathair heard the door close and he tried to keep his breathing shallow and light so as not to make any audible noise.

"Master Fenn, you are one of the foremost wizards of our time, and I know you have been doing quite a lot of research."

"I try to remain sharp, Headmaster," Master Fenn said.

"Well, what do you think of Nagar's Blight?" Herion asked. "Is it truly a curse that will last forever? Or, will it fade over time?"

Master Fenn laughed. "You know as well as I do that Nagar's Blight is as strong now as it was when it was created."

"Sure, sure, but can it be negated somehow?" Headmaster Herion asked. "I have heard of trees that can filter dark magic out of entire regions. Might there be something to that?"

"No," Master Fenn said. "That is nothing more than an old wives tale. Trees cannot filter out dark magic any more than wearing a colander in front of your face will save you from toxic swamp gas."

"But have you researched it?" Herion pressed. "Has anybody actually researched it?"

Master Fenn laughed again. "What brought this on?" Fenn asked. "Did that old coot of a wizard tell you that he used to fend off shades with trees?"

"You mean Cyrus?" Headmaster Herion asked.

"Yes, I mean Cyrus. I know everyone thinks he is an incredible wizard, but I find his stories about his encounters with demons and their ilk a little beyond believability. If you ask me, he is a braggart who embellishes his former glory days in order to remain relevant enough to teach here."

"Don't forget that he fought off the shade when it attacked Kyra," Headmaster Herion put in. "Cyrus is not all boasts."

"Yes, well, if he was half as good as he claims, then why didn't he kill the shade on the spot?"

"Master Fenn, I don't recall you ever slaying a shade, am I incorrect?" Headmaster Herion asked.

"No, you are correct, but I have also never claimed to have done so."

Headmaster Herion scoffed. "In any case, Cyrus is not the person who put the idea into my head. I heard it elsewhere and thought it an intriguing concept."

"It may be an interesting notion, but it has no merit," Master Fenn replied.

"And what of dragons in general then?" Herion asked. "Suppose we had no curse to deal with, do you think dragon slayers would still be necessary? I mean to say, do you think we could finally live in peace with the dragons?"

"I don't believe so," Master Fenn said decisively. "The Battle of Hamath Valley was not only fought between us and cursed dragons. There were dragons who freely chose to join the other side as well. If we want peace in the Middle Kingdom, then two races must die; namely the orcs to the south, and the dragons that remain. If either exists, then we shall be doomed to a violent existence."

"Yes, yes, orcs I understand," Headmaster Herion replied. "They endlessly seek opportunities to do battle because they value displays bravery and valor above all else. That is how they attain their own version of heaven in the afterlife, you know."

"There is no heaven for those sent to Hammenfein," Master Fenn countered. "Hammenfein is a realm made of varying levels of hell, and that is all it is."

"Yes, but you are forgetting that orcs who attain a certain degree of valor in this life are granted nobility in Hammenfein by the gods that rule the various levels of hell. Here, in the plane of the living upon the face of Terramyr, they are cursed of the gods, but in Hammenfein, they become kings so long as they have fought well here and proven their bravery."

"Which is precisely why we can never coexist with them," Master Fenn put in. "They will always war with us, for that is all they value."

"But what about dragons?" Herion asked. "They have nothing of that sort to gain from destruction. So why do you say we cannot coexist with them?"

"Because they are too powerful. They will always turn on humans. To be sure, the Ancients may have led an era of peace and prosperity over this land, but once the dragons grew in numbers, they even turned on themselves. They are beset by the same vices as men, such as greed and jealousy, the only difference is the fact that these vices befall them more easily, and they cause much more destruction when they turn feral."

"Surely not all of them turn wicked," Herion said. "I should like to think that they have some semblance of decency and honor."

"No," Master Fenn said. "From everything I have read, and from my time with the dragon slayers, I would say the opposite is true. A dragon always turns against humans. Whether because of the curse, or a simple function of time, they all turn in the end. No human can tame or coexist with a dragon. Eventually, it will look upon humans as food. They see us as we see cattle. We are nothing more than beasts that are good for food and labor, but we are not considered equals."

There was silence for a few moments. Kathair tried to process the words he had heard. Did this mean that Leatherback would turn on Kyra? Kathair couldn't believe that. The dragon had helped her through so much already. Could it possibly turn against her? Then again, everything Kathair had ever heard pointed to the fact that eventually Leatherback would succumb to Nagar's Blight. The curse would turn him feral and he would wreak havoc.

Kathair held his breath as Master Fenn spoke again.

"Why do you ask me these things?" Fenn said.

"No reason in particular," Headmaster Herion said. "I have been conversing with the priests from Valtuu Temple about their beliefs and customs. It is quite fascinating.

However, I would assume anything they said about dragons to be biased, of course."

"Of course," Master Fenn said. "I have studied the matter thoroughly, and I have given you my unbiased conclusion that I believe any intelligent man would come to if presented with the information I have gathered over my lifetime."

"And that is why I asked to see you, Master Fenn. That is exactly why I asked for your advice."

"Is there anything else?"

Headmaster Herion replied, "No, thank you. You may go."

Kathair heard feet shuffle toward the doorway and then the door was pulled closed.

Kathair forgot about replacing the book and pulled himself up to the larger beam as quietly as he could. He decided that he would go with the dragon slayers on their patrol. Maybe they could shed some more light upon this issue for him and help him understand whether Kyra was in danger, or if it might be possible that Leatherback would remain loyal and kind to her.

*****

While Kathair was sneaking around inside the bowels and inner spaces of Kuldiga Academy, Kyra had skipped her session with Cyrus to return to the aspen wood. She had packed food for the day, as well as a few books to keep her company while she sat upon the boulder in the clearing and waited.

After a couple of hours, a great shadow fell over the clearing. Kyra looked up, but was disappointed to see nothing more than a large, gray cloud.

Great, all I need to round out the day is rain.

She stuffed her book back in her bag and slid off the boulder to move to a more covered location, but she took only one step before the cloud itself fell upon the grove. The heavy fog surrounded her and she couldn't see more than a foot in front of her face.

The next thing she knew, the ground shook and rumbled.

"Don't be afraid," Njar called out. "It's us, I was using the cloud to conceal our flight."

The cloud vanished and Kyra jumped with joy when she saw Leatherback's grinning face. The dragon bent its head down and Kyra reached out and hugged his snout.

"I missed you, I was worried about you!" She pushed back from him and pointed at him. "Don't do that ever again!"

"That's my fault, Kyra," Njar said. He pointed to his leg and then gently slid off the dragon's back, wincing and stooping when he hit the ground. "I was wounded in the fight, and he had to carry me back to my home."

"He carried you back to Viverandon?" Kyra asked. She turned to Leatherback and smiled. "Then, can he fly to the north?"

Njar shook his horned head. "No, Viverandon is only a couple hundred miles from here. To reach the next continent to the north, he would have to fly twenty times that distance, and he would have to do it without stopping for rest. That's to say nothing of the mountains that surround this continent. His lungs likely aren't developed enough to make that flight."

"Why didn't you send me a message?" Kyra asked.

"I barely was able to open a portal back to here," Njar explained. "I think I fell before I could even walk through it."

"I pulled him through," Leatherback confirmed. "Njar was weak. I helped him. I was like Gorliad."

Kyra smiled wide and nodded. "Why didn't you fly back to tell me?" she asked.

"That's also my fault," Njar said. "I put him under a spell to help him sleep. The problem was, I lost consciousness shortly thereafter. Leatherback didn't wake until the village healers had helped me. Then, we came here as fast as we could."

"Why not use a portal?" Kyra asked.

Njar frowned. "I am still pretty weak," he said. "I could likely open a portal big enough for me, but not for him. We had no choice but to fly. I couldn't let him chance being seen either, so I went with him and created the cloud for cover."

Kyra smiled and hugged Leatherback's snout again.

"Did Headmaster Herion receive my letter?" Njar asked.

Kyra's smile faded and she nodded. "He did, but…"

"Did he ever send anyone to help?" Njar pressed. "I was right about the trap, you know. The shade was there."

Kyra looked at him curiously. "The shade was there?"

Njar nodded. "He attacked with three wraiths. I killed the wraiths, but I think I only managed to injure the shade. If we can find him soon, then we can strike him down before he recovers fully."

Kyra shook her head. "First, I need to ask you something."

Njar stood straight and nodded. "All right, what is it you wish to know?"

"Headmaster Herion said that he was there on Kelboa Island, summoned to a peace conference with you and your people. He said that you ambushed them with four hundred warriors and murdered the king."

Njar's face seemed to lengthen as the satyr frowned. His ears dropped and he closed his eyes and sighed. "No, that was not my doing," he said. "I can explain, if you let me."

Kyra nodded. "I need to know everything."

Njar leaned heavily upon his staff. "In those days, King Jarek was keeping company with warlocks, shadowfiends, and necromancers in his court. I believed that he was being misled, and that the dark wizards deceived him. I called the summit, and invited the whole of his military and magic officers, so I could expose the evil deceivers. However, I was not the chief of my tribe then. I was only an elder. The chief agreed with my plan, and allowed me to take a few of my advisors. However, I did not know that he had his own plan. He waited until the meeting had only just begun, and then he and a group of powerful satyr wizards opened portals for the army to march through. They began slaughtering the humans without warning. I tried to stop it, but there was nothing I could do.

King Jarek was slain early on, and from that point on neither side could be calmed.

"I fled with thirty others back to the ship we had arrived upon. All of the others died there in that hall, including our chief. After that day, I became the new chief of my tribe. I tried to send letters to King Mathias over the years, but they were never answered. I knew Herion would not accept my help, but I hoped he would at least heed my warning."

Kyra smiled and nodded. "He sent others to Caspen Manor," she said. "I don't think you should count on reconciling any time soon, but for what it's worth, I believe you."

Njar bowed his head. "I will help restore balance any way I can. Unfortunately, even satyrs are not immune to greed and anger. Thus, I can only offer help from a distance, but I will always be there for you." Kyra put out her hand. The satyr took it in his furry hand and shook it. Then he looked to Leatherback and smiled. "However, we do have something to announce, don't we Leatherback?"

Leatherback grinned wide. "We found garunda beasts!"

Kyra's eyes opened wide and her smile curled upward and made her cheeks flush red. "You did?!"

Njar nodded with a smile. "There is one that prowls alone in the south. As far as I can tell by what I saw in the Pools of Fate, it is not with the shade at this time. Rather, it is hunting in the mountains."

"What does it seek?" Kyra asked.

Njar frowned. "It is near the cavern where your mother was held. It is possible that it is a remnant from before, or it could be that the shade has sent it to scout the lair. According to the Pools of Fate, if we wait for two days, it will be on its way out of the lair. We can surprise it then, and overpower it.

Kyra smiled and nodded. "I will need to tell Lepkin," she said. "He will be happy to hear of this." She almost told Njar about the werewolf, but decided it was better not to worry the satyr more than necessary.

CHAPTER 13

Kathair stoked the fire as Dengar and the other dragon slayers finished plating their meals. The men were busy talking about how they would kill whatever beast it was that was terrorizing the countryside. Kathair listened for a while, trying not to smile too much as he recalled how he and Kyra had actually taken down the werewolf, and how Kyra had told him she and her dragon had destroyed the Wylkins. Two second year apprentices were managing the work of dragon slayers as a bit of summer entertainment. His thoughts soon drifted back to Kyra and her dragon. He knew what the dragon slayers had been teaching him in the months since he had been assigned to work with them, but he couldn't help thinking that Kyra was right about her dragon. Now that Leatherback was helping her hunt down the strange beasts that were infesting the nearby lands, Kathair was more convinced than ever that the creature would never harm anyone, other than perhaps taking a sheep or two for himself, but even Kathair had to agree that was fair payment for his services.

"Have any of you ever heard of a dragon that could escape Nagar's Blight?" Kathair called out when it seemed there was a lull in their conversation. "I mean, I know that we have to hunt the dangerous ones, but are they all dangerous? Is the curse really so powerful?"

"It is here," Dengar said. "There is no dragon in the Middle Kingdom that can ever escape the curse forever. Sure, the stronger ones take longer to turn, but they all fall in the end. That's why we hunt them."

Kathair nodded. "What about other lands? Are dragons

all over Terramyr affected by the curse? Surely there have to be some that are friendly somewhere."

"Dragons are a terrible lot," Britner spat. "Even in other lands they cause problems."

"Tell him about Alerik," Dengar put in. "That's a good campfire tale anyway, and he needs to learn that dragons can't be trusted."

Britner nodded and put his plate of beans to the side. "Do you know where Almandoor is?"

Kathair nodded. "It is in the country to the north, beyond the mountains and the sea."

Britner nodded and took a swig from his canteen. "Right, it's up in the area we call Landale. It's far enough away that the curse never touched it, but this story will show the terrible reality of dragons."

The man stood up and moved close to the fire so that the flames played upon his face and cast great shadows over him. "In Almandoor there was thirty years of peace since fang and fire were quenched from the skies above the fertile plains. Ne'er a dragon was heard, nor sign found of the volatile beasts that once plagued the land. Yet there was always rumor, suspicion, and superstition. The king commissioned patrols and warriors to protect his lands and people from all threats. For decades, men rode atop valiant steeds with no enemy to face, and no threat to quell. The people rejoiced and prospered, and the king spent his days relaxing in his court and seeing to trivial affairs of trade and commerce."

Dengar slapped his knee and then elbowed Foman in the side. "I love it when he gets in his story-telling mode."

Britner glanced back at them, and then continued to stare at Kathair while he spoke. "Yet, every king knows, there is no such thing as an everlasting peace in the world of mortals. As the king waxed old and his brow grew heavy with age, his nightmares returned to plague him once more.

"A dragon, or perhaps some other fiendish beast, had found its way to the mountains along the kingdom's borders to the east. Farmers reported missing sheep, and fields smothered in smoldering ash and bubbling blood. So, one night, the king called forth his patrols and commissioned a party of men to hunt down the dragon.

"As the men filtered into the court, the king eyed each of them carefully. The shining armor, the sharp swords, and the grim faces were almost enough to rekindle the king's hope. But he knew better than to put his confidence in men when faced with such a beast. As the last of the men entered the chamber and knelt, the king sighed heavily. 'There are only eighty-five of you,' the king said."

Dengar stood up and marched up beside Britner. "'We are more than a match for any dragon!' claimed Captain Terrelius as he stood and waved an arm toward his men."

Britner turned and his face grew sour. "Oi! Are you telling it, or am I?"

Dengar sniggered and returned to his seat, forking a bite of beans into his mouth as he continued to laugh at himself.

Britner shook his head. "As I was about to say, a great man named Captain Terrelius stood and answered the king saying, 'We are more than a match for any dragon that might be foolish enough to return to these parts.'

"But the king shook his head and explained that decades before, when the first dragon appeared, there were more than twice their number, and all but one of them died. Captain Terrelius claimed that his men had better training and equipment, but the king was not convinced. The king held up his old, leathery hand and shook his head, asking if there were any additional warriors to be found.

"Captain Terrelius folded his arms and shook his head. There were no others to call on such short notice. Even if they summoned the men from the nearby villages, they would not have the same training that Captain Terrelius and his men had. Captain Terrelius said, 'Fear not, we are prepared for this.' His men all echoed his response to their king.

"Still the king was not convinced. 'Have you ever seen a dragon?' the king asked. He rose from his golden throne and pointed to the group, staring at each of the men with his icy blue eyes." Britner pointed across the flames at Kathair and glared at him, as though he were the king. Kathair couldn't help but notice Dengar behind Britner, laughing quietly while Foman tried to shush the man. Britner continued despite Dengar's mocking. "The king pressed the question again. 'Have any of you ever seen a dragon?' But, no one answered him. His questions were met with silence. Not even Captain Terrelius spoke. The king knew that the men would need help from someone who had not only seen a dragon, but fought one and lived to tell the tale. He told the men to go and find Alerik.

"The king, knowing that Alerik was not located in or near the capitol city, explained that he had given Alerik a bastion in the woods after he returned from the first dragon's nest those many years ago. He also said that Alerik now commanded a mighty cohort of men as well.

"Captain Terrelius nodded dutifully and turned to his men, informing them they would leave at once. Waves of clanking armor and boots filled the court, echoing off the granite walls and marble pillars. After the men had all exited, save for Captain Terrelius, the king cleared his throat and beckoned for Terrelius to come closer to him.

"The king said, 'Our kingdom has grown rich in these years of peace. Perhaps it is the gold that brings the new serpent near, I do not know. Or perhaps it is our flocks and herds that whet its beastly appetite. Either way, I promised to grant five hundred thousand gold pieces to all survivors of the first army that faced the dragon. I offer the same reward now. Send word of the reward and see if we might gain additional recruits."

Kathair nodded. "So, even without the curse you are saying they would terrorize humans for gold and food?"

"The gold calls to them," Dengar said, the levity gone from his voice. "And, once they have grown to their full size, hunting shepherds' flocks is easier than tracking herds of elk or deer."

Kathair nodded.

Britner cleared his throat, calling Kathair's attention back to him. "Captain Terrelius nodded and left the court without another word. When he reached the courtyard in front of the palace he saw his men waiting for him. With a simple whirl of his hand in the air, all of the men fell into line. Some sat atop horses while others formed marching ranks. Captain Terrelius mounted his horse and led the men out from the city and to the north east, to the Gray Wood.

"They travelled for three days and two nights before arriving at the edge of the wood. Even though they were still several days west of the mountains, they occasionally heard the unmistakable shriek of a dragon coming from the horizon. They never saw it, but that didn't stop the men from nervously looking over their shoulders or to the skies.

"Captain Terrelius pushed on through the overgrown road in the Gray Wood, showing no sign of fear to his men. He stopped only when the road opened up into a large field of grass and poppy flowers. In the middle of the field stood a tall, crenelated wall of black stone. Beyond the wall rose a great bastion, round in construction and easily twice as tall as the wall, granting a vantage over the tree tops. A golden flag flapped in the breeze from the top of the sturdy tower.

"They had arrived at Alerik's Bastion, a veritable fortress in the middle of the Gray Wood. Captain Terrelius advanced toward the gate and had no sooner come within twenty yards of the portcullis than the iron barrier was lifted and out came an old man on horseback. He wore brown trousers tucked into black, knee-high leather riding boots, a tunic of forest green hemmed with golden embroidery and a tan cloak that lazily flittered in the wind behind him as he trotted his horse out to greet them. A thick, gray and copper beard covered his face, and a mat of neatly brushed, sand colored hair sat atop his head. The man smiled and waved a gloved hand at Captain Terrelius.

"The man was Alerik, and he welcomed the party in and offered to feed them and house them. Captain Terrelius refused, saying they were not come as guests, but on a mission from the king. Alerik nodded and smiled wider, a furry brow arching up over his green eyes. He explained that he knew why they had come, but insisted they could not fight a dragon without a full night's rest and food in their stomachs. Alerik looked up to the sky and said, 'The sun will descend in the west long before you can exit the Gray Wood again. It is best if you stay with me now, and then depart in the morning.'

"Captain Terrelius nodded and trotted his horse up to Alerik. 'We have come to ask for your support,' he said frankly, but Alerik shook his head and explained that he was beyond his sixtieth year and not one able to fight dragons anymore. He then said that whatever he had to offer, he would do so freely and gladly."

"Captain Terrelius didn't let Alerik off easily, though. He explained that the king had ordered Alerik's compliance and then said, 'We need your wisdom, and the strength of your company.' Alerik smirked and brought a hand up to stroke his beard. Finally, he agreed to help by giving his wisdom, but he cautioned Captain Terrelius that his house was lacking in strength. 'I have only a handful of servants in my home of fighting age. Most of the rest are far beyond their prime,' Alerik explained.

"'What of the men who built your bastion?' Captain Terrelius probed. 'I heard there were hundreds of workers who came to you throughout the years, and that none of them ever returned. Where did they go?'

"Alerik looked to the ground and the twinkle in his eye vanished, replaced by a grim longing and a rigid frown. 'The Gray Wood was not always the safe place it is now,' Alerik said. 'Many died trying to clear the forest of scamps and savage beasts brought by the dragon's presence. Many more died erecting the great defense you see before you now. It seems even the land of this forest fought against us. Those who lived remain with me still.' Alerik took in a deep breath and put his smile back on his face, albeit not as large as the one before, and then he beckoned them to come inside the bastion.

"Captain Terrelius signaled for his men to advance, and

the troop followed into the keep through the portcullis. The Captain noted only a handful of guards along the walls. Most of them looked to be well into their forties, if not in their fifties. Gray hair and wrinkled faces seemed to be as common as swords among Alerik's guards. Disturbed by this, Captain Terrelius called out to Alerik, saying, 'The king said you had a mighty host at your command.'

"'Mighty in valor and honor, yes,' Alerik replied swiftly. 'We rely more on tactics and strategy than upon our numbers.' Alerik showed the guests into the main hall of his bastion, allowing them to rest their legs and remove their armor. Many sat along the fur rugs lining the walls, while others went immediately to the several long tables in the middle that had already been set with food enough for a king's feast. Three hearths glowed brightly with lively fires that spread warmth throughout the hall. A few maidens continued to bring out bread and cakes to set before all of the men while Alerik invited everyone to the table to feast upon duck and roast pig. 'I have only one rule,' Alerik said as he sat at the table and beckoned for Captain Terrelius to sit at his right. 'No one leaves the bastion at night.' Captain Terrelius turned a quizzical gaze at Alerik. 'The Gray Wood may be safer now than before, but it is still not the place one should go traipsing around after dark. There are creatures out there that are unpredictable, and I am not talking about the great serpent that plagues the eastern mountains.'

Britner turned from the fire then and reached down for his canteen. He took a long drink before continuing with the story. "Captain Terrelius agreed to the rule and insisted that they would leave at first light. Alerik nodded, seeming to agree with the idea, and. then he signaled for his piper and fifer to play music for them as the men all ate their fill. It was not long before the hall echoed with laughter and loud, merry conversation. As the night wore on and the food was picked clean from the table, one of the men finished his fourth cup of wine and stood to address Alerik.

"The man demanded to hear the story of Alerik slaying

the first dragon. Many of the warriors rapped their knuckles on the table and voiced their agreement. Captain Terrelius watched as Alerik's jovial expression again melted away and became distant and melancholy. Alerik the Dragonslayer rose up from his wooden chair and shook his head. He said, 'That is not a tale I enjoy telling.' His raucous guests were quick to boo and jeer him, but he remained steadfast. 'I lost many friends, and all of my brothers,' he continued. 'But if you must hear it, then I will send my bard out to tell the tale. I shall retire for the night.'

"Captain Terrelius watched as Alerik promptly left the chamber through a door off to the side. A moment later a middle-aged man came out with a lute. The man introduced himself as Thoron Derinis, son of Master Jofar Derinis. He spoke in a loud voice and jumped onto one of the tables amidst the warriors' thunderous applause. He began, saying, 'I will tell the tale of how Alerik slew the great dragon, as it was passed on to me by my father. Listen well and keep ye still, for the tale is one of horror, of fright, and hell. I will show you the valor of my lord, the great Alerik, and the swiftness of his blade to end the plague that haunted this fair land some thirty years ago.'"

"Let me tell this part, Brit," Dengar pleaded as he stood up again.

Britner was obviously annoyed, but motioned for Dengar to proceed. Kathair laughed as he watched Dengar jump up on a log and get into character, clearing his throat and grabbing at his collars as if he truly were a bard.

Dengar's hand swept out over the air in front of him and he smiled wildly at Kathair. His voice was deep, but not entirely unpleasant as he sang the tale. "Black was the night, and red was the morn, when dragon appeared with white fang and red horn. Maidens did faint and strong men did lose heart, as beast slew all life with its fiery darts. Down from the mountains it flew to our land, our flocks, knights, and wizards struck down by clawed hand.

"Consumed most by grief, king did see from his throne,

'spite of tears as kingdom fell to ash and to bone. At once he did summon the most skilled of warriors, but none were a match for the foul beast's furor.

"Lands ravished, laid waste, o'er the land blood was let, a great price of gold and of glory king had set. To him who could slay the draconian bane, would go title, lands, a fortune and fame. Thus into our story of woe and of grief, comes our marvelous savior and surest relief.

"A band of heroes two hundred men strong, approached the good king with boast and a song. 'The foul dragon's head we surely will take,' cried the heroes as a solemn oath they did make.

"So, horde of champions set out to the Gray Wood, jaws set as behind steel shield they stood. The great dragon reared its horned, ugly head, a bright flash of hellfire and scores lay there dead. Onward with boldness our heroes did press, stabbing and slashing the beast's stony breast.

"Though valiant as friends did fall in the fight, not one could withstand dragon fire or bite. A few of the heroes attempted to flee, but were felled as a woodsman does strike down a tree.

"Flames and fangs, tail and claws did strike them each down, and it seemed none was left to protect king and crown. Embattled 'til all knights were dead save just one, sweet Alerik the Great, a good nobleman's son. Into the fire with sword and with spear, the young man did charge, with no thought for fear.

"Through the wood rang the echoing clang and roar, as the dragon was pressed back more and more. The battle rolled on to the southern plane, engulfing all life in the dragon's flame. Battered and worn, he was yet still alive, Alerik the Bold would not give up the prize.

"For the glory was great, and the gold was better, if the hero could free our land from this fetter. None quite knows how, there were none left to see, by dawn the next day, he did claim victory.

"Songs of joy and of praise, with alms and thanks, were

offered at sight of the dragon's bloody shanks. The demon, consumed, it is said, by his fire, proved no match for him who my lute did inspire."

Dengar then bowed as Kathair clapped.

"Yes, jolly good there, Thoron the Bard," Britner teased. "Now go sit back down."

Dengar bowed repeatedly while backing away to his seat. Foman raised his canteen to salute Dengar's performance and then took a drink.

Britner turned back to Kathair and continued his tale. "As the bard struck the last chord on his lute and let the note hang in the hall. No one moved, each lost in his own thoughts. Even the bard fell into silence at the song's conclusion. As the minutes dragged into hours, one by one the men would move off to find a place in the hall to lie down and sleep.

"Captain Terrelius was the last to leave the table. He waited until all had found places to rest and then he went to the door at the end of the hall. His hand reached out for the door tentatively, but he paused when he saw someone approaching out of the corner of his eye. He turned to see the bard. 'The master has instructed we are not to go out at night,' Thoron the Bard said flatly. He reached up and pulled down a beam into its metal brackets, effectively barricading the door. 'What's out there?' Captain Terrelius asked. Thoron sniggered. 'You mean besides the dragon?' the bard said. 'Is that not enough?' The bard then nodded to someone else who quickly came to the door and inserted a large iron key, turning it several times to lock the portal closed. The bard and the servant left without another word, but Captain Terrelius stood near the door, wondering what might have the entire house so scared when they all slept under the watch of Alerik the Great.

"Just then, a horrid shriek, unlike anything he had ever heard before, erupted outside. Captain Terrelius reflexively went for his sword at his belt and watched the door. Another squeal was followed quickly by a deep, rumbling roar. It wasn't the dragon, he knew that much. It wasn't powerful enough to be the great beast he was after. Yet, whatever it was, made the hairs at the base of his neck stand on end.

"The captain stood there, watching the door and waiting for the unseen horror to come and attack, but it never did. The shrieks and cries would rend the silence of the night every few minutes, but it never came closer to the door. Still, it was several hours before Captain Terrelius allowed himself to relax and sleep.

"Alerik was sitting at the table before Terrelius woke the next morning. The captain threw off his blanket and sauntered over to the table, still shaking the sleep from his steps as he navigated through the floor full of sleeping bodies. Terrelius immediately inquired of Alerik what had made the strange noises outside during the night.

"Alerik frowned. 'The Gray Wood has many dark corners and crags,' he said. 'Best you not worry yourself about it.' Alerik clapped three times and in rushed a line of servants, each holding a platter of freshly baked bread. They were followed by a few women holding pitchers, and then finally by several more servants carrying platters of fruits and eggs. 'Eat your fill, you will need your strength,' Alerik said.

"Terrelius insisted that he and his men should leave, for they yet had a long way to travel to reach the dragon. Alerik nodded in agreement, but implored Captain Terrelius to wait but one more day, claiming he had a few more things to prepare before they should depart.

"Captain Terrelius allowed his men to pass the time that day whittling and swapping stories with the people in the tower, but all the while he stared at the front door and thought of the dragon. The few moments he spent thinking on anything else came upon him as his mind would recall the horrid sounds of the previous night.

"After supper that evening, the men resumed the same sleeping positions they had taken up the night before. Again, just a short while after the others were asleep, the terrible screams and howls erupted outside. This time Captain Terrelius went for the door. The large portal was locked as it had been the night before, but there was a panel that he could open to peer out. He reached up to the brass knob and pulled the panel open. The cold night air wafted in, bringing with it the scents of the forest. He waited a moment for his eyes to adjust to the black night. He scanned around, but saw nothing. Not even guards moved outside of the hall.

"Alerik snuck up from behind and said, 'It would be better to keep the door closed entirely.' Captain Terrelius jumped away slightly, caught off guard by Alerik's sudden appearance. He apologized, and then explained that he heard the same sounds again in the night. 'Curiosity killed the cat,' Alerik said with a smile as he brought a steaming mug of mulled wine up to his mouth.

"Captain Terrelius closed the panel securely and stepped away from the door. He asked Alerik once more what was outside. Alerik shook his head. Saying only that it was best that no one venture out after sundown. Alerik shrugged and then said, 'Simply follow my instructions and this is one danger that will not bother you or your men. You have my word.' The large man gestured to the hall with his open hand and told Captain Terrelius to get some rest. 'We leave tomorrow, yes?' Terrelius asked. The lord of the tower didn't reply. He just walked through the hall and disappeared into another doorway. Captain Terrelius sighed and forced himself to sleep.

"The next day proceeded much the same. Terrelius suggested the group depart, but Alerik came up with more excuses, holding them all in his tower again while he went about seeing to his so-called preparations. The third night brought even more shrieks and howls in the forest - wo many that all of the men woke and reached for their weapons. Terrelius tried to calm them, saying he had heard the sounds before, but the men all remained awake. A pair of Alerik's guards stood on the inside of the door, each holding wicked pole-axes that had hooks on the back."

"What was out there, the dragon?" Kathair asked as he stared at Britner through the smoke of the fire.

Britner shook his head, signifying that he would not reveal the end of the story early. He continued on. "Terrelius couldn't be sure whether the guards were there to protect them from something breaking in, or to keep them from going out. Alerik was down in the hall the next morning before the first rooster's crow. He woke Captain Terrelius and then laid out a map on the table. As the rest of the men began to stir, Alerik pointed the way the group should take through the wood. Again, Terrelius asked about the sounds in the night. Alerik nodded. 'It was a bit louder than usual,' Alerik replied. 'But it sleeps now,' he quickly added. 'We can travel to the edge of the wood without fear.' Terrelius placed a hand on Alerik's shoulder and asked, 'But what was it?' Terrelius asked. Alerik replied that it was better Terrelius didn't know. Alerik then said that he would meet Terrelius and his men in the courtyard. Captain Terrelius asked how many of Alerik's men would be joining them, but Alerik turned on his heels and shot Terrelius a look that nearly froze the man's blood in place. 'None,' was all that Alerik would say.

"Captain Terrelius opened his mouth to protest, but the words never found their way to his mouth. The old dragon slayer threw open the bolt, unlocked the door, and stormed out of the hall before Terrelius could find the courage to say anything.

"Once the men were ready, and had eaten their fill of eggs and bread, they marched out to see Alerik dressed in oiled leather armor, with a simple helmet on his head. A greatsword hung on the left of his horse while a bow was slung over his back and he held a spear in his right hand.

"Like in the song," Kathair called out to Dengar. "He fights with sword and spear."

Dengar winked at Kathair and raised his canteen to his lips.

Britner continued the tale, without pausing. "Alerik pulled the reins off to the left, urging his horse into a healthy trot out through the gates and into the wood. Captain Terrelius quickly issued the command and the rest of them did their best to match pace with Alerik as they took the winding trail out of the wood and toward the southeast.

"The birds sang and deer bounded through the brush at the sight of the troop. Rabbits nibbled clover near the edge of the road and the trees swayed in the warm breeze. It was as if nothing had happened the night before, but Terrelius knew it had. He kept his eyes peeled for the mysterious beast, but he saw nothing more dangerous than a pair of hawks circling high in the sky. His ears, on the other hand, picked up the thunderous roar of the dragon from afar off. 'Sends a chill down your spine, does it not?' Alerik asked after a particularly long dragon roar. Terrelius nodded. 'Does it sound as large as the one you slew?' he asked.

"Alerik narrowed his eyes and sighed, looking off in the direction of the sounds and waiting for the next cry. A few moments later, when the horrible cry tore through the air, Alerik nodded his head. A sour grimace crawled onto his face, turning the corners of his lips downward and causing a tense knot to form between his brows. 'It is the same as I remember before,' Alerik said somberly. 'You may wish to let your men have one last night of revelry before we move on to face its wrath.'

"Captain Terrelius turned on him sharply. 'My men are not cowards,' he declared. Alerik shrugged and said, 'The brave die as quickly as anyone else. I am just pointing out that these may very well be the final hours of their lives. Perhaps we could try to make them a little lighter.' Captain Terrelius shook his head, his impatience turning to anger now. He turned to Alerik and said, 'You tried to keep us in your tower, and now you would ask me to make camp before we should. We have a long way to travel yet, and our foe does not wait for us. It will devour our people if we linger.'

"Alerik pulled his horse to a stop and instantly all of the men behind stopped as well. 'The dragon will devour its prey whether you face it a few hours early or not,' he said. He then pointed to a large cave. 'I propose we make camp there, it is where I made camp with my group of heroes some thirty years ago.'

"But the captain was not having any more of Alerik's

tricks. 'No,' Captain Terrelius said. 'We should press on. We still have daylight left, and we can make better time if we use all of our light.' Alerik shook his head. He explained that the rivers near the base of the mountains were flanked by thick brush and trees that grew close together. Beavers had felled many trees, not only making dams, but also making the path treacherous. Alerik informed Terrelius that even if they somehow managed to get through that before the sun fell that day, they would find themselves in an open field, with nothing else between them and the dragon they hunted. Alerik said, 'The cave provides shelter from the weather, and fortification against a dragon's flame. Remember, even though it takes you a day to cross the valley, the dragon can fly over this area in a matter of only a couple of hours.'

"Terrelius shook his head, still not willing to listen to the experienced dragon hunter. 'We should go farther. We can camp in the wood near the rivers,' he said. Alerik turned his horse off the road and shouted over his shoulder. 'The dragon hunts at dusk, and doesn't sate his appetite until well into the night. You do what you want, but I am pitching camp here in the cave.' Captain Terrelius turned back to his men. He could see the looks on their faces. There would be no way to convince them to press on. Ultimately, he agreed to camp with Alerik, calling out to his men saying, 'We leave before first light. Set up rotating watches and post a guard at the entrance of the cave.' The lieutenant nodded dutifully and blew a short blast on the horn. 'You heard the man, move it, move it!' the lieutenant shouted.

"Captain Terrelius pulled his horse up along that of his lieutenant and watched his men break ranks and make for the cave. 'I am starting to have my doubts,' he said to his lieutenant. The lieutenant turned and offered a curt nod. 'Three days in the bastion and now he slows us down and instills fear in the men,' he said. 'Makes me wonder if he slew the dragon, or if he ran and the dragon just happened to succumb to its wounds.' Captain Terrelius nodded his agreement with the lieutenant's sentiments.

"Terrelius spat on the ground and turned a sour face to the cave. 'I suppose we will uncover the truth soon enough.' Just then, Alerik shouted from up the hill. 'Come, Captain Terrelius, you will not want to be outside of the cave when night falls.'

"'Again with his ghosts of the night!' Terrelius grumbled.

"'Permit me to take a few men and camp out in front of the cave,' the lieutenant requested. 'Let me show the men there is nothing to fear from Alerik's monster stories.'

"Captain Terrelius sighed and shook his head at first, but upon the lieutenant's insistence, Terrelius gave permission for a few of them to camp outside. The lieutenant quickly rode off and selected a few men to join him. Then they returned to make camp. Alerik saw them and came down the hill from the cave. He walked up to Captain Terrelius with a most disapproving frown.

"'The men should come into the cave,' Alerik said. 'It is not safe out there.'

"'If the dragon comes, we will spot it, and retreat to the cave,' the lieutenant said. 'Then we can rouse the others and emerge to fight it.' Alerik shook his head. 'You cannot fight a dragon at night,' he said. 'They can see clearly as day, but we cannot cut the darkness with our eyes.'

"'We have fire,' the lieutenant said. Alerik smirked. 'So does the dragon.'

"'We are staying,' the lieutenant said defiantly. Alerik shook his head and waved a dismissive hand at him. 'It is not the dragon that should worry you here at any rate,' he said. 'Then what?' Captain Terrelius asked pointedly. 'We are no longer in the Gray Wood, what monster roams the valleys out here?'

"'I can't say,' Alerik replied. 'Because you don't know,' the lieutenant stated. 'Are you Alerik the Great, or are you a coward?'

"Alerik arched an eyebrow and slowly folded his arms across his chest. He then decided to let the men seal their own fate. He denounced them as fools who sought glory and riches but lacked the brains or courage to find either.

"Captain Terrelius grew enraged and told Alerik, 'You have proven neither brave, nor wise so far along this venture of ours, and you have offered only one feeble old man when we asked for the strength of your warriors.'

"'My men have spent their lives for the last thirty years battling the dangers of the gray wood. They have faced danger enough to earn them the right to live out the remainder of their lives with their families,' Alerik replied. 'They will not now walk into the fire. That is for me to do, and me alone. In fact, all of you should turn back. Let me face the dragon alone. You can even keep the riches if you like.'

"'What game are you playing at?' Captain Terrelius asked.

"Alerik shook his head again and walked away. 'Wouldn't believe me even if I did tell you,' he mumbled into the wind.

Kathair rubbed his shoulders and then drew his knees up to his chest as he watched Britner continue the tale. It was longer than he had expected, but now his mind was captivated by the riddle. What *was* Alerik hiding?

Britner took another drink from his canteen and then moved to the other side of the fire where the smoke was a bit thicker and lowered his voice before continuing the tale. "A couple of hours after the group had eaten their supper, they went about dousing the fires and preparing for sleep. They were going to rise early, so they laid down before dusk had fully faded into the black of night. The night was peaceful, calm, and cool. Only the wind howled against the mouth of the open cave. The stars were out, and the half-moon provided a bit of light with which to see. Captain Terrelius leaned back against the wall of the cave's opening. He knew he should sleep, but he kept watch on his men in the valley. The lieutenant and another warrior stood watch, each trading places and pacing around as they normally did to avoid exhaustion as the night wore on.

"It proved unnecessary, as there was nothing to be seen. No beast had followed them from the Gray Wood, no dragon dropped down from the skies, not even a bear roamed the area. All was tranquil. As the lieutenant woke another warrior to take his place in the rotation, Captain Terrelius allowed himself to drift into sleep. His eyes grew heavy, and his breathing slowed. He pulled his thin blanket up to his shoulders and tucked into the wall as best he could, turning his head into a small curve in the rock. A horrid scream jolted him from his slumber not more than a few seconds after he had closed his eyes. He looked out and saw a flash of darkness swirling about the men and his lieutenant.

"'To arms!' Terrelius cried. He jumped to his feet and pulled his sword. He took one step out of the cave and then a hefty arm wrapped around his chest and yanked him back. A second hand clasped over his mouth, tight as a vice.

"'Keep still!' Alerik whispered harshly. 'To venture out is to die!' Captain Terrelius struggled against him, but Alerik was much stronger, despite his age. 'Order your men to stay here. I will go,' Alerik said.

"Alerik released Terrelius and ran out into the night, fast as a fox. Terrelius ran out a few paces after him, as did several of his men. Others were clambering about deeper in the cave, but they were too far away to lend any immediate support.

"Another cry rent the air and a warm liquid splattered across Terrelius' face and neck. He stopped and looked to his right, but nothing was there. A moment later something heavy and scaly slammed into his chest, hurling him to the ground. It was all he could do to maintain consciousness. He heard snarls and screams all around him. Occasionally someone would shout, but Terrelius could not make out the words.

"A terrible roar shook the valley and then all went utterly quiet.

"Terrelius fought against his burning lungs and throbbing torso, struggling to rise. A hand slipped in under his armpit and hoisted him up the rest of the way to his feet.

"'I told you to stay in the cave!' Alerik shouted. The old warrior yanked Terrelius up, half dragging him back to the shelter of the cave. As soon as they crossed into the opening, Alerik threw Terrelius down. 'All of you back into the cave.

From here on out, you listen to me. I am in command, unless you prefer to die by this idiot's strategy.' Terrelius didn't argue this time. Alerik left the cave once more and strange sounds could be heard in the darkness. Terrelius peered out into the darkness beyond the cave, trying to see what had become of his men, but the moon hidden her light behind a cloud. It was many hours after silence had fallen over the area and Alerik had still not returned. Terrelius could no longer bear the wait and gave in to exhaustion and sleep.

"In the morning, Terrelius was the first to wake. He rose to his feet, dreading what he would find. His heart nearly stopped as he surveyed the scene. A bloody hand lay on the ground, still clenching a spear near the spot where he had fallen in the night. Flies lighted on the grotesque smear of blood on the ground. He stepped out, knowing there would be no survivors left outside the cave. He found only a boot, foot and ankle still inside, a helmet with large claw marks through it, and the tattered remains of blankets and armor scattered along the ground. Some of the armor was slick not only with blood, but also a thick, yellowy slime that smelled of sulfur and refuse. Captain Terrelius bent over and vomited, his stomach heaving only burning acid, and cramping violently in protest to the sights and smells he had taken in.

"'I told you to stay in the cave,' Alerik said as he came up slowly from behind.

"Captain Terrelius turned to see his men still hovering near the entrance to the cave. 'What evil have you wrought upon my men?' Terrelius demanded.

"'If I tell you, I will need a blood oath that you will keep my secret, on pain of death, and that you will follow my orders without hesitation from here on out.'

"Terrelius straightened himself and nodded his head, giving Alerik his word. Alerik leaned in and whispered to Terrelius. The man's eyes went wide as he listened carefully. Suddenly he pulled away. 'You should have told me the first night!' Terrelius shouted."

"Told him what?" Kathair asked eagerly, leaning in

anxiously.

Britner smiled wide, teeth illuminated by the fire's orange glow. He continued the tale without answering the question. "Alerik shook his head slowly, explaining that he had needed to know he could trust Terrelius. Terrelius shook his head and protested, 'You cannot expect us to go on like this!' Alerik placed a hand on Terrelius' shoulder and squeezed hard.

"'You must,' Alerik said. 'If you do not, then my secret will be exposed and the dragon will have the advantage.' Alerik sighed and looked up to the cave, then back to Terrelius. 'Let us fight as comrades. They are the other edge of the single sword we wield against our foe. Fight with me, and we can succeed. Desert now, and all is lost.'

"Terrelius asked Alerik to tell him how he had accomplished his secret feat, but Alerik would only agree to tell if they survived their encounter with the dragon.

"What secret?" Kathair shouted. "What did Alerik tell Terrelius?"

"Pipe down and let him finish," Foman called out.

Kathair blushed as he realized how silly his excitement must have made him look to them. He settled in and listened to Britner, biting his tongue and waiting as patiently as he could for the story to unfold and reveal its secrets.

"Alerik went for his horse. The entire group was quick to fall into place, often glancing around them and behind them at the grotesque scene left from the previous night. They moved along at a grueling pace. The men on foot almost had to jog to keep up with Alerik as he led them through the winding valley, across streams and around the thick brush and birch trees flanking the mighty river that had been siphoned off in places to make beaver ponds. The going was tough, pushing through sticky branches and grabby vines, but they made it to a small, rock outcropping that jutted out from the base of a large hillock.

"'We sleep under this tonight. Then, just after dawn, we will go for the dragon,' Alerik said.

"'It is still mid-afternoon,' Terrelius protested. 'Why not

go for the dragon now?'

"As if the beast could hear them, a mighty roar shook the valley. All of the horses, except for Alerik's, bucked and shied away. Two threw their riders to the ground and ran off, but the others were soon calmed. Alerik turned a wicked grin at Terrelius and glanced down to his horse. Then he pointed back to the clumps of birch trees they had just emerged from. 'Have your men cut down enough lumber to create pikes and poles. We will ring the rock outcropping with a palisade of birch wood. That will keep us for the night. We can fit our entire group under the rocky overhang, so the dragon will not spy us from above. The pikes will keep out other unwanted guests.'

"Terrelius clenched his jaw and his nostrils flared. 'It had better,' he growled before turning to relay the orders to the men. Alerik dismounted and went under the rocky structure. As he went farther back and the ground rose up slightly closer to the rock, he put his hand up and let it slide along the smooth, black surface. As he felt the pits and bumps in the rock he recalled the previous night he had spent here. The men had been strong, valiant warriors all. There had been no singing, no games, and no story telling among them. They had all sat quietly, each pondering fires within their own souls while watching the orange flames from the campfires around them.

"After a few minutes, Alerik found the very spot where he had slept. He remembered it clearly because there was a dip in the ground, with a large gray stone covered with orange lichen half buried in the dirt. He set his sword and over cloak down near the rock and slowly turned to slide into the depression in the dirt. No sooner did he lie back, than he could see the faint images of his past comrades - those who had depended upon each other, upon him, to fight the dragon. Here he was again, lying in the same dirty hole, preparing to march against a dragon. Only this time, he had fewer men at his side, and none of them seemed to match the prowess of their predecessors who had perished in those earlier hot, white flames. He could still hear their screams and cries, and he could still smell their burning flesh. A shiver ran up his spine and then down his forearms. He flexed his fingers, trying to break free from the memory. He leaned his head back on the rock, adjusting around until the smooth, convex curve fit the groove of his neck, and then he closed his eyes, meditating upon the morrow until sleep overtook him.

"When his eyes opened again, it was night. A couple of camp fires smoldered nearby, with the smell of roasted meat still lingering in the air. He sat up and bumped a small, wooden plate with a bit of meat and beans on it. He took the food up and tore off one bite, but the meat had no flavor to him. Perhaps on another day he would have enjoyed the meal, but not on this night. His stomach protested and his mouth refused to produce any saliva. It was as if his entire body was revolting against the morsel, so he spit it out.

"He crawled up from his spot and picked his way through the men, careful not to wake them. He made his way to the north, heading for the same small crevice that he had used on that night so many years ago to escape from the camp unseen.

"Unbeknownst to Alerik, Terrelius only feigned sleep. He was watching Alerik through half-closed eyes from a spot only a few yards away. When the large man disappeared from the camp, leaving his sword and over cloak behind, Terrelius felt a sour, gripping ache tear at his stomach. He sat up slowly, looking around at his men, and offered a prayer to the old gods for help. Just as he finished his prayer, that same, strange growl erupted in the night from somewhere beyond the outcropping. Unlike other nights though, the sound only was heard once. Terrelius stayed awake, listening carefully for any sign of the beast that had attacked his men the night before, but if it was nearby, he was not for knowing.

"He soon rose to his feet and spent the rest of the night pacing about the camp under the rocky overhang, half dreading and half longing for the golden dawn. When Alerik had told Terrelius of a plan as he had whispered his secret to the captain the day before, he had also explained where the beast would be. Alerik was to sneak out during the night, undetected, and then Terrelius was to march to the agreed upon spot in the morning. He struck a fist into his open palm and hoped to the gods that he had made the right decision in trusting the old man.

When the first rays of light finally broke the darkness, he began rousing his men and getting them ready. There was no breakfast this day. The men just donned their armor, checked their swords, and fell into lines under the rock. It wasn't long before they noticed Alerik had disappeared, but none of them mentioned it. Terrelius paced before them, waiting for the last of them to be ready, and then he addressed his men briefly.

"'I know we are fewer now than when we began, and I know we face something that a force twice our size barely beat. However, do not fret, we have Alerik, the Dragonslayer. He left in the night so that he might get close to the beast. While we attack from the front, he will sneak to its rear. We will be like a mighty hammer, and he will be our anvil as we strike the dragon down!' Terrelius shouted.

"A cheer broke out among the men and then Terrelius gave the signal to march out. They ran out from under the rock and turned down to the south, toward the dragon's last known location. Terrelius shouted at them as they passed by, swearing at some, encouraging others. This was no time to let his men have doubts, even if he still did.

"With the last of the men on the road, Terrelius quickly mounted his horse and tore off to lead the group. They marched for just over an hour before they came upon a blackened, charred land filled with scraggly, ashen tree stumps and covered in embers and soot. The normal smells of the forest were replaced by a thick, heavy sulfuric odor that made the men cough and hack. They slowed their pace as they approached a large, black hill. This was where Alerik had said the dragon would be, lying in slumber on the other side of a hill, nestled in his bed of coal and ash. The troop moved up, swords slowly sliding out of their sheaths and spears leveling with their points facing forward.

"Terrelius' heart skipped a few beats and his throat clogged when he caught sight of the massive beast. The head was easily twenty feet long, covered in scales the size of bronze shields and armed with fangs the size of a man. The nostrils flared lazily as the beast slumbered heavily. Its eyes were closed tight. The dragons brown, leathery wings were tucked in tight against its back, revealing its heaving belly as it breathed. Terrelius pointed to the underbelly and his men nodded. Despite the fact that even this area looked strong as steel, it was their best hope of slaying the beast. Across the dragon's back stood plates and horns made of bone, ending in a tri-tipped spiked tail. Each of the dragon's feet also bore claws at least as long as the dragon's fangs.

"'We do not fight a beast,' said one of the men. 'We are fighting an army, at least a thousand strong. We are no more able to slay it than we could break down a castle with a hammer and chisel.'

"'Be silent,' Terrelius reprimanded. 'We strike while the beast is asleep. Onward!'

"The men picked up the pace and charged in. A few peeled off from the group, kneeled in the ash and soot and drew their bows back, aiming for the dragon's head. The rest went for the underbelly. Axe, spear, and sword struck against scales of granite, damaging the weapons more than anything else. The beast drew in a great breath, and with unearthly speed it rose to all fours and lashed out with its tail. It skewered three men and flung their bodies away. Arrows glanced off its head and neck. It turned and blasted the archers with a wave of orange and yellow flame that reduced them to dust.

"'There, men, strike there!' Terrelius shouted as he pointed his blade to an opening near the underside of the dragon's tail. It looked to be the only vulnerable area on the animal's body.

"Within seconds, one of the warriors heaved a battle axe through the air, and the blade did in fact bite into the scales near the orifice, showing that it was indeed a soft spot. The dragon bellowed madly and crushed a group of men with her rear left foot. Then she bathed the ground in flame, forcing the group to retreat or die in her fiery wrath.

"The tail came down, crushing a man on horseback to the ground, merging both broken bodies together like some sort of fleshy pancake. Then the dragon reared her neck back, like a snake might do, peering down at the men before her."

Britner cleared his throat and bellowed out the next part loudly. "'What is this?' the dragon sneered. 'A handful of babes in skins and metal think to destroy the mighty Garnuthak?' The dragon laughed heartily and struck out lightning fast with her left foreleg. She seized a man in her grasp and brought him closer to her eyes for inspection. 'What hope have you now?' Terrelius watched helplessly. The man squirmed to get free, cursing at the beast all the while.

"'What do we do?' one of the men shouted. 'We can't pierce her hide.'

"'Where is Alerik?' shouted another.

"Terrelius stood silently, eyes fixed on the man in the dragon's clutches. Finally, her eyes caught his gaze and she dropped the man as a child might drop an old doll when given a new one. She brought her face low to the ground and extended her neck out. Terrelius' men trembled and backed away as the dragon slightly opened its fang-filled snout, revealing the ever-hot, orange glow in its throat.

"'You lead this band against me?' the dragon asked. 'Why?'

"Terrelius stood firm, matching the gaze in the dragon's left eye. 'I cannot let you terrorize this land. You must be stopped.'

"'Ha!' she sniggered as she snapped her head back to survey what was left of the group. 'You have only thirty men left. I have killed scores more than that in a single spurt of my fiery breath,' she claimed.

"'What do we do?' the men asked again. 'Do we attack?'

"'No,' the dragon answered. A low, rumbling growl formed in her throat and her very eyes burned with anger. 'You will die!' Out poured searing flame, catching all who were too slow to evade its fury. The dragon tramped around the ashen land, seeking the men out one by one. She bit some, stomped others, and crushed others under her tail. The men fought as valiantly as they could, but there was nothing they could do to stop her onslaught.

"Terrelius charged in, yelling a final war cry and beseeching the gods for strength. The few remaining men joined him, rushing forward to give their last efforts. The dragon laughed heartily, almost smiling at the challengers. She sat back on her hind legs and prepared to strike again.

"'GARNUTHAK!' came a shout from behind the dragon. 'Have you forgotten your oath, you foul demon?'

"The dragon's sneer vanished from her face and she whirled around to face her newest rival. Her tail whipped up dust, soot, and ash, forcing Terrelius and his men to stop. Terrelius could just make out Alerik's outline atop a hill beyond the dragon. He stood alone, with a gleaming spear in hand.

"'You,' the dragon hissed. 'I thought you would be dead by now.'

"'A mortal's life is short,' Alerik agreed. 'But I am still here, dragon.'

"'And you, did you break *your* oath to me?' Garnuthak probed. 'You did give me your word of honor.'

"Alerik pointed to the base of the hill. Terrelius and his remaining warriors took a collective step back when a second dragon came around the hill, standing almost as tall as Garnuthak, and certainly just as deadly. 'I never break my oath,' Alerik shouted.

"A second dragon!" Kathair shouted. He couldn't stifle the excitement he felt. Dengar and Foman laughed, but Britner continued as if he hadn't been interrupted at all. He stalked around the fire and crouched low as he spoke in his impersonation of the dragon's voice. "'Then how is it you are still alive?!' Garnuthak hissed. She turned to the dragon and lowered her head, gazing into the second dragon's eyes.

"The second dragon growled and clawed the ground, but stood mostly still.

"'He does not know you,' Alerik shouted. 'The years he

spent forming in his egg, I sang to him. I sang the very song you sang before I took the egg from your nest. He recognizes me as his family now, not you.'

"'Impossible!' Garnuthak bellowed. She turned and swiped the ground before Alerik, tearing the earth and stone apart. "He should have killed you once he hatched!" She turned and looked to the other dragon one more time and then looked back to Alerik. 'For your treachery, I will kill you myself!'

"Alerik held up the spear and shouted, 'You cannot!' He pointed the tip at her throat. 'You swore to me, gave me a dragon's oath, that you would never lay a hand on me so long as I protected your son from death.'

"'You *stole* him from me!' she hissed. 'What else could I say?'

"'You also swore never to return so long as your son lived!' Alerik bellowed. "'Do you remember the punishment for breaking that oath?'

"'You cannot enforce the rules of a dragon's oath, you are but a human!'

"Alerik set the butt of the spear on the ground and then pointed to the second dragon. 'But he is not. Your son is a dragon, and he can enforce the dragon's oath.'

"Garnuthak's eyes widened and she backed a few steps away. She set her gaze back to the other dragon. The two locked stares for what seemed an eternity. Then, Garnuthak bowed her head. A misty, green vapor rose from the ashen earth, enveloping her form. The fire in her throat was quenched in one breath, and her scales began to fall off, revealing soft, pink skin underneath. Her fangs broke and fell from her snout, as if they had been rotting for thousands of years, her claws became brittle and snapped under her weight. All of her horns and spikes shed from her body as easily as though it were a dog breaking free from its winter coat. The mist then fell back to the ground and vanished.

"Garnuthak humbly lowered herself to the ground. 'Are you satisfied now, human?' she hissed resentfully. 'My shame is more than I can bear.'

"Alerik tapped his spear on the ground three times. 'A dragon's oath is more than a man's,' he said. 'It is an oath sealed by great magic.' The second dragon rolled over onto its back and extended its young, still tender neck.

"'What are you doing?' Garnuthak asked.

"'The second part of your punishment, should you break your dragon's oath. Do you not remember it?' Alerik started walking down the hill.

"'No!' Garnuthak bellowed. 'Let him live!'

"Alerik stopped and turned. 'You gave me a dragon's oath,' he said. 'Your oath was to never return so long as I lived. In return, I gave you an oath to never harm your son. The terms of your oath were clear. Should you ever return, I would be able to call forth your shame, and I would be set free from my oath.'

"'I never thought my son would willfully obey your command,' she said. 'I thought he would tear you asunder!' She desperately turned to the other dragon and grunted, gesturing with her head for him to rise and fight back.

"Alerik nodded. 'I would be willing to let him live on one condition.'

"Garnuthak turned to him. 'What is it?'

"Alerik raised his spear to the air. 'Surrender yourself to Captain Terrelius and his men. Now that you have no scales, they can make a clean death for you, and you will trouble our lands no more. Do this, and I will again be bound by my oath to never harm your son.'

"Garnuthak looked to Terrelius, then to Alerik, and then back to her son. She closed her eyes and extended her long, scale-less neck toward Terrelius. 'Strike fast and true,' she said as a single tear welled in her eye.

"Alerik tapped his spear on the ground three times. The second dragon rolled over to sit on its haunches. As Terrelius and his men closed in, the young dragon sang a song that caused the ground to shake. He continued singing until Garnuthak's spirit floated out from her body, and into the heavens from which it had been born. Then, all was silent.

"Alerik gathered the water of Garnuthak's tear into a vial, and then looked to Terrelius. 'I am glad that you trusted me,' he said.

"Terrelius looked to his remaining seven men and nodded. 'And I am glad you held to your word.'

"'You knew about this?' one of the men asked as he pointed to the young dragon.

"Terrelius shook his head. 'Not until after the night by the cave.'

"'How do you control a dragon?' one of the warriors asked of Alerik. 'And how did you know this dragon's name?'

"Alerik's head sunk low and then he sighed. 'Did you not hear the discourse between me and Garnuthak?' he asked. 'Thirty years ago, I could see that we were heading to our doom. So I snuck out at night, careful to track the dragon without being seen. I found its nest, and inside I found an egg. I stole it, and hid it from Garnuthak. Five of the other warriors went in with me on the plan. I brought the egg to them and they took it to the Gray Wood. I then approached the dragon the next day. I was too late to save the other warriors, but my five companions and I survived and struck a deal with Garnuthak.'

"'But how did you know it would work?' Terrelius asked.

"Alerik smiled slightly. 'I had spent a lot of time reading of dragons,' he explained. 'Have you ever heard of The Compendium Drakonis?' Terrelius shook his head. Alerik smiled and looked back to the young dragon. 'It is the largest work about dragons ever compiled by man. It discusses every aspect you could ever think about.' Alerik then held the vial up in the air with the dragon's tear and swirled it in the light. 'Now, we should discuss what we do from here.'

"Terrelius stepped forward. 'Before we do that, I want to ask something.' His stern gaze met Alerik's and the captain slid his bloody sword back into its hilt. 'If you could control the dragon, why did it attack my men outside the cave, and why did you not let us out in the Gray Wood at night?'

"Alerik frowned. 'I don't control the dragon,' he said honestly. 'I have formed a bond with him, so that he views me as family. This took decades to do, and even now I do not understand exactly how strong the bond is, and what might break it. While my song usually calms him and makes him listen to my commands, he is still a wild beast at heart, and there is no knowing when our bond may dissolve.' He paused and then glanced at the other men. 'He hunts at night, as did his mother. While I have been able to teach him not to hunt the people that live with me in the Gray Wood, I have not been able to break him from attacking strangers who wander into his territory.'

"'So when he reaches adulthood, he will hunt like his mother did?' one of the warriors asked.

"Alerik nodded. 'And that is why we need to discuss what happened here,' he said. 'No one can know that this dragon exists.' Alerik turned and looked at the young dragon. 'Nor can anyone know that I survived. You six will return, claim the reward for yourselves, and live out your lives however you like. I ask only that you let me and the dragon depart out to the east, and never reveal our secret.'

"'Where will you go?' Terrelius asked.

"'Best that you not know. I will say that it will be far enough away that even after I die, this beast will not return. There are lands that are yet savage far out to the east, where hunting is plenty, and he will be happy there.'

"'We could kill it,' one of the warriors put in.

"Alerik scoffed. 'You couldn't slay him any more than you could pierce his mother's scales, but there is no need to find out. Everyone put forth your left hand and we will take an oath. The men put forth their hands and Alerik used the spearhead to slice their palms. As the blood dripped to the ground below they each swore an oath, vowing never to speak of how the dragon had truly been defeated, or reveal that Alerik yet lived.

"Then they parted ways. The six began their journey back to the king, carrying bloody dragon fangs from Garnuthak as proof of her death. Alerik rode upon the young dragon's back as the beast took to the sky and flew out to the east, disappearing over the mountains, never to return.

"When the six finally arrived at the castle, they were welcomed with a shower of rose petals and lilies. The king held a grand feast for seven days. One day to celebrate each of the living heroes, and one more to honor the fallen. When the feast was over, the king brought out the promised ransom, and divided it among the six. The five warriors each set out on their separate ways, retiring from battle and taking up more peaceful lives in countryside villas.

"Captain Terrelius returned to the Gray Wood. He used his treasure to build up Alerik's bastion where he became friends with the young bard, who, he discovered, was the son of one of Alerik's five companions who had helped him to hide away Garnuthak's egg those many years ago. After telling him the whole of the true story, the bard composed the tale a great battle which told of how Alerik died while delivering the final deathblow to the terrible dragon. He swore an oath to Terrelius to proclaim this story throughout the kingdom until the day of his own death. Terrelius then gave a portion of the treasure to the bard for the young man to use as he traveled around the kingdom singing praises to Alerik the Dragonslayer. So it is told, from village to city, and kingdom to empire, that Alerik the Great slew the beast whilst entangled in its jaws, saving all by offering his own life. None were ever to know the truth as it really happened."

Kathair screwed up his face and shook his head. "Then how do you know?" he asked.

Dengar laughed. "He's a quick one, isn't he?" he said.

Britner patted the air. "The young bard wrote the true account down in his journal. After his death, it was discovered by his grandson. From then on, the true account has been known. Either way, this story isn't about how Garnuthak died. It's about the savage nature of dragons."

"You see," Dengar put in as he pointed to Britner. "Alerik's baby dragon hunted humans too. Even as tame as it was, Alerik could never break it from its monstrous appetites. So, to answer your question, a dragon might come to like a person or two, if a bond is formed at birth, but it will always be savage on the inside. Just like that night outside of the cave, a dragon could turn on anyone at any time."

"What happened to Alerik?" Kathair asked.

Britner shrugged. "No one ever heard from him again."

"Probably eaten up by his own dragon," Dengar said. "Come on, let's turn in and get some sleep."

Britner nodded and turned a narrowed pair of eyes on Kathair as he held up a warning finger. "Even *if* a dragon lives beyond the reach of the curse, they can't be trusted."

Kathair spent the rest of the night playing the tale over and over in his mind. At first he thought the others might be right, but then he thought about it more and he came up with a different idea. If even the mother would give an oath for the life of her unhatched egg, then dragons weren't all that different from men. Bigger, more deadly perhaps, but greed beset men just as easily as dragons it seemed. What mattered to Kathair was two things. First, the love that Garnuthak had for her offspring and second, the fact that the young dragon did in fact learn to let everyone in Alerik's bastion live. More than that, it had not attacked Terrelius or the others at the mountain. In fact, it sounded as though the young dragon followed Alerik's commands.

So what did that mean for Leatherback? Would he remain loyal to Kyra, or would he someday become more animalistic? Kathair wished he could know how Alerik spent the rest of his years with the young dragon. Still, he took the tale as a sign of hope. If Kyra and Leatherback could get the dragon beyond the mountains and the sea, then he could escape the curse.

CHAPTER 14

Kyra waited in the library, reading her books and pacing back and forth from the table to the window overlooking the courtyard. She knew that Lepkin had gone on patrol with the dragon slayers, but he was due to return today, and she was more than anxious to tell him the news about the garunda.

It was well after noon before she saw them ride into the courtyard below. Kyra nearly squealed with excitement and turned to rush toward the door, but stopped short when she saw Feberik standing there, watching her. Kyra's smile vanished and her stomach flipped.

Feberik offered a half-smile and he glanced out to a window near him. He sighed and then held out his hand. "I thought we could have an early dinner tonight," he said.

Kyra had been so excited about the garunda that she had entirely forgotten about her weekly dinner with Feberik and Janik. It wasn't exactly an event she enjoyed going to, but she had never been able to excuse herself from one before either.

She wanted to ask the large warrior why he was doing this. Why was he still going through with the betrothal? She wanted to tell him that it was never going to happen. Even if Leatherback could never fly north, away from this land, she was never ever going to marry Feberik, of that she was certain, but the words would not come to her. Instead, she stood there, silent and unmoving while Feberik held his hand out for her.

"Are you not hungry?" Feberik asked.

Kyra sighed and shook her head. "Perhaps we can skip this week," she said.

Feberik winced and his eyes looked pained. His hand

slowly fell to his side and he looked out the window again. "Tell your friend that he owes me a horse," Feberik said out the corner of his mouth before leaving the library. "Also, you should give the vial of werewolf ashes to Headmaster Herion."

Kyra held her breath. She hadn't told anyone about hunting the werewolf, and she knew that Lepkin hadn't either. She was a more than a little surprised by Feberik's reaction, and had no way of knowing exactly when he had figured it all out. She stood there, watching the empty doorway for some time after the large warrior had left. As much as she hated the idea of him as her fiancé, she couldn't help but feel a little sorry for the man. She had never before seen him so crushed and defeated.

Fortunately for her, Lepkin came through the doorway, rushing in and smiling as he always did.

"I thought I might find you here," Lepkin said.

Kyra smiled wide. "Njar is back, and he found a garunda!"

Lepkin stopped in his tracks and his eyes widened as his brows shot up. "And you're sure it isn't another werewolf?" he teased.

"Njar doesn't make mistakes like that," Kyra fired back.

"Ah yes, it was an amateur mistake on my part, I see that now," Lepkin said as he folded his arms and feigned insult.

"So, are you ready?" Kyra asked.

"Now?" Lepkin asked.

She nodded. "It's a long way from here, so we will need to ride Leatherback."

Lepkin nodded nonchalantly and then the words sank in and his face lit up and his eyes danced above the biggest smile Kyra had ever seen. "Wait, I get to ride on a dragon?!"

Kyra nodded again. "Meet me at the nest, and I will bring him to you."

Lepkin clapped his hands together and nodded enthusiastically. "This is going to be amazing," he said as he turned around. "I'll gather my things and head out now!"

Kyra smiled and watched him run out from the library. The young sorceress then opened a portal to the aspen wood and stepped through. She found Njar and Leatherback waiting for her patiently.

"Is he back?" Njar asked.

Kyra nodded. "We need to give him some time, but he will be at the nest fairly soon."

Njar nodded. He tossed Kyra's staff to her. "Make sure to take this. We are going after dark creatures today. We shouldn't take any chances."

Kyra nodded and examined the staff. She could feel it vibrating slightly and hear the hum of the power inside. "Did you augment it again?" she asked.

Njar nodded. "Leatherback has been out of the grove much more than before. I want to be sure he is kept safe."

Kyra smiled and looked to Leatherback. The large dragon peered back at her with his sky-blue eye and then winked at her.

"I have an idea," she said suddenly. "We have some time before Lepkin will be at the nest, so why don't we go back to that pool?"

"A pool?" Njar said.

Kyra didn't give the satyr time to reject the idea. She quickly moved toward Leatherback and hopped up on his neck. She then looked down expectantly at Njar. "You coming?"

Njar pointed to his leg. "Better to not get the wound wet. It isn't fully healed yet."

Kyra shrugged and then patted Leatherback on the side of the neck. "Let's go," she said.

Leatherback launched them into the air and within a few short minutes they were back at the pool they had made together. Kyra instructed him to land nearby, but Leatherback only grinned and dropped them both directly into the pool, splashing a great amount of water out onto the nearby trees.

Kyra slapped Leatherback and then let go to fall into the water. The two played in the pool for a long time. She would swim side to side, and he would twirl about in the middle. He even found a fish that had been trapped in the pool and snatched it up for a quick snack.

The two played for roughly an hour before Kyra clambered out over the side and took her clothes off to dry, laying them out in the sun as she sat in the grass nearby and watched Leatherback continue to play. He was fun to watch as he dipped below the surface and tried to spin about in the pool. It was just large enough of an area that he could float along the length of the pool so long as he kept his legs tucked up under himself.

Kyra had only barely dried off in the sun when Leatherback dipped below the water, came up with a mouth full of liquid, and spurted it all out at Kyra, soaking her to the bone and knocking her backward.

"Leatherback!" she cried out as she slung her hands out to the side. "I was warm already!"

The dragon sniggered and let out a puff of smoke as he twirled around, pretending not to hear her complaints.

Once she was dry for the second time, she gathered her clothes up and put them on. They were still a bit damp, but it wasn't anything a short flight wouldn't take care of. Getting Leatherback out of the pool, however, proved to be a feat all its own.

"Time to go," Kyra said.

"No," Leatherback replied evenly. "I am swimming, like Gorliad."

Kyra had to remind herself that despite his size, Leatherback was still very much a child. Njar's magic had amplified Leatherback's growth, but the truth of the matter was that he hadn't even reached his first anniversary yet. By all accounts, he was in fact a baby. She had to ask him three more times before Leatherback finally responded, and even then she had to tap her foot impatiently while the dragon pretended to slip back into the pool twice.

When they were finally back in the grove, they were met with an impatient Njar, who was sitting upon the boulder and stamping his staff into the ground.

"Ready?" he asked gruffly.

Kyra nodded. "We're ready if you are," she replied.

Leatherback bent his neck toward Njar and the satyr scrambled atop the beast as best he could. Njar then summoned a cloud to hide them as they flew up and made their way to the old rock nest where Kyra had first found Leatherback's egg.

They found Lepkin waiting for them, pacing back and forth upon the gray rocks. He looked up with eyes filled with wonder and mouth hanging open as the cloud dissipated and he saw Leatherback.

"He's huge!" Lepkin said. "What have you been feeding him?"

Leatherback smiled. "Elk," he said happily.

"You ready?" Kyra asked.

Lepkin nodded, and then looked to the satyr. "You must be Njar," he said.

The satyr nodded. "And you must be the young boy who mistook a werewolf for a garunda," Njar said.

Lepkin frowned and looked to Kyra. "You told him about that?"

Kyra sniggered. "We had to talk about something on the ride over here."

Lepkin shook his head. "Where do I sit?" he asked.

"Behind me," Njar replied evenly.

Kathair Lepkin nodded and rushed over to climb up onto Leatherback's neck.

"Hang on," Kyra cautioned. Everyone was thrown back a bit as Leatherback leapt into the air. Lepkin shouted and hollered all the way up, giggling and laughing so loudly that Njar had to put his ears down. The cloud reformed around them and they sailed, hidden in the sky toward the lair where Njar had found the garunda.

The flight was nearly three hours long, and Lepkin was laughing for all of it but the last half hour. He probably would have continued laughing the entire trip, but Njar had threatened him that it was either silence, or he was going to be thrown off from the dragon's back. Lepkin chose silence.

Kyra felt her stomach twist into knots as they approached the lair. A copse of pines grew atop a small hill overlooking the entrance to a dark cave. Leatherback landed upon the hill and the three riders dismounted. Lepkin reached up to help steady Njar while Kyra walked toward the cave and surveyed the area.

She couldn't see any sign of the garunda beast, but she had expected that. She knew from her reading that they were nocturnal creatures. It was likely inside the cave sleeping until the sun set. What was odd, however, was the lack of other life in the vicinity. There didn't appear to be any birds or squirrels in the trees. All was silent. It was something both strange and familiar. The feeling of death hung in the air. She looked around and realized that if they waited for the beast to come out, then it would be stronger, for the darkness of the night would empower it.

She knew they would have to go in after the creature. Kyra turned to the others and motioned for them to catch up. When they approached she announced her decision.

"We should go in now," she said.

"We should wait," Njar countered. "It will come out during the night, and then we can attack." Njar turned and pointed to Leatherback. "He could kill the beast himself."

Kyra shook her head. "Something is wrong," she said. "What if it's a trap?"

"What do you mean?" Njar said.

"You said the shade laid a trap for me at the manor. Maybe it knows we are hunting it. It knows we have a dragon. Now it knows that you are on our side, which means he might know about the Pools of Fate. What if he set this up so he could ambush us at night?"

Njar shook his head. "No, that isn't possible, he would have to be able to tamper with the Pools of Fate. Even he is not that strong."

Kyra frowned. "What if he is?"

Lepkin stepped forward and pulled his sword. "If it were me, that's what I would do. He already nearly killed you once, Kyra." Lepkin glanced down to Njar's leg. "And, by the looks of it, he fared well against you also."

Njar sighed and nodded. "Very well. Stay behind me. We'll go in after it."

The group moved into the cave, Njar leading, Lepkin in the middle, and Kyra bringing up the rear. She had tried to be second, but Lepkin wouldn't let her. He insisted on standing in front of her. They wound their way down through the cave until they rounded a curve and lost the light of the sun.

Njar summoned a great orb of white light that hovered in the air above them. They continued walking through the cave. There were scratch marks along the walls, but no signs of life anywhere. It wasn't until they came to an eerie staircase that any of them heard the rhythmic breathing coming from further in the cave.

They descended the stairs slowly, watching for the beast. The tunnel around them changed from being a simple shaft in the ground to a grand cavern meticulously carved from stone. The floor was cracked and the place had seen better days, but even now it was impressive to look upon.

As they reached the bottom of the stairs, they again pressed forward, but they fanned out instead of walking in a single line. They passed over strange bones, noting spiders and centipedes that crawled away from the orb of light as they passed.

Suddenly a roar was heard. Kyra saw the beast, but not until after it stood on its hind legs and let loose with a strange spell that sent a shockwave through the air. Njar tried to fend it off, but wasn't fast enough. He was launched through the air and tumbled across the stone floor, screaming in pain.

The garunda charged like black lightning, zig-zagging as it ran so as to avoid Kyra's spells.

Lepkin stepped close to Kyra, his sword at the ready. The black, gigantic cat-like creature leapt the final fifteen feet between them as if it were a short hop. Lepkin pushed Kyra aside and then somersaulted forward, ducking and rolling under the great beast. He then shot up to his feet and reached for his mini-crossbow. He fired the weapon and the bolt struck the beast in the chest.

The garunda appeared to smile as it stalked toward him, unfazed by the crossbow attack.

Kyra launched a fireball, but the garunda turned and knocked the spell away with a psionic blast that redirected the fireball toward Lepkin. The young swordsman was forced to dodge out to the side.

The garunda then turned and shrieked in a scream so loud and so shrill that Kyra backed away, covering her ears with her hands. She barely saw Njar push himself up to his feet and rain magical hail upon the garunda, for her head was pounding furiously and she reflexively closed her eyes. Only when the garunda stopped screaming, could she open her eyes once more and try to focus.

The beast was now facing Njar, hunkering down as if preparing to leap toward him.

Kyra saw Lepkin charge in from behind. The young man shouted loudly, distracting the garunda from Njar.

"Now!" Lepkin yelled.

Everyone attacked simultaneously. Njar fashioned a spear of ice and hurled it toward the beast with magical precision. Meanwhile, Kyra lifted the garunda with a cyclone that she formed directly under the monster. The garunda spun up into the air and the magical ice-spear corrected its trajectory and flew up to pierce its flank just as Lepkin ran in below it and shoved his sword deep into the garunda's chest. Njar sent two smaller ice-spears toward the garunda, one catching it in the neck and the other going straight into its skull. The garunda then fell to the ground dead.

Lepkin smote off its head, just to be sure it was dead, and then Kyra quickly filled three vials with the beast's blood, careful not to spill any of the green liquid on herself. When they had what they needed, Njar burned the body.

"You're hurt," Kyra said as she noticed that Njar's wound had reopened. Blood was oozing down his leg.

"It isn't as bad as last time, he said quickly. "Come, we need to get out of here."

"Let's get back to the grove," Kyra said. "We can drop Lepkin off at the rock nest on the way back, then you can get back to Viverandon."

Njar nodded.

Lepkin put Njar's left arm over his shoulders and helped the satyr hobble his way out of the cave. Exiting the shaft took considerably longer, given that they had to stop every few paces for Njar to catch his breath. Yet, even as his legs grew weaker, Njar refused to rest until they were out of the cave. Only then did he use any magic to help reclose the wound. His healing spells took several minutes to complete, but once they were done, the blood had stopped trickling out and Njar seemed to be in better spirits.

"I'm afraid I won't be any good for the fight with the shade," Njar said.

Kyra nodded. "That's all right. I think we have what we need."

Lepkin shook his head. "We don't have any dwarven armor or weapons yet," he said.

Njar looked at him curiously. "What do you need those for?"

Lepkin replied, "In the accounts we read about defeating shades, the dwarven items help protect against the shade's magic."

Njar nodded. "Do either of you know where to get something like that?"

Lepkin nodded. "I know of a place," he said.

"All right, then it's settled. We'll go tonight and get the rest of what we need, then tomorrow night we will attack the shade."

Njar shook his head. "No, you can't go after the shade, not without me. He'll overpower you. He is too strong."

Kyra grinned slyly. "No, I have a plan."

Lepkin returned her smile and his eyes twinkled. "Setting a trap for the shade?"

Kyra nodded. "Precisely."

CHAPTER 15

Leatherback huddled down low to the grass. Kathair checked the forest around them while Kyra petted Leatherback's snout reassuringly.

"I'll be back soon," Kyra promised.

Leatherback purred and tried to settle in even lower into the ground. The tall pines would conceal him, exactly as Kathair had promised, but there were no aspens nearby. Kyra placed her staff next to the dragon, and then hurried to catch up with Kathair.

"I don't see anyone around," he said with a dutiful nod. "Leatherback should be safe here."

Kyra offered a half smile and then glanced back over her shoulder. "He would have told us if anyone was around before we landed," she informed Kathair. She looked up at the night sky. "We need to hurry so we can make it back before dawn. We can't risk being seen."

Kathair nodded. "Let's go."

Neither of them spoke again until they reached the gates of Buktah. Kyra watched the walls seemingly grow in the darkness as the two of them came nearer. The towers loomed over them, with guards inside each one. The orange light of the torches reflected off their armor and cast shadows over their faces. The gatehouse was simple, but formidable. With the light shining from a set of large braziers on either side of the road leading in, and sconces along the walls flanking the gates themselves, Kyra noticed that large spikes protruded out from the center of each iron gate.

"How do we get in at night?" Kyra asked.

"Like I said," Kathair began, "I know the guards."

Kathair took her up toward the gate and stopped in place when one of the guards from the wall commanded them to identify themselves.

"I am Kathair Lepkin," Kathair said.

Before Kyra could even open her mouth, a guard approached quickly from the gatehouse and held his arms out wide.

"I didn't think I would see you back so soon!" the guard said. The large man turned and waved to the archers above. "It's all right, he's one of the good guys," he called out.

"He must not know about your habit of breaking into other people's offices and stealing things," Kyra whispered out the corner of her mouth.

Kathair didn't miss a beat. "Anything to help a damsel in distress," he said cockily.

"Damsel?" Kyra echoed.

Kathair was already moving away and shaking hands with the guard.

"What are you doing walking around outside in the dark?" the guard asked.

"I came to see you, Berklin," Kathair replied. "Can we come in for a bit?"

"Uh-huh, sure you did. I remember the last time you were here. Running another errand for the dragon slayers are you?"

Kathair nodded. "Something like that. I need to see Al."

"Ah," Berklin said with a grin. "Well I am sure he is still awake and working hard as usual."

The guard nodded and motioned for Kyra to come with them as he turned and led them to the gate. He knocked twice, banging the bottom of his fist on the solid iron gate.

Rattling chains filled the air with their song and then the doors began to swing inward toward the town. Teams of oxen, attached to long, thick chains that creaked and groaned at the strain of the heavy doors pulled the portal open.

"Why do the doors open inward?" Kyra asked. "Shouldn't they open outward to offer more protection against battering rams?"

Berklin laughed and thumbed at Kyra. "See, if only the powers that make the decisions had as much sense as your lady friend, Kathair, then we would be in fine shape."

Kyra smiled at the compliment and then followed Kathair through the portal.

She could smell the ox dung as they passed through, but the odor quickly gave way to the smells of dust and roasting meat.

They walked for several minutes down an old, dusty road dimly lit by candles housed in glass cases atop wooden poles just a bit taller than Kathair. They soon turned down a path that was narrower than the main road and was flanked by short, brown wooden buildings. The doors were simple and there were usually one or two windows facing the street, but occasionally there were buildings without windows. All of the buildings were scrunched up against each other, some taller and some shorter, but none with an inch of space between them. Most had candles that could be seen through the windows, but some were entirely dark inside.

A short, fat woman came out into the street from one of the buildings on the right. She shot Kyra a sour look and then tossed a dead rat into the street. Kyra paused momentarily as a couple of stray cats seemed to materialize from the shadows and rushed in to fight over the prize.

"Disgusting," Kyra said as they continued walking.

"Afraid of rats?" Kathair teased.

Kyra shook her head. "No, I simply find them revolting."

They came to a road of cobblestones that crossed the dirt path they were on. Kathair pointed to the left and then motioned for Kyra to keep up.

Kyra saw several signs. Some were ornate with fresh paint or elaborate engravings. Each sign was cut in a different shape and hung above the front door of an inn. There was the Rosewood, the Midnight Traveler, The Spotted Owl Inn, and then there was one plain sign that simply had the word "Inn" etched lightly into its side. All but the last one had their doors cast wide open. Kyra could hear the many different songs emanating from the buildings and out to mix in the street. A bard played a lyre in the Midnight Traveler. A small band of fiddlers created a lively tune in the Rosewood, and someone was singing and playing a piano in the Spotted Owl Inn. Kyra smiled then. A flood of memories came to her mind. The music brought memories of dancing with her mother at the mid-summer festival each year for as long back as she could remember. She closed her eyes and, for a moment, could see herself dancing with her mother again.

Her mother's hair spun out behind her in a wide flare. The two of them laughed and held each other's hands as they began to spin faster and faster, their feet struggling to keep pace with the fiddlers. Then they fell to the side, crashing into a soft pile of hay and laughed aloud.

Kyra opened her eyes and the memory was gone.

She reached up to wipe a tear and then blushed when she noticed that Kathair was watching her.

"You all right?" he asked.

She nodded.

"Thinking of your mother?"

Kyra smiled. "She loved to dance," she explained.

Kathair stopped and held out his hand. Kyra looked at it and arched a brow.

"Come, I'm not much of a dancer, but I can show you something fun," Kathair said.

Kyra was about to protest, but Kathair reached forward and took her hands in his. "Hold on," he said as he stepped in close. "I used to do this back in Tualdern, it drove the elders mad because it always disrupted the dances the others were doing."

"What do I do?" Kyra asked.

"Lean back, and try to keep up," Kathair said.

Kyra found her heart racing with joy and heavy with sorrow all at the same time as Kathair smiled and then let out a laugh as he leaned back to his arms' full length. The two began to spin. It was the same as when she used to do this with her mother once they had tired of dancing, but it was also different. Kathair's hands were warm and strong, holding Kyra locked in the spin, whereas Kyra's mother had always had soft hands. After only a moment, Kyra was laughing as well and the two spun and spun until their feet tripped upon themselves and they tumbled down to the ground.

It was not the soft landing that Kyra had always been used to, but it didn't seem to matter. Kathair had done something that Kyra could not do for herself. He chased the grief away from the memory, and gave Kyra the chance to enjoy thinking about her mother without feeling overwhelmed with loss.

She turned her head and looked at him, his chest and stomach heaving as he laughed wildly, lying upon his back in the middle of the road. He struggled to sit up and put a hand to the side of his head.

"It's been a long time since I have done that!" Kathair exclaimed. "I don't remember the ground being so hard before."

Kyra nodded as she rose to her feet. Everything around her was still spinning slightly, but she closed her eyes and counted to ten, and then focused on a single spot in front of her. The only thing was, when she opened her eyes to focus on something, she found her gaze locked with Kathair's blue eyes. For the first time, she noticed how deeply blue they were. She was beginning to realize that there was much more to this young man than a sword. She smiled and turned away almost at the same moment that he averted his eyes.

"Come on," Kathair said. "We should keep moving so we get back on time."

The two walked to the inn with the plain sign and then Kathair motioned for her to follow him through a small alleyway to the back. The two of them had to turn sideways as the space between the inn and the building next door was very narrow. As they came around the back of the inn Kathair pointed to a blacksmith shop that was joined to the back of the inn. "That's where we're going."

Kyra could see the orange and yellow glow from the forge. Smoke rose up high over the chimney, somehow darker than the night sky itself. "Your friend is here?" she asked. "And you are sure he will have a dwarven charm I can use?"

Kathair smiled. "I think you are going to enjoy this," he said with a wink. He reached back and seized her hand, pulling her behind him as he walked into an open area where the coal for the furnace was piled higher than either of them were tall. Kyra could feel the heat coming from the open door of the shop, but what surprised her was that she could smell the heat. The only other time she had ever smelled heat was when Leatherback used his fire breath. In such a confined space, the odor made the air inside the forge heavy and somewhat difficult to breathe, but it had an alluring quality to it as well. She followed Kathair, allowing him to pull her by her hand until they found someone standing near a work table.

"What are you doing out of bed at this hour?" the blacksmith asked as he turned around.

Kyra eyed the blacksmith with wonder. There before her stood not a human, but a dwarf! He was only a little over three feet tall, with a red beard that swept the tops of his boots as he walked. His long, red hair was pulled into a single plait in the back. He wore a black apron and held his massive hammer in his left hand.

"You're a dwarf," Kyra said without thinking. She turned to look at Kathair's beaming smile and told him, "Your friend's a dwarf!"

"I might have guessed a girl was involved," the dwarf said as he shook his head. "Kathair, you can't just use your connection with me to impress all of your lady friends."

Kyra looked back to the blacksmith. "*All* of his lady friends?" she echoed.

The blacksmith nodded and turned to set his hammer down on the work table with a *thunk!* "Oh yeah, once or twice a week he brings a new little lass around to impress them."

"Stop it, Al," Kathair said sternly. "You know that isn't true."

"Aye, but she doesn't," the dwarf said with a wink at Kyra.

Kyra then noticed the dwarf's eyes land upon her hand, which was still gripped inside Kathair's. The dwarf then winked again and wiped his hands on his apron. The young sorceress pulled her hand away and moved it up to brush her hair back.

"Al, allow me to introduce Kyra Dimwater," Kathair said as he held a hand out to indicate toward her.

"Enchanted," the dwarf said with a bow. He then stepped in close and stuck out his meaty hand. "My friends call me Al," the dwarf said. "I am the finest blacksmith in Buktah, and probably the entire Middle Kingdom."

"Humble too," Kathair put in.

Al shrugged. "There might be someone better than me inside Roegudok Hall, but in terms of blacksmiths that live above ground, I'm the best there is."

"That doesn't sound like a dwarf name," Kyra noted as she shook Al's hand.

"Well, that's the thing about tall folk. In the three hundred years since I have been above ground, I haven't found a single person who can say my name correctly. I guess your tongues don't work well enough to pronounce it. So, I shortened it."

"What's your full name?" Kyra asked.

"Aldehenkaru'hktanah Sit'marihu," he said with a wide smile. "Would you like to try to say it?"

Kyra gasped slightly and put a hand to her mouth. "Are you a prince?" she asked.

Al balked and glanced to Kathair.

Kathair shrugged and stared at Kyra blankly.

"No, I know that name," Kyra insisted. "That is the royal family's name, isn't it? That is the line of the kings of Roegudok Hall."

"And what would you know about the dwarves of Roegudok Hall? You can't be more than fourteen, scarcely eligible to begin your time in the scholar's school at Kuldiga

Academy."

"I'm nearly fifteen, I belong to the sorcery school, and I know plenty about Roegudok Hall." Kyra began hotly, "I've read several books over the last year about the dwarves of the middle kingdom, including the story of how your people were first made from the Black Mountain by Hiasyntar Kulai, the great golden dragon, and your first king, Persais, was chosen for his valor in rescuing the crowned egg. I've even translated the first of the Chronicles of Kendualdern from the original Peish, which is how I know that the runes on the hammer you carry there say that you are the crowned prince."

For a moment, Al stood flabbergasted, then he turned his gaze to his hammer and ran his fingers across the runes. "This was a title meant for me in another life. Standing at the forge is where I belong, not buried away in a throne room, bound by ceremony and convention. You'll find me burdened under a crown and stuffed in ceremonial armor when the Wealth of King's is found." He finished with a hint of sarcasm.

"I thought that was lost ages ago?" Kyra questioned.

Al wrinkled his nose and tugged on his beard. "I like her, Lepkin, she's smart. You better make sure you hold onto her."

"Hold..." Kathair said slowly as he drew his brow together. Sudden realization must have dawned on him, for his brows shot up and he opened his mouth to speak, but Kyra beat him to it.

"No, Al, we are just friends, that's all," she said quickly.

Al looked them up and down and sniggered. "Right," he said as he turned around and moved back toward the table.

Kathair and Kyra shared a glance before the young man spoke up.

"We are looking for a dwarven charm," he said.

"What for?" Al asked as he retrieved his hammer, slid it into a special holster hanging from his belt, and then moved around the table to pull up a short sword.

"I am going to hunt a shade," Kyra said bluntly.

Kathair shot her an angry look and shook his head.

Al looked up and set the blade on the table. "I'm sorry,

dear, I think I misheard you. What did you say?"

"I need protection from a shade," she repeated.

Al's eyes shot open as wide as saucer plates. He looked to Kathair and shook his head. "Never mind, Lepkin, she may not be that smart after all."

"It killed my mother," Kyra said fiercely. "It now hunts me."

Al screwed up his face and tugged on his beard. "It hunts you?"

Kathair stepped into the conversation then. "She's already fought it once," he said.

"And lived?!" Al cried out. He shook his head in disbelief. "Stonebubbles, what does it want with you?"

Kathair answered before Kyra could get a word in edgewise. "We don't know. It seeks something. The masters at Kuldiga Academy are doing their best to help her, but it isn't enough."

Al took in a deep breath and then finally nodded. "I have something that will work. I made it myself, so I know the runes are done right. It doesn't just protect from shades, but from all manner of dark creatures." He turned around and started shuffling toward a door. "Wait there a moment."

He returned after a couple of minutes with a silver amulet resting upon a strong chain. It seemed to glow in the firelight as the rectangular amulet twirled this way and that. Al held it up for them to see and then he offered it to Kyra.

"How much?" Kathair asked.

Al shook his head. "This one's on me," the dwarf replied solemnly.

Kyra smiled and reached out to take it. She grasped the chains with both hands and then slipped it over her head. She opened her mouth to thank Al, but as the amulet touched her breastbone, she felt a strange, tingling sensation run through her body. Her legs grew weak and her knees gave out.

Kathair was only barely able to catch her and help her back up to her feet. "Are you all right?"

Kyra couldn't think straight. Her mind went foggy and

her strength seemed to evaporate away as if she had none at all. The runes on the amulet glowed brightly.

Suddenly, something tugged at the back of her neck. She felt a sharp, momentary pain, and then the clouds seemed to dissipate from her mind and she breathed in short, quick breaths as her strength returned to her legs.

"Oh, deary, you should have told me about that," Al said. He turned and put the amulet on the work table.

"Should have told you what?" Kathair asked.

"I'm afraid you can't use this amulet," Al said pointedly to Kyra.

"Why not? Tell me what happened!" Kathair shouted.

"Because," Kyra began softly as she pushed Kathair away, "I am born of a vampire."

Al nodded grimly. "As I said, any charm that works upon shades, works upon other creatures imbued with dark magic." Al shook his head and sighed. "This charm works against shades, vampires, shadowfiends, and some demons. If you are even partly of vampire lineage, there is no way you can wear this."

Kyra nodded and reached her hand up to touch her skin just below the neck where the collarbones meet. The area was sore and stung fiercely as she lightly brushed the pad of her finger against it.

"Let me see something," Al said. He slipped the amulet around his neck and tied the now broken chain behind his head. "Go ahead and try to hit me with a spell."

Kyra nodded, blinking her eyes and rubbing her left temple to massage away a headache. She extended her right hand and tried to send a small bolt of lightning from her finger. The spell leapt from her and darted out, but then fizzled to nothing in the air several feet away from the dwarf.

"Now try him," Al instructed, pointing to Kathair.

"I'm not wearing an amulet," Kathair pointed out.

Al nodded. "Keep it to a small jolt, don't want to fry your friend," Al said.

Kyra turned to Kathair and pointed her hand at him. The

small tendril of blue electricity snaked out and bit into Kathair's shoulder. The young man jumped and grabbed his shoulder.

"Ouch!" he cried out. He rubbed his arm and then pointed to Al. "Al, stand next to me," Kathair said.

The dwarf shot him a curious look.

"Please," Kathair pleaded.

Al shuffled over and stood next to Kathair.

"All right, Kyra, fire again," Kathair said.

Kyra reluctantly took aim and fired. As it had when she cast the spell at Al before, the lightning lost its power a couple of feet before it struck Kathair.

"There, see?" Kathair said. "If I go with you, then I can wear the amulet. I will accompany you into the shade's lair. We can defeat it together."

Al shook his head. "Not so fast, Lepkin," he said. Al moved across to stand beside Kyra. "Try it again," he said.

"What?" Kathair shouted. "We already know she can hit me if you aren't close to me."

Al lifted a finger to his mouth and shushed Kathair.

Kyra cast the spell again, but this time nothing happened at all.

"As I thought," Al said. "If the amulet is even close to you, it will prevent you from using magic."

"Then I cannot use the amulet at all," Kyra said somberly. She stepped away from Al, though whether she could actually feel the amulet's power or was just afraid of it, she wasn't sure.

"Then let me go," Kathair said quickly." We have the garunda blood. Give me the charm, and I will slay the shade."

Kyra shook her head. "No, you will never survive," she said. "It's too powerful."

"But if the charm prevents it from using magic, then I just have to stab it with some garunda blood on my sword. I can do it."

Kyra shouted, "No!" She looked to Al for help. "I have seen the shade," she told the dwarf. "It's too fast for him."

Al's brows shot up. "Too fast for Lepkin?" he questioned.

"That is something," he said. "But, I don't doubt it, shades are very dangerous creatures."

"So what do we do now?" Kyra asked.

Al held up a finger and then hurried through the door once more. He came back less than a minute later with a wicked-looking crossbow in his hands. "This is an experimental weapon," he said as he turned it to the side and presented it to Kyra. "It has three slots for the bolts. Each one has its own separate arms, string, and trigger." Al held it up higher so Kyra could see it. It looked almost as if someone had sandwiched three crossbows together, and then set the three triggers in a row. "Behind the stock you pull on this metal handle to cock it. The downside is, you have to load three bolts at a time, because all three arms move with the single handle. However, you can fire the bolts separately, or together. Watch."

Al pulled up a quiver of bolts and slid three of them into place. Then, with his left hand on the stock and his right hand on the metal handle in the back, he pulled the limbs into place with a loud *cl-click!* He then turned to the pile of coal nearby.

"First I will demonstrate single-fire." He lifted the weapon and pulled the first trigger. The top bolt flew out and exploded into the coal. He then pulled his finger out and put it back on the second trigger. He pulled it and the middle bolt fired. He then slipped his finger back to the third trigger and pulled it. The bottom limbs snapped into place and the last bolt flew through the air.

"Now I will show you the rapid-fire method." Al loaded three more bolts, and then held the weapon up to take aim. This time, Kyra watched as the dwarf pulled the trigger back hard enough that his finger slipped straight back, hitting the second and then third trigger in less than half of a second. The three crossbow bolts blasted into the coal at nearly the same moment.

"I can loan this to you," Al told Kyra. You can both go in and hunt the shade. He can wear the amulet, which will protect you both, and you can use the crossbow."

"I have never used one before," she said.

"It ain't difficult," Al commented. "You just pull it up and look down the middle at what you want to hit. When you see this little knob over the target, you pull the trigger." Al pointed to a short, oblong metal protrusion on the front of the crossbow. "Just don't waste all three shots unless you know they are all going to hit the target."

He held the weapon out for Kyra.

She took it and turned it over in her hands.

"If you ever dry fire the thing, the limbs will break," Al warned. "Always load all three bolts."

Kyra nodded.

"How much for the weapon?" Kathair asked.

Al shook his head. "Just don't get yourselves killed," he groused. "Also, I am looking for an apprentice. What do you say, Lepkin?"

Kathair shook his head. "No, you know I am bound for the dragon slayers."

Al shrugged and then held his hands out to the side. "Worth asking," he said. "It's hard to find good help in Buktah."

Al then moved to a shelf on the wall and retrieved a large, canvas bag. He went to Kyra and took the crossbow from her, setting it into the bag along with the quiver of bolts. "Don't want the guards seeing this and confiscating the only one I have."

Kyra smiled. "Thank you," she offered.

Al shook his head. "Don't thank me unless you live. Frankly, I wouldn't face a shade unless it had hunted me down and had me cornered. I think the two of you are on a fool's errand. Why not just wait for the masters to take care of it?"

"They can't track it," Kathair said.

"And you can?" Al quipped.

Kathair just looked at Al and nodded.

Al frowned. "Oh," he said. After a moment, he removed the amulet and handed it to Kathair. "You sure I can't convince you to reconsider?"

Kyra shook her head. "We'll have help," she said.

The two of them made their way back to Leatherback. Kyra sighed with relief and rushed up to hug Leatherback's snout when she realized he was resting safely where they had left him.

"How do you feel?" Kyra asked.

Leatherback grinned. "I feel good."

Kyra picked up her staff and then climbed atop the dragon's back.

Kathair stopped for a moment and removed his shirt. Kyra was about to ask what he was doing, but then he wrapped the amulet in the shirt and stuffed it into the back of his left boot as best he could.

"I don't know if it will help," Kathair said, "but I thought it might be worth a try."

"Thanks," Kyra offered. She couldn't help but notice Kathair's wide shoulders and muscular chest as he approached and scrambled up to sit behind her. He wrapped his hands around her waist and then Kyra took the reins.

"Let's go home," she said.

Leatherback launched into the air. Moments later Kyra smiled while Kathair giggled and laughed uncontrollably. It sounded as though he was having far more fun than Kyra had ever had while riding Leatherback.

They flew back with great speed, the wind blowing into them hard and forcing the pair to hunker down atop the dragon as he beat a furious path through the night sky with his wings. There was no way to be sure, but the flight seemed to be nearly half what it had been on their way to Buktah.

Before they knew it, they were landing in a forested area, setting down upon a valley of rocks. Kathair slid off from Leatherback and patted the dragon's side.

"Thanks for the ride," he said.

Leatherback turned his head and bowed it slightly while emitting a short purr.

"He likes you," Kyra said with a smile.

"Of course he does," Kathair said as he swept his arms out to the side. "Everybody likes me."

Kyra shook her head and pulled on the reins.

"Wait, before you go, what is the plan?" Kathair asked.

"Meet me in the library tomorrow," Kyra said.

"Promise you won't go tonight," Kathair demanded.

Kyra nodded. "It's too late even if I wanted to. We would lose the cover of night in a few hours."

Kathair smiled and looked to Leatherback. "Make sure she doesn't go anywhere but home tonight, okay? It's important."

Leatherback grinned and then turned his head away.

"See you soon," Kyra said. Then she tugged on the reins twice and Leatherback launched into the air.

The first beat of the dragon's wings bent the trees away and Kyra could hear Kathair coughing as clouds of dust erupted around him. She smiled at her friend as he quickly disappeared below her.

Soon, she and Leatherback were landing back in the glade. Leatherback let out a satisfied growl and Kyra slid off to the ground and then patted Leatherback's shoulder.

"Get some rest," she said. "Tomorrow night we will go after the shade."

"Hunt the shade," Leatherback snarled.

Kyra nodded. "Do you still feel all right?"

Leatherback nodded.

"Kyra," a voice called from the darkness.

She spun around, alarmed, but Leatherback identified the speaker and calmed her.

"Njar," he said reverently.

The satyr conjured a magical orb of light that hovered above his staff and approached them. "I wanted to check on Leatherback again," he said. "I know you have been out longer than this before, but with the frequency and distance from the grove you are travelling, I thought it best to be cautious."

Kyra nodded. "He says he is fine, but I understand."

Leatherback took a step toward the satyr and then bowed

his head low.

The satyr put out a furry hand and placed it upon Leatherback's forehead. A green glow emanated between them and Njar began to hum as he closed his eyes and leaned toward Leatherback. The dragon purred softly, closing his eyes as well.

Kyra was never entirely sure what was happening between them, but she felt much more at ease with Njar's tests than the priests from Valtuu Temple. Knowing that Njar had once been friends with Leatherback's parents made it seem better, safer somehow.

The exam took several minutes, but Njar broke the spell soon enough and smiled, seemingly pleased.

"Still no evidence of the taint. I will work tonight to strengthen the aspen wood as much as I can."

Kyra nodded. "Is there anything I can do to help?" she asked.

Njar pointed to her staff. "Leave that here with me as well. I will try to enhance its powers.

Kyra moved to hand him the staff. She then asked, "Are you sure you know the shade's location?"

Njar nodded. "After you slayed the first beast, I was able to hone in on a second using the Pools of Fate. I saw it emerge from its den. It is there that we will go. If I am wrong, then at least we will eradicate another garunda monster."

Kyra glanced back to Leatherback. Finally she would have answers. Cyrus may not believe her ready to fight on her own against the shade, but she was not alone. She had good friends to help her.

Kyra opened the portal and walked through without another word.

She appeared in the rocky nest, only a few feet from where she had left Kathair.

The light of the moon was enough to see her way from here. She went toward the tree line, but something moved in the darkness in front of her.

"Kyra, is that you?" Kathair whispered.

Kyra squinted, trying to distinguish her friend from the

shadows.

"Kyra?" Kathair repeated.

"It's me," she said.

Kathair came rushing out from the bushes, waving his arm for her to come to him. "Quickly!" he said. "The priests are coming."

"The priests?" Kyra asked.

Kathair rushed forward to take her hand and pulled her to the bushes. "Come on, we don't have much time."

Kyra resisted. "Why are they out here?"

Kathair shook his head. "I don't know," he said. "But I saw them with Dengar, he is one of the dragon slayers I have been working with. After you dropped me off here, I left the forest, but I found the priests with Dengar just beyond the trees. Dengar left the priests, going back to the academy I think, but the priests turned and walked toward the forest. So, I rushed back here to find you first."

"We can't escape from them," Kyra said. "They see auras. They will find us no matter where we hide."

Kathair shook his head. "They can't see through walls," he said. "There is a hollowed out tree just over here. I found a large rock I can roll in front of the opening, we'll be concealed."

Kyra stopped him and pulled her hand back. "No, a tree is a living thing. It has an aura that they can see. Either they will see our auras inside of the tree, or it will somehow signal to them that we are there."

Kathair stopped and shook his head. "But, we have to hide somewhere," he said.

"Why?" Kyra asked. "They have done no harm to us."

Kathair shook his head. "I could hear Dengar talking. I think he has caught on about Leatherback. He was asking about the priests, what they were doing here, and whether they had found a dragon."

"Why would he ask that?" Kyra asked.

"Because, he has seen you scampering about like an imp," a voice called out from the darkness.

Three men in long robes emerged from the tree line and walked steadily over the rocks.

"They're fast," Kathair whispered out of the corner of his mouth.

"Just because our eyes do not work like yours, that is no reason to suspect that we do not have full control over our other faculties," the priest said. "We have come to warn you, that is all."

"You aren't going to hurt Kyra or Leatherback?" Kathair asked as he took a half step in front of Kyra.

The young sorceress glanced at Kathair, surprised that he should be so protective.

"We have only come to warn you. The dragon must be moved. Dengar has seen you walking in this direction, Kyra. He has also seen us when we have left the academy for our inspections."

Kyra's heart sank. The priests had promised to be careful. How could they have let a dragon slayer see them?

"Perhaps this will help you trust us," the priest said. "If you were to move the dragon, and then from that point on we used your portal to conduct our inspections, then the dragon slayers would have nothing to follow. They would only see us enter your room. Or, perhaps we could convene in the headmaster's chamber."

Kyra nodded. She didn't know what to say. Njar was reinforcing the magic of the grove. If they had to move now, then they would have to start over. That was not a risk she wanted to take. For half a moment she thought of fighting the dragon slayers, but that notion left her mind nearly as quickly as it had come. Such actions would only bring more dragon slayers to the area.

"With your permission, we will go and tell your dragon of the danger."

Kyra shook her head. "I'll go first." Kyra opened the portal and before anyone could protest, she stepped through and it closed behind her.

The sound of Kathair's laughter filled the rocky clearing

as the priests grumbled to each other and began walking again.

CHAPTER 16

Lepkin and Kyra waited anxiously for the daylight to fade away the following day. They waited in the old rock nest, in the spot where Guardian, a special lizard that had watched over Leatherback's unhatched egg, had been killed by a wraith. Kyra had hidden the special crossbow near a large rock, well out of sight to anyone but her. She had tipped the three bolts with garunda blood. Lepkin had also smeared the blood across his sword.

The young swordsman was hiding a couple feet away, lying under a large, flat rock in the same place that Leatherback's egg had once been hidden from passersby. This way, it appeared that Kyra was alone when in fact, Lepkin was close enough that the dwarven amulet he wore could protect her as well. The dragon was crouched in the forest, and would take to the sky after dark so he could circle from above.

Kyra took in a nervous breath, fidgeting with her feet as she waited for darkness to fall over the rock nest. She hoped her plan would work. She had opted for luring the shade to her instead of trying to find its lair and go after it. She didn't know what to expect, but at least she felt as though she maintained some amount of control over the battle.

Her mother's killer would be here shortly, and it was up to her to bring him to justice for what he had done. Kyra cracked her knuckles and prayed silently to her mother in that moment.

Watch over me now, Mother, as I avenge your death and end this plague of evil that has befallen our family.

The final hour before darkness passed by agonizingly

slowly, as if it were itself an entire day. Then, as darkness crept over the land, she took in a steadying breath. She jumped when she heard Leatherback take flight, his massive wings bending the trees and kicking up dust. Kyra glanced over to the large, flat rock that she had so many times used to cover Leatherback's egg. Now Lepkin was crouched beneath it, waiting to spring out and attack the shade.

"Ready?" she called out to him in a tone that was little more than a whisper.

"Ready as I'll ever be," Lepkin said.

Kyra waited a few minutes, more out of nervousness than anything else, before she pulled a knife from her belt. She cut a thin line across her left forearm. It was nothing serious, but enough to draw blood from and squeeze upon the ground. She had tried this before, and it had nearly ended in her death. She could only hope that this time she would be ready. She let the droplets fall upon the ground and then waited.

Only a few seconds passed before a silvery mist wafted into the rock nest. It brought a deathly chill along with it and then the shade appeared.

"Did you bring the dagger?" the shade asked.

Kyra shook her head. "I don't have it," she replied.

The shade shook his head and made a clicking sound to show his displeasure. He then split into two, then three, and then four images of himself. Each shade continued to divide itself until she was surrounded on all sides.

"You do remember how this went the last time, yes?" the shade hissed.

Kyra nodded. "If you kill me, you will never find the dagger," she said, trying to sound confident.

The shades all moved in closer, all speaking in unison. "There are spells that can bring you to the edge of death, and make you feel such pain that you will give up the dagger just for release.

The shades all raised their right arms and sent great, silver balls of fire hurtling toward Kyra. The young sorceress made a motion as though she was casting a ward spell, but of course she wasn't, the amulet Lepkin wore would have prevented the ward had she tired. More importantly, the amulet protected her from each of the fireballs. They each fizzled out a few feet away from her and she laughed as though she had countered the spells.

The shades' mouths dropped open and a look of disbelief was painted clearly on each of their faces.

"You have grown stronger," the shades said. "No matter, I will finish this with my bare hands!" The eight-foot tall shades all ran toward her simultaneously. Kyra spun around, hoping she would end up facing the true shade when all the illusions were dispelled by Lepkin's amulet.

The shades sprinted toward her, hands raised and long, claw-like nails ready to strike her. Then, to her great relief, all but one faded away. The final shade stopped, stunned and confused by his lack of power. He raised his hand to fire another spell, but he was standing a few feet away from Lepkin's hiding spot, so nothing happened. The shade roared and rushed toward her.

Kyra screamed and went for the crossbow.

Kathair burst out from under his rock and took a swing at the shade.

The nimble creature leapt into the air, flipping over Lepkin's blade so deftly that only a few hairs were severed by the young man's sword. The shade landed before Lepkin could recover from his powerful swing and sent a savage back kick to Lepkin's side. Lepkin spun through the air and crashed on the rocks some ten yards away.

The shade rushed in.

Kyra came up with the crossbow and pulled the first two triggers without hesitation.

The shade threw up his arm and summoned a ward. To Kyra's horror, the ward spell worked and the crossbow bolts shattered against the magical shield with absolutely no harm done to the shade. Kyra screamed as the shade prepared a massive mess of lightning bolts, but instead of blasting her with it, the shade hurled it at the sky.

Leatherback dodged the first spell and returned fire with his flaming breath. The shade vanished and teleported to the other side of the rock nest.

"Clever girl," he said as he sneered at her. "But I have a few tricks of my own."

The shade fired a series of magical orbs at her. Kyra turned and ran, carrying the crossbow with her. The first orb struck a few feet behind her, and exploded. Hunks of stone flew out in every direction. The second did likewise, but the third dissipated in the air as she got close to Lepkin once again and his amulet dispelled the shade's magic.

Lepkin sat up and blinked as he rubbed his side. He took one look at Kyra and then stood on his feet, sword at the ready once more.

"Come down here and face me like a man," Lepkin taunted.

The shade laughed and shook his head.

Leatherback sent another stream of fire at the shade, but the shade vanished again.

He was nowhere to be seen now, though Kyra could hear his sinister laughter filling the area around her.

Snapping and ripping sounds were then heard in the forest. Kyra turned her eyes, and the crossbow, toward the sound. Her mouth fell open when she saw that a horde of trees, walking upon great legs made from their trunks and swinging ball-like clubs on the end of each branch, were advancing on them.

"Leatherback!" Kyra screamed.

The dragon blasted the trees with his fiery breath. The trees fell over upon the rocks, unable to get anywhere near the trio, but still the shade laughed.

The flames on the trees then grew into animate beings of fire and turned upon Kyra and Leatherback.

"What do we do now?" Lepkin asked.

The flame golems turned on each other and began combining themselves. Each time they joined, they grew taller and thicker, until a giant fire creature the size of Leatherback stood before them.

Kyra turned to the dragon and waved for his attention. "Go up, don't fight it."

The dragon looked at her for a moment, but then did as he was told. Leatherback flew up into the air, far out of the fire-creature's reach and disappeared into the sky as he soared away as quickly as he could.

"You may be able to dispel my magic, but let's see you dodge this," the shade said. The flame-creature bent down and picked up a great stone. The rock became red hot in its hands and then it hurled it at Kyra and Lepkin.

Lepkin pulled Kyra out of the way just as the stone crashed into the mountainside behind where she had been standing.

"We have to stop it!" Lepkin said.

"I can't use my magic!" Kyra replied.

Just then a great beat of wings fanned the whole of the rock nest. The flame-creature looked up and then hissed as Leatherback flew in with a mouthful of water and doused the flame-creature. The fires died down until the creature was only the size of a man.

Lepkin jumped up and sprinted out toward it. "This is my chance!" he shouted.

Kyra tried to grab him, but Lepkin was too quick. He sprinted straight for the creature. The fire golem saw him coming and ran at him too, but as its life was tied to the shade's magic, it disappeared when Lepkin got close.

"I got it!" Lepkin shouted.

Leatherback gave a triumphant roar, but Kyra could only scream as she saw the shade reappear next to Lepkin.

"Here I am," the shade said. It pulled a sword out of the air and then engaged Lepkin. The shade struck down with a chop, but Lepkin blocked and spun out to the right. The young man slashed at the shade, but the shade leapt away long before the sword could connect.

Kyra raised the crossbow and took aim, but the two were too close. She couldn't pull the trigger for fear of striking

Lepkin.

Leatherback roared into action and rushed downward. The shade nimbly avoided a swipe of Leatherback's claws, and then dodged a massive tail swing. The shade then rushed out from under the dragon and attacked Lepkin once more.

The young swordsman blocked one, two, then three lightning-quick stabs, but he never saw the roundhouse kick to the temple before it connected with his head and sent him cartwheeling across the ground.

Kyra jumped up and took the shot.

The crossbow bolt flew straight and true, but the shade turned and caught it in his hand. The shade sneered, and then gasped in horror and threw the bolt down. He looked at his hand and then glowered at Kyra.

The shade ran toward her, but Leatherback landed between them and engaged the shade. The dragon struck down with his claws, but the shade vanished once again.

Kyra shrieked audibly once she realized that the amulet was too far away to stop the shade from casting spells. Worse than that, Lepkin was not getting up.

Leatherback roared and spewed fire all around them, lighting the trees on fire and illuminating the shadows that the shade could otherwise hide in so easily.

"This ends now," the shade said. Suddenly a fist of stone erupted from the ground and caught Leatherback in the stomach. The dragon flew upward from the force of the blow, and then fell to the ground, heaving for breath.

"NO!" Kyra screamed. She turned on the shade and threw her own ball of fire at the creature. It waved its hand and dispelled Kyra's attack. Kyra rose to her feet and marched toward the shade. She threw fireball after fireball, alternating hands as she kept her spells coming in rapid succession. The shade put up a magical shield and let the fireballs slam into it as he continued his attack on Leatherback.

The shade pummeled the dragon in the side with another fist of stone. Then he lifted boulders and pounded the top of Leatherback's head with them. The dragon dodged to the right, then to the left, and then finally collapsed onto his stomach.

Kyra broke into a run, but it was no use. The shade turned to her for an instant and raised a stone in front of her face. The rock slammed into her with such force that she didn't even realize she had hit the ground until she tried to move her feet again. Her head turned to the side and she saw Leatherback taking blow after blow from the shade as he magically formed many giant fists of stone to pummel the dragon.

Kyra tried to get up, but she couldn't. Her legs wouldn't respond.

Then, she saw Lepkin push up from the ground. He rushed toward Leatherback, leaving his sword on the ground and sprinting for everything he was worth. The stones continued to assail Leatherback, but as Lepkin neared the dragon, the stone fists split apart and the spells became ineffective.

Lepkin pointed to Kyra and shouted out. "Now! Attack now!"

The young sorceress finally was able to get her feet under herself and rise once more. She engaged the shade with everything she had. Lightning, cyclones, and fire. Nothing penetrated his shield. The shade then turned his attention to her and began gathering a massive sphere of silver lightning between his hands.

Kyra heard a might roar and glanced to her left just in time to see Leatherback launch Lepkin with his tail. The young swordsman was flying through the air, amulet in hand and heading straight for the shade. Kyra turned back to the shade and redoubled her efforts, hoping that the smoke and sparks she created by blasting the shade's magical shield would provide the cover Lepkin needed.

Lepkin soared through the air and then, as he neared the shade, Kyra's spells dissipated around him. The next thing to fail was the shade's magical shield. The shade looked up and apparently tried to teleport, for he jumped in the air, but frowned when he landed back where he had been standing.

Lepkin connected with the shade a half second later. The two tumbled over the rocks, slamming each other and bouncing along the nest. Kyra rushed in to help, feeling powerless as she watched the shade dig his nails into Lepkin's back.

Lepkin cried out, but then pressed one hand to the shade's face. Kyra stopped in her tracks when she realized what was happening. The shade released Lepkin and fell to his back on the ground. Pressed to his cheek was Lepkin's amulet. The shade was weakening in exactly the same way Kyra had when the amulet had touched her.

Lepkin's right hand went up in the air, and then came down in a heavy arc and the shade twitched. When Lepkin shifted his weight on the shade, Kyra saw the dull end of a crossbow shaft sticking out from the creature's forehead. She glanced back to where the shade had last stood after it had kicked Lepkin. The bolt was no longer on the ground where the shade had dropped it. Lepkin had picked it up and used it to attack the shade.

Leatherback grabbed Lepkin's sword and then dropped it in front of Kyra.

Kyra took the hilt in her hands and then stormed up to the barely breathing shade.

"You will never win!" the shade hissed.

Kyra looked down and pointed the tip of the sword at the shade's heart. The green garunda blood hissed and bubbled as she plunged the blade into the shade and ended his life.

The hole in the shade's chest widened and then emitted a ghastly green glow that erupted into flames. Lepkin jumped back and watched the shade turn to ash.

Leatherback roared triumphantly and let out a large column of fire into the air. For a moment Kyra and Lepkin just stood there, breathing heavily. Kyra wiped her hand across her face, and then put both hands to her heart, trying to calm its frantic beating. She startled slightly when she heard Lepkin whoop loudly and jump while he thrust his fists into the air around him several times. Catching on to his excitement, Kyra began to laugh a bit hysterically, and then more naturally as she watched Lepkin run to Leatherback and plant a big kiss on his muzzle. Leatherback snorted once in response, and then blew an enormous ring of smoke into Lepkin's face. Lepkin took a few steps back, coughing, and then fell to the ground, still breathing a little heavily and laughing sporadically.

"It's done," Lepkin said.

Kyra nodded, staring into the green flames as the shade continued to burn away into nothingness. "My mother is avenged," she said, hardly daring to believe the words. In an instant she replayed the last year in her mind: the first of the strange attacks at Caspen Manor, her arrival at school, the day she had first seen Lepkin, the day Leatherback had hatched, her first battle with the shade, and now this moment, knowing that this creature which had sent the demons to hunt her had now been silenced forever. Then, her smile slowly faded away as she recalled that even this creature had been sent by another.

Kyra walked over to where Lepkin was lying on the ground and knelt down next to him. "We killed a shade. A *shade!* And you were amazing, but it is not done yet."

Lepkin sat up a little and leaned on his elbow. He looked to her with a questioning stare, and then his impish grin returned and his blue eyes sparkled once more. "Time to hunt the vampire?"

Kyra nodded. "It's time to cut the head off the snake, and it seems I have a dagger to find."

If you enjoyed this book, then be sure to pick up the other books in the Sorceress of Aspenwood series!

Book One   **Book Three**

You can also learn more about the girl who becomes Lady Dimwater in The Dragon's Champion Series, and discover whether Al the dwarf ever does return to his mountain kingdom, as he said, when the Wealth of Kings is discovered!

For the latest updates, follow Sam's Amazon Author Page, read his blog, www.talesfromterramyr.com, and follow him on Twitter @Author_SamFerg and Facebook

Other Books From Dragon Scale Publishing

ABOUT THE AUTHOR

Sam Ferguson is a fairly average guy.
That's it.
No, really, that's it.
Oh- you are actually reading this?

Well... the truth is that Sam is a very *lucky* guy. He juggles work in such a way that he makes sure to spend enough time with his loving wife and sons. He loves being a fulltime writer and enjoys sharing his workspace with two bearded dragons. If he can carve out an extra hour for himself during the day, he'll hit the gym to try and regain the body he used to have in his youth (but he eats too much junk food to ever accomplish that goal).

He spent nearly five years serving as a U.S. Diplomat and absolutely loved the experience, but decided to move back home. Outside of the U.S. he has lived in Latvia, Hungary, and Armenia. He speaks Russian, Hungarian, and Armenian. (He used to speak some Latvian too, but he has no one to practice with anymore...)

He also has two dogs.

He plays the Elder Scrolls series.

His favorite superhero is Wolverine, but Batman is a close second.

If the kids go to bed at a reasonable hour, he will cuddle up with his wife to watch Scrubs reruns, the Big Bang Theory, Castle, and Burn Notice.

See, really just an average guy after all.